Close Encounters of the Curd Kind

BOOK THREE IN THE AT WITS' END COZY MYSTERY SERIES

KIRSTEN WEISS

Cover artist: Dar Albert
Cloud Photo: Kirsten Weiss

Visit the author website: www.kirstenweiss.com

Misterio Press mass market paperback edition / September, 2019
http://Misteriopress.com

ISBN-13: 978-1-944767-43-3

ACKNOWLEDGEMENTS

No book is written in a vacuum. I would like to thank ███████████████████████████████████ for her assistance in researching ██████████████████████████████████ and for pointing out the strange connections between this book and the events chronicled in Doyle Witch book #6, *Fate*. I would also like to thank █ ███████████████████████████████████ for his informed take on the ████████████████████████████ ██████████████████████████████████. Dover and Jayce ███████████████████████. And finally, thanks to the ██████ ████████████████████████████████ California on December 19th, 2019.

CHAPTER 1

Most days, it's easy being an optimist. The sun shines. I have people who love me.

Life is good.

But other days, something else is waiting, a shadow just behind my left shoulder. If I let it, it grabs, bites, digs in.

Not even Arsen knew about the shadow. I haven't let it catch me for a long time – not since my grandmother died. But I felt its presence as I stared from the porch steps, my muscles tensed.

"Something crashed." My cousin Dixie craned her neck. Her gaze traveled past the turrets and gables of my B&B, Wits' End, past the decorative UFO in the tile roof, past mountain peaks, blackberry in the twilight.

A streak of cloud like an airplane contrail bulleted toward the earth. A poof of white, an explosion of some sort, lingered at the base of the contrail. The exclamation point glowed bright and faraway against the darkening western sky.

And it made my heart race and skin itch.

I glanced at Dixie, in her camo shorts and black tank top, the tips of her dark hair tinted green. Helpless love and worry for my reckless young cousin swelled in my chest and throat. When it came to Dixie, to Arsen, to the strange glowing light in the sky, I was not in control. But I was damn well going to control the pieces of my life I could.

I jammed my hands into the pockets of my capris and clenched my fists. It had to be something natural.

I hoped.

Beside my sneakers, Bailey gently whoofed.

I bent to scratch the beagle.

"Something came down," Dixie said, "and it exploded."

Bailey's whoof turned to a growl.

Two male guests in shorts and baseball caps with the *TRUE MEDIUM* logo staggered onto the porch. The crewmen, Bob and Mahir, carried a long, black case.

"Shush, Bailey," I scolded. "You know they're guests." He never growled at guests. What was wrong with him? He knew who paid for his dog biscuits.

The beagle's growl turned menacing.

"I believe your dog is growling at me," said a masculine voice from somewhere near my left hip.

I jumped, startled.

A tiny stranger grinned up at me. He swept off his top hat in a low bow and handed Dixie a flyer. A t-shirt reading CIRCUS OF IMPOSS— peeked beneath the v of his blue-satin blouse. Beneath his top hat, his black hair was slicked-back like a cartoon villain's.

Bailey's lips peeled back.

"Sorry." Scanning the driveway for more surprises, I knelt and grasped Bailey's collar. "I don't know what's gotten into him."

Dixie examined the flyer and wrinkled her pert nose. "The Circus of Impossible Things?"

"We thought of calling it Improbable Things." He eyed my dog. "But by definition, a circus is over the top." He replaced his hat and winked. "Or under it, the big top, you see?"

I forced a smile.

"Locals' discount," the little man continued. "Ten percent off on opening night."

"Thanks," I said.

He handed one of the cameramen, Mahir, a flyer and strode from the yard. His top hat bobbed behind the roses, headed toward my neighbor, the colonel's house.

When he was out of earshot, Dixie snorted. "A circus? How lame." She eyed me. "So, I guess you'll be going?"

I snatched the flyer from her hand. "I'll post this in case any of our guests are interested." And yes, I'd probably be going. Doyle was a small town. You had to grab what entertainment came your way.

I glanced from the sky to the purple flyer. When was the last time a circus had come to Doyle? "This is turning into a very weird day."

"This is Doyle." Dixie folded her arms over her black tank top. "Every day's a weird day."

"Susan, this place is marvelous!" A slim, middle-aged woman in jeans and a *TRUE MEDIUM* t-shirt emerged from the B&B and waved at me. She joined us on the lawn. "I can feel your grandmother everywhere."

I felt my grandmother around the B&B she'd left to me too. She was in every rose bush. Every grainy UFO photo.

Danella Jones, the true medium of the eponymous TV show, continued. "Is it okay for our van to be here for loading? We won't be much longer." Lines fanned outward from her lips, marking a lifetime of cigarettes. Their odor hung in her thick, gray-streaked brown hair.

Dying to ask her more about my Gran and determined not to, I swallowed and rolled the flyer into a tube. "It's fine."

A van door slammed.

The medium turned and stared upward, tracking Dixie's gaze. "Oh." Her hands clenched and unclenched. "That is strange. And disturbing. Are clouds like that... normal for the mountains?"

The men strode past us and into the B&B.

"No." I tried to inject some optimism into my voice. "We get a lot of lenticular, UFO-shaped clouds, but I have no idea what that is."

Dixie snapped a picture with her phone.

The medium shivered and rubbed her lips. "A bad omen. But since the whole town can see it, it's probably not a bad omen for you, specifically." She smiled brightly.

"So... good news?" I said.

Her brows puckered. "I just hope..."

We stared at the cloud. The wind had blown the top of the contrail into an elongated question mark.

"I need to check my cards." Danella hurried into the B&B. The twin screen doors slammed behind her.

"Check her cards?" Dixie asked.

"Maybe Tarot?"

"So much for the Age of Enlightenment." She rolled her eyes. "Why did that medium have to come here? We're a UFO B&B. We're about science. Not the supernatural."

That was debatable, but I'd learned long ago not to tussle with Dixie on UFO-related matters. She was a true believer, her trailer fitted with radio equipment to catch alien communications. I was an agnostic on the UFO front, which probably wasn't the best position for the owner of a UFO-themed B&B.

It was complicated.

Small-town Doyle was complicated.

The last glimmer of sunlight flared across the Sierras, glimmered off the UFO in the mansard roof.

"Space junk, falling to earth?" Yeah, that made sense.

"Space junk's one way to describe it." Dixie lowered her head. "The other way is an acronym that starts with *U* and ends with *O*. The middle letter is *F* in case you don't—"

"I get it, I get it."

A shiver of alpine air rustled the pine boughs. The trees swayed and soughed, and a flutter of fallen rose petals drifted past my feet on the lawn.

Bailey whined. His tail wagged once, tentative.

I bent and picked up a soft petal, rubbing it between my fingers to release the rose's odor. Its sweet scent bloomed in the air.

Gran had always been able to chase my odd anxiety away. Now me and my self-help books were on our own. My happy-go-lucky best friend, Arsen, had recently become my boyfriend. I wanted to meet him halfway and loosen up. But only halfway. I still had a business to manage.

So did Arsen. But Arsen's idea of managing was to float through life and let things come crashing down where they may.

Like whatever had caused that weird cloud.

The B&B's front door slammed. Danella trotted down the porch steps behind the two men. Her smile was uneven. "Are you sure you don't want to watch the taping? The camera would love you. Good figure. Blond hair. All-American good looks."

My face warmed. "Thanks, but no."

"Your loss." She shrugged and sauntered to the van.

The three got inside. Buckled up. Backed out.

And drove into the driveway of the A-frame cabin next door.

My brows lifted in surprise. The colonel's house? I couldn't imagine Colonel Fitzgerald and his gossipy wife, Marion, having anything to do with an online psychic. The colonel was a hard-edged man, rigid and controlling, and kept to himself.

His wife had even petitioned the town to make me remove the UFO from the Wits' End roof. But Gran had parked that UFO in the Wits' End roof since before the Fitzgeralds had moved in next door. It had squatter's rights.

And Marion had failed in her quest. Doyle was experiencing a UFO-related tourism boom.

"Clare," Dixie said, her voice thick with disdain.

I shot her a startled look. "What?"

"She's moved back into her father's house." Dixie nodded toward the colonel's shingled A-frame. "Didn't you know?"

Clare's arrival had been hard to miss. She'd been there six weeks. "All right. I'll bite. Has it got something to do with *True Medium*?"

"Duh. You don't think the colonel called them in? Clare thinks she's being haunted or something, because – get this – she's been waking up in strange places."

"Weird."

"You're telling me."

"You'd think these shows would need more than six weeks to set up a visit," I said.

She tossed her emerald-streaked hair. "*That's* what you think is weird? We live in the UFO abduction capital of the world, and Clare thinks she's being kidnapped by ghosts. Ghosts!"

I shrugged. "UFOs aren't the only explanation for disappearances. Some people think it's fairies doing the kidnapping." Some people will believe anything.

Dixie threw her hands in the air. "I need to check my radios." She swiveled on her hiking boots and strode through the white-painted front gate.

Dixie and her radios. Some things, at least, would never change. Grinning, I watched her vanish down the street. But there *were* odd similarities between the old stories of fairy encounters and today's UFO abductions. Bright lights. Lost time.

Probing.

Yech.

"I won't have it!" Colonel Fitzgerald, a tall, straight-backed man with cropped gray hair, stormed from the house.

"Dad! Wait!" His daughter streaked through the door after him and onto the porch. She touched his arm. Although Clare was pushing forty, she still had a gamine, fey vibe. "Please."

Jaw tight, he turned to her with military precision. His nostrils flared. The colonel was a "my house, my rules," sort of guy. I didn't think she had a chance.

Clare stepped smartly backward and straightened. She'd moved to Doyle years after the colonel and his wife, and I didn't know her well. If she'd sprung *True Medium* on him as a surprise, I couldn't blame him for being annoyed. She said something in a voice too low for me to eavesdrop on.

Colonel Fitzgerald's posture softened.

She hugged him, and the two returned inside the cabin.

I blew out my breath. So, Clare had won this round. Maybe the grumpy colonel was mellowing? He'd actually smiled at me last week.

Venus emerged, glittering low above the mountains. The contrail was dissipating, widening, but still it glowed, baleful.

I shivered in spite of the summer warmth.

Bad omen, indeed.

CHAPTER 2

The next morning, I bustled about the octagonal breakfast room and stacked dishes in my arms. The blue-flowered curtains breathed at the open windows.

Arsen stuffed the last bites of cinnamon roll casserole into his mouth. He kept his head low over the plate as if I might snatch it away before he'd finished. His golf shirt showed off the sinewy muscles in his arms. A breeze through the window rustled his whiskey-colored hair.

I was noticing those details more frequently, and not just because Arsen was good looking. I was also trying to pay more attention to the present moment instead of thinking about the future or the past. It was an anti-anxiety technique, and it worked.

His foot thunked against something, and he bent, picked up a plastic bottle of window cleaner. "Uh, is this supposed to be here?"

Heat flushed my face. "No." *Dixie!* Leaving a cleaning bottle under the table was unprofessional. But in fairness, neither my cousin nor I were cleaning professionals.

Hazel eyes twinkling, he shoved his chair away from the oval table. "Getting more relaxed with the cleaning?"

"Definitely not." I grabbed the bottle from his hand and glanced into the foyer for my wayward cousin. But the high-ceilinged room was empty. Morning sunlight cascaded through the stained-glass window above the transom. It tinted the wooden reception desk in faded reds and blues.

Arsen stretched, his shirt pulling against his washboard abs. He rubbed his hand across the logo for his security company, embroidered in one corner of the blue fabric. He grinned. "Sterling breakfast, as usual, Susan."

I smiled at the compliment. He said the same thing every morning, but I loved it that he did. "Thank you."

"So... Are your parents coming up anytime?"

My stomach tightened. "Um, no." Had I told him they might come? It didn't seem possible. My parents and I hadn't talked in... a long time.

I hurried from the room and through the swinging door into the kitchen. The white subway tiles above the sink gleamed.

Bailey looked up from his dog bed and eyed the plates for possible scraps.

"Dog food only." I set the plates on the butcher block counter. "You're on a diet, remember?"

The beagle laid his head on his paws and shot me a sulky look.

I turned to study the pot of lemon curd on the modern stove. You'd think something called lemon curd would involve curdling. But it's supposed to be smooth. Big gloppy lumps marred the surface of my pot.

The kitchen door swung open behind me. "What's wrong?" Arsen strode inside.

"I can't get this lemon curd not to curdle." I moved the pot to the counter. "My scones bake up fine, in spite of the altitude. What do lemons have against me?"

"I meant your parents."

"Oh." I scrutinized the lumpy yellow mess. "They're busy."

He lightly batted at a wayward spider plant dangling from a wooden shelf. "They seem to always be busy."

"Yep. Busy, busy, busy." I stared hard at the lemon curd. My gran had never had to strain curds, and this was her recipe.

He slipped an arm around my waist. "They brought you here every summer to stay with your grandmother. I don't remember them ever hanging around."

He smelled clean, like soap. But I was not going to get distracted. This was important, and I loved him, and he needed to drop the subject.

"They never really liked it up here." I motioned toward the curtained window over the sink, and the mountain beyond. "Too much nature," I lied.

"Maybe we should go see them," he said. "San Francisco isn't that far away."

I turned and stared up at him in horror. He *looked* like Arsen Holiday. High cheekbones. Muscular arms. Tanned skin. So why the devil had he suggested something so... monstrous?

"They must miss you," he continued blithely.

"No," I said. "No, they don't." A chill touched my upper back, as if a shadow had fallen across it, and my stomach tightened.

"That can't be true." His handsome brow furrowed. "They're your parents. They love you."

"Yes, of course, but—"

"It's starting to get weird," he said. "We've been seeing each other for months—"

There was a shout from next door.

"What was that?" Eager for the interruption – any interruption – I walked to the kitchen sink and peered through the window.

Arsen came to stand beside me. "Trouble?"

Colonel Fitzgerald glowered from the top of his porch steps. Two steps beneath him stood a round, ruddy-faced man. It was my neighbor on the other side of the colonel's house, Rufus Berghoff. The lawyer's neck muscles strained against the collar of his button-up shirt. The men shouted, their words impossible to decipher from my spot at the window.

"Not again," Arsen said. "I had to separate them outside Ground the other day."

"They were fighting?" I asked, startled. "Fist fighting?" The colonel always seemed so controlled and correct. I knew the two neighbors didn't like each other, though the why's and wherefores were unclear. But actual fighting?

"Only yelling. I thought one of them was going to have a heart attack."

I frowned, worried. They both *did* look pretty red in the face.

Arsen made a move toward the kitchen door. "I'd better—"

The A-frame's front door swung open. A man in his late thirties and wearing a sheriff deputy's uniform strode onto the porch – Rufus's son, Emmery.

Emmery walked down the front steps. He stopped between the two men, his hands outstretched, pacifying.

The colonel shook his head and stormed into the cabin, slamming the door behind him.

"It looks like I won't have to," Arsen said, easing backward.

Emmery said something to his father.

Rufus made a rude gesture toward the A-frame. He stormed down the driveway and into the court.

"I guess that's that then." I turned from the window and leaned against the counter.

"Yup. All's well that ends well," Arsen said. "And it's time I meet your parents."

I sputtered. "That's not—"

My cell phone rang on the butcher block counter. I lunged, answering without checking to see if it was a telemarketer. I was that rattled. "Wits' End, this is Susan Witsend speaking."

"Hi, this is Cameraman Bob."

My shoulders relaxed. Not a telemarketer. "Hi, Bob. What can I do for you?" *Please let there be something I can do.*

"Hey, I left a lens in my room that I need, and I've got my hands full here. Is there any chance you can bring it next door?"

"We are a full-service B&B, so I'd be happy to. What's it look like?"

"It's in a black case about the size of a lunch box. I think I put it on the floor by the bed, beside the window. It's sort of hidden. That's probably why I forgot it."

"No problem. I'll grab it and be right over."

We said our goodbyes and hung up.

"Duty calls," I said to Arsen.

His eyes narrowed. "Gee, Susan. It's almost like you're avoiding this conversation."

"What conversation? Hey, you wouldn't mind cleaning up in here while I—"

"Whoops." He checked his dive watch. "Client meeting. Gotta go." He strode manfully from the kitchen.

"I didn't think so," I muttered, but I smiled.

I hurried into the reception area. Kicking flat the edge of the faux-Persian rug, I grabbed my master key from inside the battered reception desk. I jogged up the stairs and down the green-carpeted hallway lined with UFO photos to room number five.

I found the lens case right where Cameraman Bob had said it would be and walked next door to the Colonel's house.

My footsteps sounded hollowly on the wooden steps. I knocked on the front door.

It sprang open beneath my fist. The other crew member, Mahir, peered out and pressed a finger to his lips. He grasped my elbow and tugged me inside the cabin before I could react.

Bob aimed a camera at Danella and Clare, seated on the couch. The taping had already started.

I pointed at the case, but Mahir had already abandoned me for his camera, mounted on a tripod. He peered through the viewfinder at the two women.

The medium's eyes were closed, a serene look on her face. One graying braid dangled over her shoulder and down the front of her red peasant top, tangling in her beads.

The medium grasped Clare's hand. "There are energies around you."

"A presence?" Clare rubbed one palm on the thigh of her jeans. "Then I was right? I knew I really felt something." Her reddish hair was tied in a loose bun, coppery wisps coiling around her slender neck.

Emmery, the top button of his sheriff's uniform undone, raked a hand through his curling, brown hair. His eyes were a startling blue against his olive skin.

Feeling out of place, I hugged the wall and tiptoed to stand beside the colonel.

He stood out of the camera's line of sight, against a wall. Knuckles white on his silvery travel mug, he nodded to me, his expression grim.

Danella shook her head. "No, these energies are the remnants of something else, a portal."

Frowning, the colonel sipped something green from the tumbler. It smelled faintly of mint.

"A portal?" Clare squeaked.

Danella opened her eyes and frowned. "Oh. This is complicated."

"Complicated?" Clare laughed shakily. "That doesn't sound good."

"I believe what we're dealing with are interdimensionals."

There was a soft snort to my left. Marion, Clare's stepmother, stood in the kitchen doorway. Her green eyes blazed against her tanned skin. Or maybe she was just spitting mad.

"Interdimensionals?" Clare parroted.

"Interdimensional aliens," Danella said.

My brows shot skyward. I hadn't expected that twist, and I'm considered something of a local alien expert.

Marion tossed her short, frosted hair.

"For God's sake," the old colonel burst out. "I've had enough of this nonsense. I told you this would come back to aliens."

One of the cameras swiveled toward him.

Danella smiled serenely. "*Interdimensional* aliens."

"It's garbage," he said. "I won't have it in this house."

"I'm afraid what you will or won't have has no effect on the aliens," Danella said. "They come and go as they please."

"Get out," the colonel said. "All of you. This is still my house, and I won't have this insanity."

His wife straightened off the doorway.

Emmery cleared his throat. "I think those papers you signed means they get to finish, sir."

The colonel's face reddened. "There was nothing in those papers about this having to take place inside my home. I'm done. I'm–" He made an odd, strangled sound and clutched his chest. His face contorted.

"Colonel?" I grasped his arm, my heart in my throat. "Are you all right?"

His eyes rolled up in his head. The colonel collapsed to the wood floor.

CHAPTER 3

Emmery brushed past me. The sheriff's deputy dropped to his knees and performed CPR on the colonel. "Clare," he said, "call an ambulance."

"Daddy?" Clare reached out a trembling hand to her father.

The medium sat pale and frozen beside her. The two crewmen lowered their cameras and looked worriedly at each other.

"Ted?" Marion pushed past the cameramen. One hand on the wood-plank wall, she slid to her knees and grasped his hand. "Ted?"

"Clare," the deputy snapped. "Call an ambulance."

She shook herself and fumbled in her purse.

"I've got it." Silently cursing my own stunned inaction, I pulled my phone from the pocket of my capris. I called nine-one-one.

The dispatcher promised help would be there in ten minutes.

"Ten minutes," I told the room, my voice a quaver.

Clare fell to her knees beside Emmery and took her father's hand. "It's okay," she whispered. "It's going to be okay."

Emmery's mouth flattened, but he said nothing.

Horrified, I edged backward, out of the way. The colonel didn't look like he was going to be okay. His face was slack and gray.

My heart gripped. My Gran had died from a heart attack. "I'll wait on the street for the ambulance."

No one responded.

I jogged out the front door, down the steps, and to the court. Had it been a heart attack brought on by stress? I glanced at the mid-century modern home on the other side of the colonel's, where Rufus Berghoff lived.

A siren wailed in the distance.

One of the stoners who lived in the house across the street ambled from their driveway. He saluted, shirtless.

I waved back half-heartedly.

Poor Clare. But what my dark, selfish heart really felt was *poor me.* My throat closed. If the colonel died, it would be the end of an era.

The colonel and Gran had been friends. I remembered the summer I'd come to Doyle after he'd first moved in. I remembered the shock of seeing his cabin on the lot where Arsen and I had once built a tree house. I remembered him shouting at Arsen and me to get off my Gran's roof. I remembered he and Gran arguing good naturedly about aliens over the fence separating their properties. They'd always gotten along. Grumpy or not, he'd been a good neighbor.

A few minutes later, an ambulance followed a sheriff's SUV into the colonel's drive.

Sheriff McCourt stepped from the car, and I blinked. She was our small town's big cheese. What was she doing at the scene of a heart attack?

She jammed her wide-brimmed hat over her spill of blond curls and scowled. "Witsend."

Two EMTs bustled past. "Where is he?" one asked me.

"Inside. Front room." I nodded at the porch steps.

They climbed the steps and jogged through the open front door.

"What happened?" Sheriff McCourt asked me.

"It looked like a heart attack. He was upset–"

Her cornflower blue eyes narrowed. "You upset him?"

"No," I said calmly. The sheriff knew me. We were friends. Compadres. I was practically her secret weapon in crime solving. "Why would I upset him?"

She gave me a look.

"We had very good… pretty good relations. It was the internet show." I motioned to the *True Medium* van in the driveway. "They're filming Clare. The colonel was uncomfortable with it."

"You said *upset.*"

"I don't know. Exasperated. Well, kind of angry." Should I mention the argument with Rufus?

No, it couldn't matter.

"And what's your role in this lunacy?"

I rolled my eyes. Her overwrought suspicion was only a little game she played. She pretended we were adversaries, but I knew the truth. Some people just had a hard time getting close.

"Nothing," I said. "I mean, the medium and crew are staying at my B&B."

She groaned.

"They needed a lens they'd left behind." My voice rose slightly, and I cleared my throat. I glanced toward the cabin. They couldn't have restarted filming in there, could they? "So, they called me, and I brought it over."

"How helpful of you."

"I try to accommodate our guests whenever—"

"Go back to your B&B. We won't talk later." She strode inside the A-frame.

Huh. Sometimes it seemed like the sheriff really didn't like me.

I made a face. But in this instance, she was right about me being in the way. There was nothing I could do here to help.

I returned to Wits' End and checked my planner. I had absolutely nothing to do that would take me from the kitchen. So, I finished my cleaning there, glancing out the side window at the colonel's house. No one emerged from his shingled cabin.

Sitting at the kitchen table, I opened my planner and made notes on what I'd witnessed. This probably wasn't a murder investigation.

But you never could tell.

The bell on the front desk dinged.

Hurrying into the reception area, I helped a middle-aged couple check out. We plotted their road trip to Vegas, and the couple, loaded down with suitcases, bumped out the door.

I followed them onto the screened front porch.

Outside the colonel's house, the EMTs wheeled a sadly lumpy body bag to their ambulance.

My chest squeezed. *Dammit. No.* The colonel hadn't made it.

Dixie walked up the steps, her gaze following mine. "Who died?"

"The colonel."

"What?" Dixie paled and took a step backward, her head bumping a hanging fern. She ducked and glowered at the plant. "How?"

"I think he had a heart attack."

"You *think*?"

"He was shouting at the medium, then he grabbed his chest and keeled over." I swallowed. Could I have done more? But Emmery was a cop and knew CPR, and I'd called for help. It just hadn't been enough.

At my feet, Bailey swiveled his head between us.

"So it *looked* like a heart attack," Dixie said.

Exasperated, I folded my arms. "Yes, that's what I said."

"They would want it to look that way," she said in a low voice.

My eyes narrowed. "They?" Alien conspiracy theories were good for business, and Dixie was chock full of them. But this wasn't the time.

"The colonel worked at Area 51."

Oh boy. I'd heard that rumor, too, but had never had the nerve to ask him if it was true.

Also, not the time! "And speaking of work, the guests in room two just checked out. Why don't you start cleaning there? I've got to do some shopping for tomorrow's breakfast."

She shrugged, the muscles on her bare arms and shoulders moving smoothly. "Whatever. Bury your head in the sand. It's what this town does best." She stomped up the carpeted stairs.

Bailey woofed and trotted after her.

Doyle's "downtown" wasn't far. But it didn't exactly feel nearby when I had to lug groceries for twelve. So, I hopped into my blue Crosstrek and drove into the town center, parking in a lot behind the bookstore.

A piercing whistle sliced the air as I turned the corner onto Main Street. Three whirling acrobats, women in bold reds and blues tumbled down the middle of the road. Twirling ribbons on the ends of long sticks, they pretzeled into liquid patterns. One leapt weightlessly into the air.

Tourists pointed and applauded, laughing from raised, wood sidewalks. The little man from yesterday handed out flyers.

But not all the watching faces looked delighted. The local's smiles were less certain, absent of mirth.

I studied the acrobats and shivered. Maybe it was because I'd been touched by the colonel's death, but there was something uncanny about the three women. The way they contorted their limbs seemed inhuman, unnatural, wrong.

The little man stopped before me and started to hand me a flyer.

Automatically, I reached to take it.

He waggled his finger at me. "You already have one. Waste not, want not!" He winked and strode away.

Nonplussed, I continued to the grocery store at the far end of Main Street and did my shopping. I returned to my car and loaded the bags. I straightened from the open door. A bird chirped in a nearby elm. Sunlight glinted off fenders. The lot was deserted.

I wanted company of the non-UFO-B&B variety. Pulling my planner from my bag, I nodded. There was time for a detour. I jammed the leather-bound binder into my bag. It had gotten thicker since I'd started assisting the sheriff with investigations. My throat tightened. I hoped the colonel's death wouldn't become another series of entries in my planner.

Rounding the corner to the bookstore, I strolled inside.

Its owner, Lenore, looked up from the counter. Tall, willowy, and blond, she looked like she'd stepped out of a Scandinavian fashion catalog. She smiled. "Hi, Susan. How are things at Wits' End?"

I winced, my footsteps slowing, growing heavy. "Not good." I wended my way through the aisles to the high counter. "Colonel Fitzgerald passed away today."

Her blue-gray eyes widened. "What? But I only talked to him yesterday. What happened?"

"It looked like a heart attack, but I'm not sure."

"Looked like?" she asked sharply, echoing my cousin. Her expression smoothed. "Of course you can't be sure what it was. But you saw it? You were there?"

"They were filming that online show, *True Medium*, at his house. The crew is staying at Wits' End." Blinking away unexpected tears, I explained about the colonel's collapse. The colonel and I hadn't been close. Why was I so upset?

The bell over the front door jingled, and we turned.

Old Mrs. Steinberg strode into the bookstore, her cane thumping the thin, gray carpet. Her blue-tinted hair was swathed in a black scarf. "I heard Fitzgerald died and you were there, Susan. What happened?" She came to a stop beside me, her black dress swaying around the ankles of her heavy boots. She lowered her Jackie-Kennedy style glasses and glared.

I wasn't super surprised Mrs. Steinberg knew I'd been there. The old lady, who worked in town records, was even more gossipy than Mrs. Fitzgerald. But Mrs. Steinberg's talent lay in collecting, rather than spreading, gossip. It was the reason no one could force her to retire. She knew where the bodies were buried.

I explained for the third time what I'd seen. Lenore and Mrs. Steinberg exchanged enigmatic glances.

"Best you stay out of this, Susan," the old lady said.

"Stay out of what?" I asked.

"Nothing," Lenore said quickly. "Because Susan's right. There's nothing to stay out of."

I bit my lip. "Well, I *am* worried about Clare. She's been under a lot of strain. And now with her father's death—"

"Clare can manage without you," Mrs. Steinberg said. "She's got that boyfriend of hers to take care of her."

"I suppose," I said doubtfully, "but—"

"There are dark forces at work here," Mrs. Steinberg said. "If you know what's good for you, you'll stay out of it."

Dark forces? In spite of everything, I bit back a laugh. Dixie wasn't the only one obsessed with alien conspiracies. In Doyle, it was part of the culture. "I'm pretty sure it was a heart attack."

"I'm sure that's all it was," Lenore said.

"Why?" I asked Mrs. Steinberg. "Did you hear something different?"

"The colonel was a man of many parts." She dug through her big black purse. "Stay out of it."

"Was there a particular book you were looking for?" Lenore asked me.

"What? Oh. Do you have anything by Danella Jones?"

"No, sorry," she said quickly.

Wow. She knew her inventory by heart?

Lenore blushed. "It's just that I know we don't have her, because the colonel asked me about the book as well."

"Thanks anyway." I ambled from the bookstore. The door swung shut behind me, and I looked over my shoulder.

Lenore leaned over the counter toward Mrs. Steinberg. They spoke, their expressions intent. They both looked toward me, then quickly away.

My insides knotted. *Ha.* If I were a suspicious person, and I totally was, I'd think they'd been talking about me. But that was just my own paranoia. I mean, why talk about me? Mrs. Steinberg's hints about the colonel were only more of her usual cryptic weirdness. She didn't actually *know* anything.

Or did she?

I wandered into the coffeeshop, Ground. Hangings fluttered against its bare brick walls, the air stirred by overhead fans. The whir of the espresso machine made my shoulders loosen. The scent of coffee always made me want to sit and linger.

But since I was on a schedule, I ordered my double espresso to-go and went to stand at the pickup line.

In spite of the full tables, the café's volume was low. But Ground being open on Saturdays was still a new thing for Doyle. Maybe this was a different and less boisterous crowd.

I surveyed the customers. Brows furrowed, people hunched over laptop computers. Clusters of locals leaned over square tables. People spoke in hushed tones. What was going on? Could they have possibly heard about the colonel's death already?

"Here you go. A double espresso and my magic coffee scrub." The owner, Jayce, handed me a paper cup and a glass jar filled with dark grounds. The scrub worked wonders on my hands after gardening, getting off all the grime. She wiped her hands on her green apron and looked past me. "It's quiet today. I'd say too quiet, but not even I'm that cliché." She laughed.

Customers turned to stare.

The café owner took a step backward, and her laughter subsided. "Seriously, is something up?"

"I don't know," I said slowly. "Though my neighbor, Colonel Fitzgerald, passed away today." I crossed my arms and looked briefly away. "A heart attack."

Her eyes, the color of fresh clover, blinked. "Oh, no. That's terrible. How's Clare?"

"I'm not sure. But she was there when it happened. I left her with Emmery." Should I have stayed? I'd felt in the way, but maybe that had been my own, selfish discomfort.

"I'll pay a condolence call later," Jayce said. "Thanks for letting me know."

"Hey, Susan," Tom Tarrant called to me from a table. The reporter had the all-American good looks Danella had accused me of yesterday. Once, I'd fallen for his wholesome country boy shtick. Tom had taken full advantage.

Never again.

"You got any comments on One-armed Frank's cows?" he continued.

My neck stiffened. "Excuse me?"

The coffeeshop fell silent. The kind of silence that has weight to it. Pregnant. Thick. And really, really uncomfortable.

My skin prickled. I looked around.

Yes, everyone really *was* staring at me.

"His cows have gone missing," Tom said.

"Why would I know anything about missing cows?" I asked.

He grinned. "You know. Alien abductions?"

"Of cows?" Cattle mutilations *were* a part of UFO lore but *not* cattle rustling. As a Doyle reporter, he should know that by now. "I don't think so." I flounced from the café and strode down the shaded sidewalk. Baskets of ferns and impatiens hung from the eaves. Dog bowls filled with water sat outside the shops, and I smiled, thinking of Bailey. If I hadn't been grocery shopping today, I would have brought the beagle.

The phone pinged in my capri's pocket, and I dug it free. I had a new text from Dixie, with a link to what looked like an online video.

Dropping onto a wrought-iron bench, I clicked the link and angled my phone, widening the video screen. In the video, Danella sat on the bed in her room in my B&B.

The medium leaned toward the camera, one long braid swinging forward. "Today," she said solemnly, "something terrible happened. While we were taping in a home where a woman was being haunted by interdimensional aliens, her father suddenly died." She pressed a hand to her throat. "Of course, we had to stop filming. But questions remain. Is this town, Doyle, California, a death vortex? Is this the influence of interdimensional aliens? In any case, further investigation is warranted."

I sucked in my breath. *Is Doyle a death vortex?* What the heck was a death vortex? I mentally paged through my encyclopedic (ha) knowledge of vortexes. Healing vortex. Sedona vortex. Vortex of eternal despair... Nope, no idea what a death vortex was.

But it sure didn't sound good.

CHAPTER 4

Pasting a smile on my face, I reminded myself the customer was always right.

Even when they weren't.

Sunday morning sunlight streamed through the blue-curtained windows in the breakfast room. I'd cleared the plates, but the octagonal room still smelled of bacon and waffles.

"But a death vortex?" I asked. "Really?"

The lines around Danella's mouth deepened. Wisps of long, brown hair escaped her loose ponytail. "You doubt? A man was murdered in this very B&B last year. And now your neighbor is dead by digitalis."

I stiffened. The murder in my B&B totally hadn't been my fault. And I really didn't like that the colonel had died from an accidental poisoning. The news had made the morning paper. The local reporter was disturbingly efficient for a small town.

"This town's murder rate is through the roof," she continued earnestly. "And they haven't been gang murders or muggings gone wrong, like in a big city. I researched the murders, read the articles. They were all personal. There's something here that's acting on people's psyches."

"Correlation is not causality, and the colonel's death was an accident."

"Then what do you think is causing this?" She brandished the Sunday morning paper. "My– My client's father died horribly right in front of us."

I forced my smile wider. "I'm just saying we don't know for sure what's going on in Doyle." *Customer's always right.* "The fact is, no one does. A lot of businesses in this town and their employees are dependent on tourism. Wouldn't it be the responsible thing to have a better understanding of what's happening before telling the world Doyle is a murder vortex?"

"Death vortex," she corrected sniffily.

"Death vortex." *Always right. Always right.*

She heaved out a breath. "Maybe you're right. Perhaps I shouldn't jump to conclusions. So." She brightened. "I'm just going to need to extend our stay to investigate further."

My hands clenched. That wasn't what I'd meant!

"But don't worry," she said, "I'll be sure to really talk up Wits' End."

And death vortexes? My mind raced. I could lie and tell her the rooms were booked. But she'd just go to the Historic Doyle Hotel, and it was most definitely not full. Early May in the Sierras isn't a huge time for tourists. The skiing is usually blah to nonexistent, and the hiking is cold and muddy. And forget about swimming.

"I'll see what I can do," I ground out.

"Thank you." She grasped my hand. "This place has a lovely atmosphere, in spite of the bodies. In fact, I sense two spirits here. One's got such a lovely, gentle aura. It must be your grandmother. The other is a bit dicey, but we haven't had much interaction. Would you like me to contact them for you?"

"No, I'd better go check on your room availability." I fled into the kitchen.

Bailey looked up from his dog bed and woofed a gentle *hello*.

Dixie, in her usual cargo shorts and tank top, leaned against the counter reading a paper. She snorted. "Get this. There was a fight in front of Antoine's last night."

"Oh?"

"Spence Shelton accused some rando biker dude of being an alien, and they got into a punch up."

Maybe Doyle was too alien obsessed?

She lowered the newspaper and studied me. "You look more freaked out than usual. What's up? And why is this lemon curd lumpy?" She nodded to the jar at her elbow.

My face tightened. Did she have to rub it in? "Because I don't know gran's secret. And what do you know about death vortexes?" Maybe if I understood what Danella was talking about, I could nudge her in a less disturbing direction.

I grabbed the bottle of lemon hand lotion from its spot by the sink and squirted air into my hands. Disgusted, I tossed the empty bottle into the trash beneath the sink. Nothing lemon was going my way.

"Hm." She angled her head and tapped her chin. "Nothing. I'm a UFO expert, not a death vortex expert. Why don't you ask one of the witches?"

"Witches?"

"Lenore or Jayce."

"Lenore or Jayce Bonheim?" Incredulous, I shut the cupboard door.

"How many Lenores and Jayces do you know in Doyle?"

"Only two, but they're not witches. I mean, just because Jayce says her hand scrubs are magic… They work wonders, but come on."

"Are you seriously that out of touch?" She dropped the paper on the counter. "The whole town knows they're witches."

The town also thought they were the victims of repeated, mass alien kidnappings. "Just because the Bonheim sisters were home schooled, doesn't make them witches."

"No, but it doesn't *not* make them witches. And don't forget Karin. They're triplets."

"I know they're triplets. Karin's a friend of mine." I wished she hadn't moved to Angels Camp, though it wasn't really that far away. Maybe I could schedule a lunch date. "But what does them being triplets...? Oh, never mind."

I walked to the sink and gazed out the kitchen window. Roses danced in the light, spring breeze. On the foxglove, the buds were just beginning to pop.

Foxglove. Digitalis came from foxglove.

I glanced down at the paper. My chest squeezed, my eyes moving past the article about the death of a local officer in a car accident. I found the article about the colonel.

"So, do I have to work today or what?" Dixie asked through a mouthful of waffle.

"Yes." I grabbed a stick of incense and matches and strode out the kitchen door.

Bailey leapt from his dog bed and scuttled through the door before it could close. The beagle picked his way down the three porch steps to the lawn. He trotted to the Thai spirit house.

Arsen had sent my grandmother the spirit house from Thailand during his "circus," a.k.a. military, days. She'd made a practice of lighting incense there daily. I carried on in her honor.

Setting the incense in its little stand, I lit a match to the stick. When the flame caught, I waited a moment before blowing it out. A thin column of smoke spiraled lazily into the air. I turned to a blossoming white rose bush.

"I wish you were here, Gran," I whispered to it, my chest pinching. "But maybe you and the colonel are catching up now." I knelt to ruffle Bailey's fur and kissed the top of his furry head. "We all miss you."

Sliding the matchbook into the pocket of my white capris, I paced along the flower bed.

Bailey trotted beside me.

The colonel didn't grow foxglove in his yard. It was unlikely the poisoned plant had come from mine. You don't accidentally pick foxglove from a neighbor's yard, but—

My heart stopped. I stared down at a stump of plant.

Someone had snipped my foxglove.

"Oh, damn." I looked up at the A-frame cabin. The colonel had been murdered.

Next door, a curtain dropped in a second-floor window.

I swallowed and hurried into my kitchen. A vacuum cleaner roared upstairs. Dixie.

I grabbed my cell phone from where I'd left it in my private sitting room and called the sheriff.

Yes, I've got her private number. Like I said, we'd worked together in the past. Not that I had any intention of getting involved in another investigation. I'd nearly gotten killed the last time. Still, I *had* assisted in bringing a murderer to justice. Plus, this was my neighbor. And my foxglove.

The sheriff needed me.

"Witsend," Sheriff McCourt snarled. "Do I have to change my phone number?"

"Someone took some of the foxglove from my garden," I said.

There was a long silence.

"Digitalis is in foxglove," I continued. "The paper said—"

"I know what the paper said. I'll be there in ten minutes."

She was here in five. A second sheriff's SUV pulled into my gravel driveway behind her.

I met Sheriff McCourt on the front steps.

Bailey barked hysterically. He had a thing about uniforms.

I dragged the beagle into the foyer and shut him inside, then returned to the porch.

The sheriff shoved up the brim of her hat. "Where?"

Silently, I led her around the corner of the Victorian to the spot in the flowerbed. "Here."

"And you didn't cut it?"

Inside the B&B, Bailey howled.

"It hasn't even bloomed yet," I said. "Why would I cut it?"

She whirled on a blond deputy I knew slightly, Owen Denton. "Why didn't you find this yesterday?"

He winced. "You told me to search the colonel's yard, not this one."

"Use some initiative! And search the rest of this garden." She turned to glower at me. "Unless you're going to ask me for a warrant?"

I backed away, my hands raised. "No. No, no. Search away. Outside," I added hastily. I wanted to keep the wheels of justice turning. But I wasn't thrilled by the idea of turning my guests' rooms upside down without a warrant. "But you know what this means."

She squinted at me.

"It couldn't have been accidental poisoning," I continued.

Her mouth compressed.

"I mean," I said, "if foxglove got jumbled up in his herb garden, that would be one thing. But to take it from my yard—"

"Stay out of this investigation, Witsend." She growled.

She knew I really hated being told what to do. I tilted my chin down to study her. "Is this reverse psychology?"

"No."

"Because you know telling me not to do something will just make me do it." Which was manipulative, but I *still* wasn't going to do what I was told. I'd been bossed for most of my life and in minute detail by my parents. I wasn't going to let that happen again.

"Don't get involved."

Of course. It was obvious. She couldn't legitimately ask for civilian help on something like this. "So, *get* involved?"

Her nostrils flared. "Don't get involved, and keep your mouth shut."

Realization washed over me. "You knew it was murder all along! But you told the newspaper—"

"Shut!"

"Sure, sure. Shut. Got it." Minutely, I shook my head.

I didn't get it.

Of course, I wouldn't blab about the murder. But honestly, if she wanted me to help, all she had to do was stop playing these silly games and ask.

The A-frame's front door swung open. Emmery stepped onto the porch. He wore civilian clothes – jeans and a t-shirt. The latter stretched admirably across his muscular chest. "Sheriff, can I help with anything?" he shouted across the fence.

"No," she said shortly.

He leaned inside the house, as if speaking to someone.

"Well?" the sheriff said to me. "What are you waiting for? A clue to pop out of the ground like a genie?"

"Uh…"

"Go."

"Right." Feeling guilty about shutting Bailey inside, I strode around the corner of the B&B to check on him. The beagle wasn't in the foyer. Upstairs, the vacuum was still going strong.

The phone rang. I handled the call – someone making a reservation – and the front door swung open.

Emmery steered Clare into the foyer. They stopped on the other side of the wooden reception desk.

The colonel's daughter looked awful. Dark shadows bruised the skin beneath her tawny eyes. Her red hair was lank, and her t-shirt and jeans looked as if they'd been slept in.

I closed the reservation book and hurried from behind the desk. "Clare, I'm so sorry for your loss. How are you doing?"

"Terrible." She hiccupped a sob. "If it weren't for Emmery, I don't know how I'd get through this."

"We saw Denton and the sheriff in your yard," Emmery said. "What's going on?"

"They're looking for the, uh, source of whatever the colonel ate," I said.

His handsome brow furrowed. "You grow digitalis in your garden?"

"Foxglove." *Seriously*? He didn't know digitalis came from foxglove? True, he wasn't a homicide detective, but no wonder the sheriff relied on me.

"Susan," Emmery said. "We've got a big ask."

"Anything," I said. I'd meant to ask them how I could help, but when you're grieving, it's hard to come up with ideas. If Emmery wanted something now, I would do whatever it took.

The vacuum quieted above us.

He glanced up the green, carpeted steps. "Can we speak privately?"

"Of course." I led them through the kitchen and into my private sitting room. Gran had been daring here, decorating the room in a sort of modern Victorian style. Black and white toile wallpaper. A fluffy white throw rug on the wood floor. A slick ebony coffee table. I motioned them to the black velvet couch and settled myself into a matching high-backed chair.

"Clare has been going through something," he said.

"I know." I braced my elbows on my knees. "Your father—"

"Not my father," she croaked. "I can't talk about my father. Emmery means before… that."

Emmery glanced at her. "Maybe you should tell Susan the reason you contacted that medium."

Clare stared at her tennis shoes.

"How did that come about?" I asked casually.

"I saw her online last month," Clare said, "and she seemed… I don't know. Comforting. Familiar. There was a contact number on the show's website, so I emailed about my problems."

"Oh?" I asked.

She drew a shuddering breath. "Lost time. I've been… blacking out and then waking up somewhere else." Clare pulled a black throw pillow to her chest. "I think I'm going crazy."

"You're not," Emmery said stoutly. "Susan, we'd like you to help us figure out what's going on."

"Me?" Emmery was a cop. Why did he need me? Had the sheriff told him about my superior investigative skills? Because, lost time *was* a hallmark of UFO encounters, and I was sort of a local expert.

"I think I'm too close to this," he said carefully.

Ah.

Clare's laugh was cold acid. "You mean you don't want to believe I'm nuts."

He took her free hand, his gaze deepening, and my heart caught. Their love for each other was clear as June sunshine.

"You're not crazy," he said, his voice thick with emotion. "But a good cop knows when he's emotionally involved. And when you're emotionally involved, you need to step back, get another perspective." He caught my gaze. "You're my— our other perspective."

"What about Danella?" I asked. "You hired her— or invited her here to figure out what's going on."

"She has her own point of view," he said. "I'm not saying it's wrong, but we'd like someone more, er, grounded as well."

"And you want me to look at it like a UFO investigation?" I asked.

"Yes," he said.

I rubbed my forehead. "I run a UFO B&B. I mean, I know something about how UFO investigations operate—"

"That's more than we do," he said.

"But I've never actually conducted one," I finished.

"You know more than we do," Emmery said. "Will you do it? Conduct a UFO investigation?"

Huh. The sheriff had told me to stay out of the investigation into the colonel's death. But she obviously hadn't meant it. And in any case, this wasn't about murder. This was investigating UFOs.

It was almost as if Sheriff McCourt had set this up.

And I could do UFOs. "Clare, are you sure this is what you want?"

She pulled the throw pillow tighter against her chest. "I don't know what I want anymore. This is so... I don't understand why this is happening to me." She swallowed. "But I want to find out. Yes. Please help us."

"Okay then. I'll be right back." I rose and went to the foyer. A collection of UFO books and paraphernalia were for sale there on a bookshelf set into the stairs. I grabbed a booklet on UFO investigations and returned to my guests in the sitting room.

"A checklist," I said. Because good order is the foundation of all things. That quote's not mine. It's Edmund Burke. "Okay, why don't you tell me what's going on, and I'll follow up with some questions?"

"It started three months ago." Clare's knuckles whitened on the pillow.

"Do you remember the exact time and date?" I asked, pen poised above the booklet.

"Um, early February?" She looked to Emmery.

"It was the seventh," he said.

"I was home," she said. "My home. Not my father's. I was in the bedroom, about to go to sleep. Things seemed to get really bright, disorienting. And then I woke up outside."

"Where outside?" I asked.

"In the woods not far from my cabin."

"How much time had passed?" I asked.

Clare blinked rapidly. "Hours."

"And you don't remember anything?" I asked.

She shook her head.

"You said you felt disoriented," I said. "Can you tell me more?"

"It's like..." Her breathing sped, her chest rising and falling in quick gasps. She clutched Emmery's hand. "It's like the world is separating. Like the light is pulling everything apart. It makes me feel sick. And then I'm somewhere else and hours have gone by."

Worried, I glanced at Emmery.

He nodded for me to go on.

"This has happened more than once, I take it?" I asked.

"Yes. I started to keep a log." She pulled a small, spiral-bound notepad from the rear pocket of her jeans.

Emmery's eyes widened with surprise. "You didn't tell me that."

"You were the one who suggested it," she said.

"Did I?" he said. "I don't remember."

I leaned across the coffee table and took the notepad. "Can I borrow this?"

"Sure."

"This is useful," I said, "thanks. What else can you tell me?"

She blinked, swallowing, and looked away. "It's horrible. I'm not in control."

The booklet crumpled in my hands. Hastily, I smoothed it on the coffee table. "Not in control... when?" I couldn't imagine anything worse. But I didn't have to imagine. I'd been there, and my stomach churned.

"When they take me," she whispered.

"You remember someone taking you?"

"I remember flying, or the sense of flying. And I remember... It's not human. Its face... It's horrible. White and black, a giant white owl. And it's so strong."

"An owl," I said, pen hovering over the page. "Not an alien."

She leaned forward. "It's just always so bright."

Emmery winced, his hand still gripped in hers. "It's okay. Breathe."

She sucked in deep breaths, calming. "Nothing looks right," she said. "I know I'm supposed to tell you it looks like an alien, and it does have those huge, black eyes. But to me, it looks more like an owl."

"You don't have to tell me what you think I want to hear," I said. "Tell me what you remember." But owls were interesting, part of the UFO mythology.

"It was an owl," she said.

We agreed I'd come by her house in the valley to check out the site of the kidnappings.

"But it happened at my father's house too." She moaned. Beads of sweat dotted the skin above her lips. "I can't escape. They follow me, know where I am." Her expression grew strained. "And now my father... Is this my fault? Did I do this?"

"Of course not." Emmery rubbed her shoulders. "It's going to be okay. We'll figure this out."

She buried her head in his chest and sobbed.

I rose, heat spreading across my cheeks. "I'm going to make some tea. Would either of you like any?"

They nodded, and I left them alone to give them their privacy.

I filled a kettle and set it on the stove. Whatever had happened, the poor woman was a wreck.

Arsen strode into the kitchen. "Why is Owen Denton poking around your gazebo?"

"The gazebo you broke last month trying to parkour off the roof?" I whispered.

"You're still mad? But I fixed it."

"I'm not mad. I'm just…" I blew out my breath. "The foxglove that killed the colonel came from my garden."

"Damn." A series of expressions flowed across his rugged face – confusion, understanding, concern, anger. He pulled me into his arms. "I'm sorry, Sue."

I relaxed against him. No matter what life spun at me, I could always count on Arsen. I don't know why it had taken me so long to figure that out.

"And why are we whispering?" he asked.

I nodded toward the closed door to the sitting room. "Clare and Emmery are here."

His brow furrowed. "Oh. How's she doing?"

"Not good. She's asked me to help her."

"With what? Does she need help planning the funeral?"

"No. Well, she probably does, but I mean with her lost time." Quickly, I explained.

He shook his head. "I don't think that's such a good idea. She's neck-deep in a murder investigation, and that drops you into it too."

"I'm not investigating her father's death. I'm trying to figure out what's going on with Clare."

"And if the two are connected?"

Then I might be helping the sheriff after all. Just like she'd planned.

CHAPTER 5

Arsen cleared the dinner plates from the kitchen table. "Outstanding steaks, Susan." The ceiling fan pushed the scent of steak and potatoes through the air.

"Thanks." At the stove, I spooned another fresh pot of lumpy lemon curd into a jar. I couldn't serve it to guests, but I was not going to waste it.

He didn't say anything. The weight of the silence filled the kitchen, compressing the air.

I looked up. "But?"

"I still think you should reconsider this UFO investigation for Clare. These people are involved in a murder." Arsen pushed the window over the sink further open.

I rested the rubber spatula in the saucepan. "*I'm* involved in the colonel's murder. I was there when the colonel died." And he'd been a friend of Gran's. "He was a good neighbor," I said quietly, "even if he was a little gruff."

"A little?"

Bailey rested his head on my foot and whuffed.

"Okay, he was Billy Goats-level gruff," I admitted. "But he wasn't a bad guy. Besides, the sheriff needs me. I've already gathered all sorts of information she doesn't have access to." And I probably should give it to her.

He winced. "Are you sure the sheriff wants your help?"

"Of course. You know she's out of her depth when it comes to UFO-related incidents. Not that I blame her."

"It's just that you and Dixie were never big fans of authority figures."

"And?"

"And I'm wondering if you helping isn't a way to sort of control things."

The spoon tipped, clattering onto the floor. Yellow droplets splattered the blue-painted cupboards and linoleum floor.

Bailey leapt from his dog bed and hurried to examine the mess.

"What?" I stooped and wiped up the lemon curd with a damp cloth before Bailey could get in more than a few licks. "No way. Sheriff McCourt and I are friends. Friends help friends." I smiled and returned to my seat at the kitchen table. Arsen was amazing, and he knew a lot about PTSD, but he was no psychologist. But that was okay. We didn't all know our limits, and that just made us stretch a little.

Arsen returned to the small, round table and sat across from me. "I'm not going to talk you out of this, am I?"

I laid a hand atop his, tanned and calloused from splitting wood.

"After someone dies," I said, "everyone asks the survivors if they can do anything to help. But no one really knows how."

He nodded.

"I can do this," I said. "I can help Clare, and the sheriff too."

"Then I'll help you."

I smiled, my heart warming. "I was hoping you'd say that. And not just because of your extensive collection of spyware." Arsen had installed all the new high-tech locks at Wits' End.

"So, what's the plan?"

"Thank you for asking." I hurried into the sitting room and returned with a tabbed three-ring binder.

He cocked his head. "That's not your planner."

"I decided I needed a separate planner for our investigation." I'd combined forms, calendars, checklists and standard operating procedures into a UFO investigation toolkit.

His mouth quirked.

"I've color-coded the times and dates of Clare's lost-time experiences," I continued. "And I've started comparing them against weather data for those nights. I've also checked with the FAA about flights over her cabin."

"And were there any?" he asked.

"No." Which didn't prove anything, but it was good data to have.

He took the binder and flipped through it. Arsen whistled. "I've seen police murder books that aren't this organized."

"When did you see a murder book?" I asked, indignant. If the sheriff was sharing her murder book with Arsen—

"Different country." He handed me the book. "What else?"

"Dixie's reviewing her records for any strange radio activity," I said, mollified. "But what we really need to do—"

A woman's long scream rent the air.

Bailey leapt to his feet. He stared at the porch door.

Our heads whipped towards each other.

"That came from outside," he said.

I gripped the folder to my chest. "Clare."

He strode from the kitchen and onto the porch.

Bailey and I followed.

Clare bulleted from the front door of the colonel's A-frame. Her red hair streamed behind her like a comet.

Emmery charged from the cabin. He caught her in his arms.

She struggled briefly and went limp against his body. Clare pointed at the sky. "They're back! They're back. Oh, God, they're back."

I looked up and sucked in a sharp breath.

Circles of lights rippled across purple, bubbling clouds. The lights flickered, moving weirdly across the clouds, their undersides like grape clusters. The effect was uncanny. I shook my head, drawing backward, toward the open kitchen door.

"Mammatus clouds." Arsen watched Clare and Emmery through narrowed eyes. "Strange. There were no thunderstorms predicted."

His words snapped sense into me, and I straightened. There was nothing supernatural about the evening sky. I trotted down the steps. "It's okay!" I shouted across the picket fence. "They're searchlights."

Clare pressed her forehead to Emmery's chest. "Why? Why are they here?" The word was a bitter shriek, raising the hairs on my arms.

Bailey howled a response.

"The lights must be from that circus," I called. But I didn't think that was what she'd really been asking. Clare still believed they were UFOs, and uneasy sympathy twisted inside me. I knew what it was to panic. I knew that unspooling that began with a tightening in the chest. I knew the quick breath, the dizziness, the unreasoning fear.

"Susan's right." Emmery's voice was soothing. "Spotlights on clouds. That's all they are. You're safe. We're safe."

Shaking, she allowed Emmery to tug her gently back into the house.

"Good Lord," I muttered. "She's scared out of her wits."

Arsen's expression hardened. "She's not stable."

"We need to clear this up fast."

"Or stay out of it."

I gripped the folder more tightly. "You said you'd help me."

"I will." His face creased with frustration. "I will. But I want to be with you whenever you're with her."

My muscles relaxed. I got where Arsen was coming from. But I couldn't leave Clare and Emmery high and dry.

A high-pitched whistle cut the air, and we started. Bailey raced for the front of the yard.

"What now?" Arsen said.

We hurried around the corner of the Victorian and to the street. Bailey dawdled by the fence. He knew he wasn't supposed to go into the street unless he was on a leash.

My two stoner neighbors across the street slouched in their driveway. One pointed at the sky with his beer can.

"It's like a giant lava lamp," Dunk crowed. He brandished his beer higher, spilling some on his blond hair.

His shirtless friend, Finn, laughed. "Aliens, man!"

I groaned. Just what we needed. An invasion party.

"I wish California had never legalized weed." Arsen eyed them, his mouth compressing.

"The legal status never stopped them before," I said glumly.

"Don't get me wrong," Arsen said. "I'm a libertarian on these issues. Live and let live is my motto. But they're just so… irritating."

Irritating, but harmless. But I tugged at the collar of my blouse, a slight chill touching the back of my neck.

"Hey, Susan," Finn called, scratching his bare stomach. "We're being invaded! Think there are any sexy alien babes in those ships?"

I rolled my eyes. "They're spotlights."

"Alien spotlights," Finn agreed, nodding.

"From the circus," I shouted across the road.

"From the alien circus," Dunk said.

"Forget it," Arsen said. "Their brains are baked."

He was probably right. Finn and Dunk were willing to believe whatever was fun. It wasn't like anyone with sense would assume an alien invasion. Sure, Clare had panicked, but that was only because of her lost-time episodes.

Uneasy, I shifted the binder in my arms.

Arsen, Bailey and I returned to my kitchen.

"Are you all right?" Arsen poured himself a cup of coffee. "You're awfully quiet."

"I was thinking about Clare."

"I'm not sure we'll ever have enough evidence to convince her there are no aliens."

I didn't respond. This was Doyle, where a pub and everyone inside had vanished, reappearing months later minus the pub. Those who'd come back had no memories of where they'd been or what had happened.

The sheriff claimed it had been caused by a gas leak, but I wasn't so sure. I wasn't so sure aliens were responsible either. Like I said, I was agnostic.

He plucked an empty cup from a hook beneath a wooden shelf. "Wait. You don't think she's really the victim of alien abductions?"

"There have been a lot of missing persons cases in Doyle," I said.

Arsen took the Disappeared and their problems seriously, but not alien abductions. I still wasn't sure what I believed. But I didn't want to be shoehorned into an opinion.

He poured a cup and handed it to me. "I don't think it's going to help Clare if she believes aliens are her problem."

"I'm not trying to prove aliens are abducting her. I'm trying to find out what's going on, whatever that may be."

"But let's face it, your investigation program is all about the aliens."

"Yes, but that also includes disproving alien interference." I rubbed my thumb against the rim of the mug. "But I guess I *am* a little worried our investigation will make things worse." What if Clare was insane and had killed her father?

"Things are going to resolve themselves one way or another," he said slowly. "And you're smart enough and caring enough not to make things worse. I just wanted to make sure we were on the same page."

I sighed. "We are."

We strolled into my sitting area, and I curled up against Arsen on the black velvet couch.

He looped a muscular arm around my shoulders. "Now," he murmured into my hair, "tell me about your plan."

"Is that really what you want to do?" I teased. "Plan?"

"We could talk about meeting your parents."

I tried not to stiffen. "Let me rephrase that. Is talking really what you want to do?"

"Hm. Good point." He pulled me closer and brushed his lips against mine.

He felt so *right*, and a shiver of excitement raced through my veins. He may not understand psychology, or my relationship with the sheriff, but he was perfect in every other respect.

Someone yelled outside, and I looked up.

Gently, he tugged my chin down, my lips to his. "Forget it," he murmured.

We kissed, his hands sliding to my hips. Time slowed. My heart thumped, my breath coming in gasps.

A door slammed hard enough to rattle the crystal chandelier over the coffee table.

"Unbelievable." Danella's voice rose. "That woman is outrageous. She has no right keeping me away!"

I untangled myself and smoothed my blouse. "I've got to…"

He groaned and flopped back on the couch. "Go."

I hurried through the kitchen and into the foyer. Danella paced in front of her two crewmen. "And you were no help at all."

I cleared my throat. "What's going on?" I asked in a low voice. "I could hear you in my rooms." I glanced up the stairs. *And so can all the other guests.*

The older woman flushed. "I'm sorry, but I just can't believe that woman."

"What woman?"

"Marion. Clare's stepmother. She threw me out," she hissed.

My limbs relaxed. Maybe I *wouldn't* have to deal with noise complaints tomorrow. "I didn't realize you were still filming there."

The medium flipped back her long, graying ponytail. "We weren't filming *people*. I simply wanted to set up cameras to film the vortexes."

"The vortexes?" I asked.

"Where the interdimensional aliens come through. And Marion threw me out! Can I help it if one is in her bedroom?"

Because who wouldn't want to hear about interdimensional portals in their bedroom? I gripped my hands behind my back. "I'm sure Marion's under a lot of stress right now. Her husband *was* murdered."

Mahir and Bob crept up the stairs to their rooms.

The medium leaned closer. "That's the thing. I believe she killed him."

"You... what?" I asked, taken aback.

"I can sense his spirit there, at the cabin. He's trying to tell me something. I made the mistake of telling *her*, and that's when she insisted we leave the house. Clare was very upset. My— She didn't want me to leave, I could tell."

"Is that when Clare ran out of the house?"

"No, that was later, when I was upstairs trying to organize the cameras. Then Clare saw those horrible clouds." She shuddered. "And then Marion told me her bedroom was off limits."

"Did you tell Clare about her father's, er, spirit?"

"Of course I did. Clare's still in terrible danger. She needs to be careful. I told her that her poor father is trying so hard to tell her something, but he's still too weak. It's difficult for spirits immediately after they cross over. This is a confusing period. But a secret is weighing on his conscience, and he won't rest until he can tell it. Perhaps in a few weeks, he'll be ready to talk. I just hope it isn't too late."

"How did Clare take that?"

"How would *you* take it? Of course she was upset. Emmery had to take her to her room. I've put crystal wards at the corners and encircled the entire room in salt. The problem is, interdimensionals are not my specialty."

No wonder Marion had chucked her out. Marion and I had never been close. Her stand on rooftop UFOs had made us adversaries. But tonight, she had my sympathies.

"Clare is right to fear the clouds," Marion said.

"They're mammatus clouds, up-lit by searchlights from the circus."

She looked me in the eyes. "*Are* they? Is that *all* they are?"

I bit my bottom lip and didn't respond. Mammatus clouds were a real thing. Arsen knew his clouds. But this was Doyle.

"They're omens," she continued. "Whatever is happening isn't done with us."

It wasn't true. Omens in the clouds? But a shiver whisked up my spine.

"Done with what?" a woman said from behind me.

I turned and yelped.

A tall, olive-skinned woman in a black business suit loomed over me. Her blue-black hair was twisted into a neat bun. She stared, her dark brown eyes expressionless, fathomless.

I gulped. *Eeep.* I knew this woman. She was an FBI agent. I'd hoped to never see her again.

I smiled unevenly. "Agent Manaj! You— You startled me."

Danella stuck out her hand. "I'm Danella."

The agent's gaze flicked to her outstretched hand. She didn't move to take it. "I know who you are."

"Oh. Well. I'll just be going then." The medium scampered upstairs.

"This is a surprise," I said. Last year, she'd taken over the murder investigation of Sheriff McCourt's ex. Since he'd died in Wits' End, it had been more than a little awkward. But Manaj's real interest had never been murder.

It was UFOs.

"I need a room," she said.

Oh, damn. "Do you have a reservation?"

"You know I don't." She stooped and picked up her plain, black suitcase. "I'll take room seven."

Which was conveniently empty, but how had she known that?

Mouth dry, I rummaged in the desk for a new key and ran it through the key-imprinting thingy. "Here you go."

She studied the plastic key card. "I see you've improved your security. Let's hope it's good enough."

My gaze followed her up the stairs. Good enough? Good enough for what?

CHAPTER 6

Arsen left, and Bailey and I wandered out to the darkened side yard. The searchlights still zipped across the sky, but the clouds no longer bubbled. They were just normal clouds again, blotting out the light of the stars.

I picked up the beagle's octopus toy. The sheriff's department had sadly decided not to confiscate it in their search for clues. I couldn't blame them. It was so mangy, even I didn't like touching its matted blue fur.

I threw it toward the gazebo, silhouetted against the hillside.

Collar jingling, Bailey bounded after the stuffed toy. The dog vanished into the gloom.

A car's tires sounded on the street outside, and my head whipped toward the sound. It was probably nothing. Just a neighbor. But I strode to the front of the yard, my muscles taut.

Rufus Berghoff's Mercedes glided past and pulled into his driveway.

I glanced back at the Victorian's lit windows. Then I crossed the street and walked to Rufus's driveway.

The lawyer grunted and heaved himself from the low car.

"Hi, Rufus," I said.

"Susan." He shifted the briefcase beneath his arm. "Has something else happened?"

I needed some excuse to talk to him, but I didn't want to throw Clare under the bus. "An FBI agent has checked into Wits' End. In other news, the guys across the street are convinced the searchlights are UFOs." I jerked my head upward, toward the circles of light sweeping across the clouds.

He snorted. "Potheads."

"Did you see the mammatus clouds earlier?"

"What? No. Really? Here? Don't those only show up when there's a tornado or something?"

"Not this time." I shifted my weight. "I've never seen anything like them before."

"There's a lot you haven't seen before. And I'm sure I haven't either," he added hastily. "But ultimately, clouds are clouds."

Not according to Danella. "You don't think others might believe UFOs are on their way?" I jammed my hands in my pockets. "People seem on edge. Spence Shelton's fight—"

"Spence is an idiot."

"I wouldn't say idiot, but his interest in aliens can't be healthy."

He snorted. "Says the woman with the UFO in her roof."

"And people are asking about One-armed Frank's missing cows."

"People? Or that fool Tom Tarrant?"

"And the colonel's death hasn't helped matters," I persisted.

"The colonel was asking for it." He eyed me. "Is the FBI involved in the case?"

Asking for it? "I don't know. She didn't say."

"She?"

"Agent Manaj."

He rolled his eyes. "Not that woman again. When is she going to leave Doyle alone? It was bad enough she wasn't able to figure out what happened to the Disappeared. But she keeps coming back."

"Well, the colonel is dead—"

"She's here hunting little green men, not the colonel's killer. But you know what people will say. The Colonel worked at Area 51, died by poison, and an FBI agent shows up? They'll connect the dots and come up with a conspiracy."

"They?"

"Doyle." He rubbed his cheek, his bristles making scratching sounds. "Did she ask about me?"

"No. Agent Manaj only checked in a few minutes ago."

He raised his brows. "I suppose you told her about my argument with the colonel, Miss Nosypants?"

"I didn't." And that's *Ms.* Nosypants. I jerked down the cuff of my blouse. "And I'm not nosy."

He chuckled. "Oh? You're worse than old Mrs. Steinberg. You stick your nose into everything."

"Only the crimes," I said, offended. And it wasn't my fault the sheriff had involved me in her cases. "Besides, I think it's safer to know what's going on."

"Keep telling yourself that." He snorted. "Look, I know you heard the Colonel and I arguing. But it was about nothing."

"Then why were you arguing?"

"Because I've been his lawyer for years, and not once has he let me in on any of his investments. I don't need the money, but it's damned insulting."

"I didn't know the colonel was an investor."

"How do you think he lived like this on an Air Force pension?" He motioned to the shingled cabin.

The Fitzgeralds' cabin wasn't exactly luxurious. But California prices *were* starting to pinch, even in the hinterlands like Doyle.

"He was smart," the lawyer continued, "I'll give him that. Fitzgerald saved his pennies and invested them in commercial real estate. But he was a greedy crook."

My breath hitched. "Crook?"

He ran his hand over his smooth head. "Figure of speech. I didn't mean—" He exhaled and thunked his briefcase against his thigh. "I'm just worried about Clare and my son. It was a mistake for her to move back with her father. Things for her only got worse."

"I'm worried too," I admitted.

"She's always been a fragile free spirit. When she moved into her own place, she seemed to blossom. Emmery fell in love with that Clare. And then she came home, under the colonel's thumb, and everything changed."

I rubbed the back of my neck. Clare might be a free spirit, but she hadn't struck me as a Victorian fainting lady. At least, I didn't think she'd been before her visions of abductions and aliens. "I thought she returned to the colonel's because of the, er—"

"Lost time?" He laughed shortly. "You're right about one thing, people *are* on edge. It's all this alien foolishness. Too many people are willing to believe." He tapped his temple. "It messes with their minds. And like I said, Clare was always vulnerable."

I tilted my head, studying him. A crack opened in the clouds, and a thin stream of moonlight shone through. "You've known her long? I thought you only moved here a few years ago?" And the Fitzgeralds weren't Doyle natives either.

"I did. I had a practice in Angels Camp before."

I nodded. Angels Camp was a larger town west of Doyle. It made sense that the Colonel had found a lawyer there after he'd left the Air Force. "I remember when he moved here."

"About ten years ago." He squinted. "I followed him three years back, and Emmery moved here last year." He grinned. "Funny thing. He thought Angels Camp was too small. But then he met Clare one day when he'd come to visit me. Suddenly, tiny Doyle was the perfect place to become a cop."

"Love will do that to you." I smiled. It was why Arsen had returned. Or so he'd claimed.

"Well, have a good evening." He glanced at Wits' End, then turned and strode into his low house.

I crossed the court. Was Rufus right? Had Clare always been tightly strung? Did it matter?

Octopus toy clenched in his mouth, Bailey met me at the end of the Wits' End driveway. The beagle shook his head, the legs of the octopus whacking him in the face.

Bailey and I played a brief game of tug-of-war. He won. Following the beagle up the porch steps, I went to bed and dreamed of dancing lemons. They morphed into yellow lights that zipped through my kitchen window and vanished in a bruise-colored sky.

*****

The alarm on my phone jerked me to sitting. Wincing, I smacked it off. Five o'clock. My gran's cherry coffee cake was delicious, but I hated getting up this early to bake.

Yawning, I swung my feet out of bed and flipped the light switch.

Nothing happened.

Annoyed, I flipped it a few more times.

Still no power.

Feeling my way to the door, my toe caught on a soft object, and I stumbled. Bailey yipped a protest.

"Sorry," I muttered and opened the door.

Bailey darted between my legs and into the sitting room.

I flipped the wall switch. The lights did not go on, and I frowned. They were on a different fuse than my bedroom. Had a storm last night knocked out the power?

Bailey weaving between my feet, I fumbled to the velvet couch. I grasped its soft back and looked out the window. The streetlights outside sent yellow cones of light toward the ground.

"Stay," I commanded.

Bailey sat.

Returning to my bedroom, I found a robe and flashlight. I made my way to the fuse box in the laundry room. Its metal door hung ajar.

I pulled it wider and studied the switches.

Weird. None of the fuses had flipped. They were all neatly aligned on the same side.

Experimentally, I pushed one to the other side.

A faint light flowed through the open door, and I stuck my head out. The chandelier now blazed in my private sitting room.

My five-AM brain and I stared at the fuse box. The fuses couldn't have all blown at the same time.

I flipped the kitchen fuse, then reached around the door and turned on the light there.

The overhead lamp illuminated the gleaming stove, the subway tiles, the blue shelves.

Belly knotting, I again shined my flashlight into the fuse box. When a fuse blew, the switches usually slipped a little more than halfway back. These switches were all the way back.

Someone had flipped them.

All sorts of unpleasant possibilities rocketed through my mind. Had a guest done this? Or had someone broken in? But I'd locked the exterior doors. I was sure of it.

Pulse rabbiting, I turned the rest of the switches to the "on" position.

I checked the porch and front doors. They were locked, and the new keypad on the front door glowed. Arsen had told me if the power went out, a battery kept the keypad running. That way, people could still use their key cards.

No one without a key could have gotten inside.

I turned, biting my lip, and craned my neck toward the stairs.

It was an inside job.

CHAPTER 7

Leaving Bailey outside, I rolled up the sleeves of my robe, twisted my hair into a bun, and started on the cherry coffee cake.

Baking didn't get my mind off the fuse box.

Turning the power off seemed silly, childish. What was the point? All I had to do is exactly what I'd done – turn it back on again.

But it had happened in the room next to the one where I'd been sleeping. That was disturbing.

I glanced out the kitchen window. In the pre-dawn light, Bailey sniffed around a rosebush.

I covered the dough and set it to rise near the oven. Its clock blinked 3:39. Ergo, the power must have gone off some time before that. I'd been up, what? Twenty minutes? Thirty?

Irritated with myself, I reset the time. I should have checked the clock sooner.

Bailey gave a soft yip at the kitchen door.

I started. Muttering a curse, I let him inside.

The beagle sat near the butcher block counter and waited for me to drop something interesting.

"Forget it," I said. "Coffee cake isn't for dogs."

I refreshed his dog bowls and returned to my heavy thinking.

Rinsing a bowl, I set it in the dishwasher. Had Danella or one of her crew members turned off the power to create some video drama? I couldn't imagine any other of my guests as the culprits. The honeymooning couple had barely left their room. The UFO hunters who occupied two of my other rooms had been here several times before. We'd become friends. They weren't the type to mess about with fuse boxes.

I returned to my room to shower and change.

A floorboard creaked above me, and my muscles twitched. *Enough.* I was in an old house full of guests. I had nothing to worry about.

Still gnawing over the mysterious switch-flipper, I returned to the kitchen. I covered the pans with clean dishcloths and set them aside to rise.

Bailey whined.

"That behavior's not attractive in a man," I warned him.

I peered at the breakfast checklist on the refrigerator door and nodded. I was on schedule. There was plenty of time for detecting.

Striding into my black-and-white sitting room, I booted up my laptop. I made myself comfortable on the velvet couch and read about Danella.

Danella became aware of her psychic abilities when she was a teenager tormented by poltergeists. This experience, and what may have been her own unwitting psychic role in it, sparked her interest in psychic phenomena.

She was mentored by world-renowned psychic Julie V. Anderson, and now she uses her abilities to communicate with the dead. Parapsychologists and skeptics have tested and studied Danella's abilities. She has conducted hundreds of investigations and house clearings.

I printed the article and clipped it behind the *suspects* tab I'd added to my investigation binder. (Color code: orange, for possible threat). A threat that might be in my home.

The gray shadow wrapped a tentacle around my ribs, squeezing. I slowed my breaths. I was fine. I could handle this.

Since I didn't understand the bit about poltergeist phenomena, I looked that up too. Poltergeists, or "noisy spirits," were believed to be generated by the psychic energy of teenage girls. Or, they were frauds perpetuated by attention-seeking teens.

I shifted on the black couch.

If Danella had pulled a poltergeist stunt when she was a teen, fiddling with a fuse box could be right up her alley.

Since I was online anyway, I searched for the colonel's name. Some background on him might help my UFO investigation.

But after twenty minutes of fruitless searching, I realized there was nothing. At all.

I jammed up the sleeves of my floral-print blouse and leaned closer to the screen. How did someone go through life without leaving some sort of online trail? The colonel wasn't even included in those stupid "people search" sites.

It was weird.

Like, UFO-conspiracy-level weird.

I typed in Clare's name.

She'd posted artistic photos of the mountains and her boyfriend, Emmery, on her accounts. I smiled at a field of wildflowers, recognizing the spot. She had real talent.

Emmery wasn't on social media, but I knew a lot of cops avoided it. It made me wonder. If law enforcement stayed away from social media, why was anyone else on it? Unfortunately, I had to be to promote Wits' End, but that was business.

Emmery was mentioned in a brief article about new recruits to the sheriff's station. Otherwise, he'd kept a low profile as well.

So much for my online investigatory powers.

But I printed that out, too, and added it to my binder.

I closed the computer and returned to the business of breakfast. Soon, bacon was crackling in the frying pans. Its scent mingled with the baking sugar and cherries.

I set the table in the breakfast room and cracked open one of the windows. Fresh, alpine air stirred the blue-patterned curtains, and I inhaled. I loved Doyle, and I sent a silent thank you to my grandmother for making this life possible.

I arranged the coffeecakes on the sideboard, and Danella wandered into the breakfast room.

She yawned and stretched. "Gotta love this mountain air."

"How'd you sleep?" I asked.

"Like a rock. You?"

I relit the candle beneath the bacon's chafing dish. The flame wavered between my fingers, but at least my voice was steady. "So well that I didn't notice when someone turned off the power last night."

Her eyes widened. "Turned off?"

"They flipped all the breaker switches in the fuse box."

"Why would someone do that?"

"I don't know." I folded my arms over my chest, half regretting I'd said anything. It wasn't like she'd admit it if she was guilty. And if she was innocent, now she had more excitement for her death vortex videos. "What do you think?" I asked.

"I think it's a very silly prank." The lines on her forehead deepened. "But I *have* been known to attract poltergeist activity."

Uh, huh. "Could one of your crew have done it to amp up the drama?" I asked bluntly.

"What? No! They'd never do something like that."

Right. Sure.

A door opened and banged shut.

Arsen breezed into the breakfast room in his usual khakis and security polo.

I relaxed a little, my heart lightening.

"Is that your gran's cherry coffee cake?" He kissed my cheek, his hand on my arm.

"Yes." I bit off the word, glancing at Danella.

"Something wrong?" He slid a piece of cake onto his plate and perused the steaming chafing dishes.

"Someone turned off our power last night."

He turned and laid the plate on the white tablecloth. His expression hardened. "Whoa. How? Not the fuse box?"

I nodded.

"That's in your private space," he said.

I grimaced. "And you told me I should put a lock on the kitchen door, I know." But having locks on inside doors in my own house seemed like prison. Who wanted that?

Abandoning the food, Arsen strode from the breakfast room.

"He's cute," Danella said.

"Mm." I followed him into the foyer. Arsen's solid presence was too comforting to leave. And I loved watching him do his security thing.

He knelt, examining the front door.

"Arsen, it must have been a guest." I wasn't sure if I wanted him to tell me if I was right or wrong. Which was worse?

"Maybe," he said. "But it would have to be a pretty ballsy guest to try that under the nose of you and an FBI agent. This lock hasn't been tampered with."

He walked into the kitchen, and I trailed after him. Arsen performed the same examination on the porch door. "This one looks okay too. Can I borrow your computer?"

"Sure. It's in the parlor." Perplexed, I followed him into the black-and-white room.

He tapped away on my computer keyboard and grunted. "You need a better password."

But then how would I remember it? Passwords were the one thing you weren't supposed to write down. "What are you doing?"

"Checking the security logs for your doors."

Logs? "You can do that?"

"I showed you how when we installed the system. Don't you remember?"

My face heated. "Um, no." Honestly, I never thought I'd need the system. Which in retrospect, probably hadn't been that smart. Doyle did have an unusual amount of disappearances. And murders.

He spun the laptop on the coffee table to face me. "The front door was open between 12:32 and 2:50 AM. It opened again at 3:13 and closed less than a minute afterward."

"What?" My scalp tingled with alarm. How could it have been hanging open that long? "A guest must have left it ajar."

"Maybe." He strode from the kitchen, and I trailed after him.

Arsen opened the front door and peered into its latch strike. He dug his finger inside the metal gap and pulled out a fragment of paper.

"What is it?" I asked.

"Paper."

"I know it's paper, but..." How did paper get in there?

"Someone jammed the lock with paper to keep it open." He scraped a hand through his thick, brown hair. "This is serious, Susan."

I swallowed.

"I told you—" he began.

"To replace the door with one that closes automatically," I said. "Yes.

You've convinced me." But again, why mess with my fuse box? Why me? What had *I* done?

At least this cleared any of my guests – they were already inside and had keys. Unless a guest had jammed the door so someone else could come inside.

Nausea spiraled through me. It was a stupid prank. No one had been hurt. No damage had been done. But I'd been vulnerable. We all had. So many things could have gone wrong.

A muscle jumped along Arsen's jaw. "I'm sorry. I hate being the I-told-you-so guy. But I hate a hell of a lot more that someone was in your private space while you were sleeping."

"It was just a prank," I said uneasily. "It could have been worse."

"That's what terrifies me. I'm getting you a new door today, and I'm staying over tonight."

Arsen, terrified? My hands went clammy, and I nodded. It would be fine. Arsen would be here, and it was only a precaution.

I was safe.

Totally safe.

CHAPTER 8

I pressed my knuckles into my aching back and arched, stretching. Cleaning was my least favorite part of the B&B gig.

I examined the sparkling bathroom. But there was a certain satisfaction to putting things in order. The Victorian fixtures gleamed, every towel hanging with military precision.

The vacuum fell silent in the bedroom outside.

"Done," Dixie called. "And I'm outta here."

"Wait." I trotted into the bedroom.

My cousin wrapped the vacuum cord around the hooks in its stand.

I twined my fingers together. "Um, there's something you should know."

"You're going to buy a new vacuum?"

"No. We have a new guest. Agent Manaj."

She stiffened, her green-tipped hair quivering, and turned to me. "Agent Manaj. My arch enemy in the FBI, a Man in Black—"

"Woman in Black." *Arch enemy?*

"The woman who's probably bugging my phone – all our phones – is staying at Wits' End?"

I had no idea where to start unpacking all that. I unknotted my fingers and slipped my hands into my pockets. "Um, I really don't think she's bugging our phones."

"Yeah. You wouldn't. When did she check in?"

"Last night."

"And you're only telling me now? What the hell? How long is she staying?"

"She didn't really say." But she had given me a credit card, so at least I knew I'd get paid.

Dixie scowled. "And you didn't ask. She's got to be here about the colonel." She gnawed her bottom lip. "I suppose when an Air Force officer is murdered, the feds would get involved. He must have known all sorts of top-secret stuff."

"Right. Like you said, he worked at Area 51." UFO fanatics believed the military stored the remains of UFOs in this not-so-secret Nevada base.

She waved a hand dismissively. "A smokescreen. But he might have known something. I mean, it is a little strange that he'd retire in Doyle. We're America's alien-abduction hot spot."

"Doyle's a great place to retire. We've got that new county hospital."

"A hospital isn't any help when you've been abducted. Or maybe she's here because…"

"What? Why?"

"I need to think." Abandoning the vacuum, she wandered downstairs.

"Okay, thanks!" I called.

That had gone better than expected.

I gathered the cleaning supplies, double-checking I hadn't forgotten any, and stored them in the narrow hallway closet. It was time for Lemon Curd, Round Three. I hustled downstairs to the kitchen. Maybe if I used a double boiler…?

I zested. I squeezed. I whisked. I double-boiled. The steam broiled my face and curled my bangs. Above me, the ceiling fan rotated uselessly.

Curdled egg floated to the top of the yellow liquid. "Dammit!"

The front door clicked open. I walked to the kitchen door and leaned out.

Arsen strode into the foyer, a gray duffel bag slung over one broad shoulder. He looked up, caught my eye, and grinned. "I've brought some equipment for our investigation."

"Does it include a lemon de-curder?"

He shot me a puzzled look and pulled me in for a quick kiss. "Kitchen?"

I sighed. The scene of another failure. "Why not?"

He walked past me and through the swinging door.

Bailey looked up from his dog bed, decided no food was forthcoming, and laid down his head.

Arsen unzipped the duffel bag on the kitchen table. "You're going to love these." He handed me a pair of goggles attached to plastic headgear.

I tried to maintain my cool and professional detachment and not squeal with excitement. "Are these—?"

"Infrared goggles."

Okay, those *were* cool.

He leered. "I know what you like."

He really did. What other boyfriend would bring infrared goggles for an alien hunt? "I was serious about the lemon de-curder." Who knew what he could turn up? The man was a magician.

"No idea what that is." He handed me a walkie talkie. "But I got you this, because cell signals can get iffy."

"No argument there." There was only one cell provider that really worked in Doyle. But every mountain valley had its quirks.

I pulled what looked like a cordless vacuum from the open bag. "What's this?"

Gently, he pried it from my hands. "A net gun. I'll manage that."

"Net gun?" I quirked a brow. "Do you think we're going to capture an alien?"

"Someone broke into Wit's End. I want to be prepared. This is for you."

He handed me a laser pointer.

I flipped it on and scanned a green dot across the cupboard doors. "Neat. I can use this in my next *History of Doyle Abductions* presentation." Every Friday night at eight o'clock.

"That's not any old laser pointer. It's a photonic disruptor. Shine it in an attacker's eyes to disorient them. The good news is it won't cause any permanent damage to their sight."

"How admirably ethical. But will it work on aliens?"

"That's for Wits' End, not for alien hunting. And speaking of defense…" He set down the weapon and pulled a thick vest from the bag. "Try this on." He handed it to me.

I staggered. The thing weighed a ton. "Is this a bullet proof vest?" Because it didn't look like the ones the cops wore on TV.

"Armor plated." He helped me into it. "That will stop an automatic weapon."

I squirmed. The vest's collar jammed up under my chin. "Automatic…"

He hitched a wide, nylon belt around my waist and clipped the walkie and goggles to it. "For the equipment." He slipped the laser thing into a pocket on my vest and patted it.

The vest was smothering, hot, unwieldy. "I don't think we'll come under automatic weapons fire," I said weakly. Sweat trickled down my back in the sweltering kitchen.

"You never know." He zipped the vest. Pulling a heavy-duty flashlight from the canvas bag, he dropped that into another beltloop. "That will double as a weapon. Hey, did you get a chance to talk to your parents?"

My breathing quickened, and not in a good way. The vest was too tight. "Arsen—"

"It's starting to feel impolite. I should have introduced myself to them by now." He snapped a canteen to my belt and slid a granola bar into another pocket.

I struggled with the zipper. Hidden in the bulky vest, the tab evaded my grip. "Arsen—"

"Or if you don't want to go to San Francisco, we can invite them here. I can take them hiking."

I staggered, ricocheting off the kitchen table. Its legs screeched against the floor.

Bailey looked up, alarmed.

"Arsen!"

"What's wrong?" he asked.

"This is too much." I gasped. "Get me out of this thing."

He unzipped me. The vest fell to the floor with a clunk.

Bailey leapt to his feet and growled at it.

"I don't need all this." I sucked in lungfuls of air. "No one's going to be shooting at me."

"But—"

"No vests," I snapped, then bit my lip. Arsen was trying to protect me. What was my problem? Aside from potential smothering by vest?

"Okay, sorry." He stepped backward, his palms raised in surrender. "Maybe I did get a little carried away. I just want you to be safe. But you're right. The odds of automatic weapons fire are low. Now the Kevlar vests are much lighter—"

"Let's get back to basics, by which I mean a plan."

He scraped back a chair and sat at the table. "Great. What's our strategy?" He folded his hands on the round table and watched me attentively.

It was obvious what he was doing.

He knew I had control issues. Maybe, someday, I'd get over them. But for now, he was letting me take charge.

It was... sweet.

And I hated to admit it, but Arsen's spyware had given me an idea.

"What?" Arsen asked.

"Clare's experiences have happened at night, when the moon is new or obscured. Tonight's another cloudy night. I think we should stake her out. With her permission, of course," I added quickly.

He nodded. "Sounds good."

"And we can use your equipment."

He grinned. "Even better."

I called Clare. She answered on the second ring. "Hello?" she asked breathlessly. "Susan?"

"Hi, Clare. How are you feeling?"

"After last night's hysteria, you mean?" She laughed shortly. "I'm not screaming my head off at funny clouds anymore."

I winced. How to respond to that? "If it's okay with you, Arsen and I would like to start our UFO investigation tonight." I explained our plan.

"Oh, that's wonderful. I feel a little strange staying out here alone again."

"Alone?" I asked, alarmed. "Aren't you with your stepmother?"

"No, I've moved back into my own place. I just couldn't stay at Dad's anymore after... after what happened. When can you come?"

We made arrangements for Arsen and me to arrive before it got too dark, and I hung up.

"We're all set," I said.

He checked his dive watch. "Great. That gives us five hours." He stood. "I'll be back at six." He hesitated. "I've been thinking about the weekend. Maybe we could make a thing of it, go to San Francisco and Napa?"

My eyes narrowed. "San Francisco?"

"So, we can stop in and see your parents."

My spine fossilized. "I'm pretty sure they've got plans."

"That's fine. We could do it another weekend."

Suddenly it felt like I was in that damned vest again. "Or we could go somewhere else," I said. "What about south to Monterey or Santa Barbara?"

He gave me a long look. "Or we could do that. I'll see you tonight." He kissed me, long and lingering, and he walked from the kitchen.

I blew out my breath. Another bullet, dodged.

For now.

And I still had five whole hours to try to defeat the mighty curd.

*****

Clare lived in a one-story, dark-wood cabin with a gently sloping roof. Her dusty Honda sat parked in the carport.

Arsen and I sat beside each other on the blue sectional sofa. Clare slouched in the matching chair opposite. A blue enamel coffee pot and matching cups filled with the steaming liquid sat on the coffee table between us.

I pushed a jar of lemon curd across the table. "Honestly," I gabbled, unsure of appropriate small talk. "You should try it. It took me forever to figure out the secret, but it's so easy. You don't combine the ingredients on the stove. Oh, no. That's wrong. The recipes lie." The curd-loving jerks.

"Uh, Susan?" Arsen said.

"You cream the butter and sugar in a bowl until fluffy." I bent and pulled the binder out of my backpack. "And then you slowly beat in the eggs, one by one."

Arsen coughed. "Susan?"

Clare's head sunk to her chest, her eyes glazed.

I leaned forward and opened the binder. "And then, and only then, do you add the lemon juice. Ha! My gran didn't write that down, because she just did it. But how was I to know? Every recipe I've ever read says to combine the ingredients on the stove."

"She worked really hard on that lemon curd," Arsen said to Clare.

"I can finally serve fresh lemon curd with my scones tomorrow." And then I noticed the dark shadows beneath Clare's eyes. Embarrassed, I grabbed a cup and gulped the coffee. Maybe my talk had gotten a little out of hand. "Sorry. Who cares about lemon curd?"

She roused herself. "No, it's fine. I love lemon curd. I don't think I've ever had fresh curd."

"Are you sure you're okay here on your own?" I asked, embarrassed by my self-centered blathering. Her cabin was isolated, at the end of a road that wound through a grassy valley. I imagined the stars here would be even more brilliant than at Wits' End. But imagining was all I could do. Outside the paned windows, clouds blotted out the night sky. Only a faint glow marked the spot of the waning moon.

"I'm surprised Emmery's not here," Arsen said.

She flushed. "He's busy. He's been working extra hours since that deputy was killed."

I scowled at Arsen. I may have bored her with my adventures in lemon curd, but at least I hadn't embarrassed her.

Arsen grimaced. "Officer March. I passed that accident on the highway."

We were silent for a moment, thinking of dangerous roads and dangerous jobs.

Clare shook herself. "So how are you going to do this?"

I consulted my binder. Next on the list was completing Supplemental Form A, a description of the site. "Can you give us a tour?" I said. "We'd like to see where everything happened."

"There's not much to show you. I fall asleep in my bedroom, and I wake up somewhere else. But okay." She rose. "Come on."

We followed her into a small bedroom. A wooden bed with a patchwork quilt sagged in its center. A scuffed armoire leaned against one wall. A tin lamp dangled from the ceiling.

Arsen tugged on the window and fiddled with its lock. He tugged again.

"It's stuck," she said, and I made a note on the form. "It's been like that since I stained the house last year."

Arsen wasn't the only one with a bag of tricks. I set the binder on the bed, opened my backpack and dug out an EMF meter.

"What's that?" she asked.

"An EMF meter to check for unusual electrical activity." They were normally used to detect ghosts, but the UFO community had embraced them. Regular exposure to high EMF fields could cause paranoia, and I wanted to rule that out. "Later, we'd like to put some motion detectors outside your house. Would you be okay with that?"

"Yes, of course. I want to know what's happening."

"How long have you two been together?" I asked, making a sketch of the room on the back of the form. "You and Emmery, I mean."

"Six months." She smiled dreamily. "It was love at first sight. I didn't think I'd meet someone in a place as small as Doyle, and then Emmery moved here. His father's getting older, like mine. He wanted to be closer to him."

A pang of longing shot through my chest. If my parents and I'd had a different relationship... But we didn't, and that was that.

"So," she said, "tell me about these motion detectors you want to set up."

"They're motion sensitive video cameras," Arsen said. "They'll start recording and upload the data to the cloud. You do have wi-fi out here, don't you?"

She nodded.

"I should install them at Wits' End," I said.

Arsen shot me a look, which I ignored. He'd wanted to set them up when he'd installed the new locks, but I'd shot down that idea. Funny how one set of switched fuses will change a mind.

My mouth puckered. Had I left the kitchen window open? I'd set a jar of lemon curd on it, just because the pop of yellow looked good beside the blue curtains. And I'd opened the window to let the breeze in…

Pensive, I turned on the EMF detector and moved it slowly over the rough, wood wall. The detector beeped as it got closer to an electrical outlet. "Someone left the front door open at Wits' End late last night," I said casually.

She colored. "Um, that might have been us."

"You?" Arsen's voice razored.

"Danella invited Emmery and me over. With Marion…" She shook her head. "It's hard to think of her as my stepmother. She's not that much older than me. But my stepmother, Marion, thinks Danella is a fraud. It was just easier for us to go to Wits' End."

"What time was this?" Arsen leaned against the wall. He crossed his arms, muscles bulging beneath the sleeves of his blue hiking jacket.

"I think we left Wits' End around midnight. Danella had wine, and we just got to talking, and… you know how it is."

"Did you return?" he asked.

"Return to Wits' End?" She sat on the edge of the bed, and the springs squeaked. "Why would we come back?"

"What did you and Danella talk about?" I asked.

"The investigation. She wants to go back into Dad's house and run some tests, but Marion won't have it. And it's Marion's house now. Danella did a chakra clearing on me and some light hypnosis. She thought it would help me recall my abductions, but I just can't remember anything."

"Hypnosis?" I glanced at Arsen. If she was having some sort of mental break, was that healthy?

"It's not like you see on TV," she said. "It's just deep relaxation."

"Someone jammed the lock on Susan's front door," Arsen said.

"Jammed it?" Her face cleared. "Emmery said there was something odd with your front lock. He was going to say something to you today. Didn't he mention it?"

Arsen and I glanced at each other.

"I guess he didn't get the chance yet," I said.

"Excuse me." Arsen dug his phone from the pocket of his khaki slacks and left the bedroom.

I passed the EMF device over another wall. "I noticed your father didn't get along with Emmery's."

"It was hard not to notice." She laughed unevenly. "At least my dad never took his paranoia out on Emmery."

"Paranoia?"

"He wasn't a trusting man."

But it's not paranoia if someone really is out to get you.

"My father never hid what he felt," she continued. "Not when it came to family." She shifted on the bed, and the springs complained beneath her.

"What exactly was the problem between your father and Rufus?"

"My dad was always a good saver. He invested in a lot of little commercial properties all over Nevada. He had his Air Force pension, but he said he wanted something more to pass on. I think it was just in his DNA to save, you know? Anyway, Emmery's dad wanted to go in as a partner, but my dad said no. It wasn't anything personal. Dad just liked going it alone. But Rufus took it badly."

Bad enough to still be resentful. But it didn't seem worth killing over.

"And now you're a proud Nevada real estate owner," I said lightly.

"Not really. Dad put his property in trust for the first five years after his death. Marion is managing my share, and she gets her half. It's only fair," she said quickly. "She and my Dad married when I was ten. She was there for all of it."

Keeping Clare's funds in trust didn't exactly seem like a vote of confidence though. I hesitated. This was delicate ground, family relationships, and I wasn't sure how to dig deeper. "Keeping it in trust like that, is that normal?"

"He told me the idea was to make sure I didn't make any sudden decisions after he... after a loss."

But it was Marion's loss too, and she was managing the trust. "This trust arrangement," I said, "is it new?"

"No." Her fair skin darkened. "It's got nothing to do with what's been happening, with my lost time. My dad was just conservative, okay?"

"That makes sense," I said, placating. But it still seemed strange. My friend, Karin Bonheim, worked in estate law. Maybe she could tell me something about the arrangement.

Arsen walked into the room and pocketed his phone. "Emmery said he noticed the door wasn't closing right. But you two were in a hurry, so he didn't really examine it. Also, he'll be here in thirty minutes."

Her shoulders dropped. "Great. He's—" Her eyes widened. She staggered backward. A thin, high-pitched noise escaped her throat, raised the hair on my arms.

"Clare?" I stepped toward her.

She spun and raced from the room.

CHAPTER 9

Arsen and I glanced at each other and charged after Clare.

She streaked through her cabin's small living room. Making an eerie half-shriek/half-wailing sound, Clare flew out the front door.

It banged loudly against the exterior wall and ricocheted against Arsen's outstretched arm.

"Clare!" I shouted.

She leapt down the porch steps, stumbling when she hit the ground. Clare turned, just outside a square of light from her cabin's windows. She scanned the dark sky. "Did you see it?"

Arsen and I joined her, our gazes tracking hers. No little green men peered back. No odd lights streaked the night sky. No UFOs hovered above the cabin's peaked roof.

"Did you see it?" she repeated.

"We missed it, Clare," I said in a low voice. "What did you see?"

"The alien." She grasped my upper arms. Even in the darkness, her eyes seemed wild. "He was at the window. You must have seen him. He was right there!"

"Stay with her," Arsen commanded. He jogged around the corner of the small cabin and vanished.

I swallowed. "Can you describe what the alien looked like?"

"Like an alien!" Her voice trembled. She closed her eyes. "Its face was gray. It had big, black eyes."

"That's helpful," I said. "What else?"

"That's all," she said brokenly. "I only saw its head, looking through the window. And those eyes…" She swallowed jerkily and turned her face toward a wall of nearby pines.

I edged toward the side of the cabin and peered around its corner. Arsen was nowhere to be seen.

I bit my bottom lip. He was fine. He could handle himself. But I suddenly felt irrationally angry at Clare for sending him off into the dark.

Swallowing my irritation, I checked the clock on my phone. It was eight thirty-three. The sun had only set thirty minutes ago, but the thick clouds turned the sky black.

"The other, er, incidents you reported were in the early morning hours," I said. "They occurred after midnight."

She whirled on me. "Do you think I'm lying?"

"No. I only wanted to confirm that there weren't earlier sightings you hadn't mention. Because if not, this is a break in the pattern, something new." And where was Arsen?

She clawed a shaky hand through her hair. "This is new. I've never experienced anything this early before. You said something's changed? What? Does this mean they're coming for me again?" She grasped my arms, her fingers digging through my light jacket. "I can't take it. I can't take it anymore."

Arsen rounded the corner of the cabin, and my shoulders loosened.

He shook his head. "No one. If there are tracks, I'm not finding them in the dark."

"Why would an alien leave tracks on the ground?" Clare asked.

Gently, I pulled free of her grip. "You saw it by the bedroom window, right?"

Arsen unclipped the flashlight from his belt and climbed the steps. "First thing we need to do is set up a motion-activated porch light."

"It is…" She frowned. "I *do* have an automatic light. Why isn't it on?"

We followed Arsen onto the porch.

He aimed the flashlight into the metal lamp above the door. Reaching up, he twisted the bulb.

The porch light flashed on.

"Loose bulb," he said.

Clare sputtered. "But—"

"Where's that bedroom window?" I asked.

"Here." She strode to a corner window with decorative eaves.

Arsen knelt and examined the porch floorboards with his flashlight. "I don't see anything," he said. "Do you?"

Clare's shoulders folded inward. "You don't believe me."

"He didn't say that," I said. "You say the alien was at the window, looking in. Where, exactly, did you see it?"

She pointed. "The lower right corner."

I studied the narrow window ledge. Lightly, I touched a half-oval of white powder on the ledge. "What's this smudge?"

"Something was here," Clare said excitedly.

My insides jittered in response. *Would* we find evidence of… something?

Arsen touched the discoloration. "Looks like dirt to me."

Clare made a face. "So, it's nothing. There's no proof I saw anything, as usual. Unless you're telling me it's alien dirt."

But Clare had seen *something*. Her reaction had been all too real. "Do you know what could have caused this white mark?" I asked her.

She blinked back tears. "Probably an animal," she said, her voice thick. "I'm sure it's nothing."

I took a photo of the smudge with my phone. "Could it have been an animal you saw at the window? An owl?" But what would an owl be doing peeking in a lit window?

"I don't know." Her breath hitched. "I don't know anything anymore. What's happening to me?"

A car drove up the drive, its tires crunching on the uneven ground. We shielded our eyes from its headlights.

"Emmery," Clare said quickly. "Don't tell him. It will only worry him."

Clare was the client, not Emmery. Though he had been there when she'd "hired" me. Uneasily, I nodded. "We won't say anything."

Arsen frowned.

A door slammed. The car's lights dimmed.

Emmery ambled up the steps. "Hi. What's going on?"

"They came to interview me for their investigation," Clare said brightly. "They were just leaving."

I glanced at her. We'd wanted to install the outdoor cameras. I'd thought she'd agreed. What was going on?

"Learn anything interesting?" Emmery stopped in front of us, and he and Arsen shook hands.

Clare shot me a pleading look.

"It's too early to tell," I said.

"Well," the deputy said, "let me know if there's anything I can do to help."

"Will do." I forced a smile. "We'll call about our next steps."

I retrieved my backpack and binder. Arsen and I returned to his Jeep Commander, and he helped me inside. "I don't like this," he muttered.

"Me neither." I hated leaving Clare in this state. But at least she wasn't alone. I waved to the couple, and Arsen shut my door.

He walked around the Jeep to the driver's side and got in. "We didn't get anything done that we'd planned."

"No. I don't know why Clare wanted to get rid of us. It's not like Emmery doesn't know what we're doing."

He reversed the Jeep, and he turned out of the driveway. We bumped up the rutted road.

"I didn't see any evidence of anyone out there," he said.

"There was that smudge by the window."

"Which could have been there for months. And don't tell me you think an alien beamed down to play peeping Tom."

I slumped in the leather seat. "No." Why was I so... disappointed? My self-help books would tell me to pay attention, be in my body. What was I feeling?

Nauseated. The idea that Clare might be lying or delusional sickened me. But why? I didn't know her well. Was I sympathizing with Clare because of my own shadow?

"Look," Arsen said, "a lot of strange things have happened in Doyle. Maybe this is a part of it. But we need to face the most likely explanation. Everything that's been happening could be in Clare's head."

I pressed deeper into the buttery leather. "Her father's murder wasn't."

He shot me a sideways look. "So that's what this is? An end run around Sheriff McCourt?"

"No," I said too quickly. "Look, Clare asked us for help. And Emmery asked us for help too. You can't believe they're both crazy."

"I believe he's in love with Clare. He may not be seeing things clearly." His hands tightened on the wheel. "She may need professional help. Psychiatric help."

"She's scared," I said. I was starting to miss the old free-wheeling, devil-may-care Arsen. "That's made her paranoid. It doesn't mean she's crazy. Besides, Emmery thought this was a good idea too."

"But I noticed she didn't want to tell him about this latest incident. Maybe Emmery doesn't have all the facts. What if we're feeding her delusion?"

My chest tightened. I'd wondered the same thing and hoped I was wrong. I twined my fingers together and looked at my hands.

"I just don't want you to get hurt," he said. "I don't want anyone to."

He was protecting me, and guilt slammed down like the cover on one of my warming trays.

Because he was right.

Right now, there was no evidence of anything but Clare's deteriorating mental health. We might be doing more harm than good. On the other hand, her father had been murdered. Could it be connected? Could someone be doing this to her? "I hear what you're saying," I said, "but…"

But all I could think about was a Nevada rancher. He'd become obsessed with the lights flying over Area 51, believing they were UFOs. He'd spent all his money trying to find the secret alien base. And then one day he'd gotten lost in the desert on one of his quests and never returned. His body wasn't found until years later.

Sometimes, an interest in UFOs could cross the line. My cousin Dixie tread near that line. She was eccentric, but not crazy. But I feared Clare had stepped across the line and into madness.

I scrubbed a hand through my hair. "I'll call Clare and Emmery tomorrow and tell them we can't do any more."

"I can tell them."

"No. I'll do it." I'd gotten us into this. I'd get us out.

"And if Emmery asks you why we're quitting?"

I *hated* quitting. "I need to think about it."

The headlights swept the dirt road.

"You'll think of the right thing," he said and paused. "This is new territory. I've known guys who lost it overseas. Sometimes I could talk them down."

And sometimes he hadn't been able to. Arsen didn't talk much about his time "overseas" in the military. I didn't ask. Maybe that was cowardice on my part, but if he wanted to talk about his experience, he would.

"But this is different," he continued in a low voice. "This isn't PTSD. At least, I don't think it is."

I reached for him, and we clasped hands.

We drove in silence to Wits' End. Arsen walked with me into the B&B.

The light on the answering machine blinked, and I pressed play.

"Hi, this is Parker Franklin. We had a reservation starting this Friday, but we're going to have to cancel. Please call or email me to let me know you got this. Thanks." He hung up.

Well. That happened sometimes. It probably wasn't anything to do with Danella and her death vortexes.

A pucker appeared between Arsen's brows. "That's a bummer."

The machine beeped, and another message played, another client canceling their reservation.

"Is that normal?" Arsen asked when the machine beeped.

"No." I glanced up the stairs. *Had* Danella's video scared off two of my clients?

I walked around the desk and checked the email. Another client had canceled. My stomach knotted. Something was definitely up, and not in a good way.

I checked Danella's video channel. The death vortex video had over thirty thousand hits.

She'd tagged Doyle and Wits' End.

Heat rushed from my face to my scalp. Anyone searching for Wits' End might have seen the video.

I couldn't control what my guests wrote about Wits' End (and that killed me). But I tried to give them the best experience possible. This wasn't fair.

The front door opened. Danella and her two crewmen breezed into the foyer.

"Thanks for recommending that restaurant," Danella said to me. "Doyle is utterly charming."

I straightened from the computer. "Danella," I ground out, "can I talk to you for a minute?"

"Sure," she said.

Arsen motioned with his thumb over his shoulder. "I'll see you in the kitchen."

Muscles I hadn't realized were tight unbunched. He hadn't forgotten his promise to spend the night.

He strode through the kitchen door. The crewmen tromped up the stairs.

"What's going on?" Danella asked.

I walked around the desk to face her. "Um, I've had three cancellations since you've put up your Doyle death vortex video."

"I wouldn't worry about that. Wherever I go, business increases. Besides, my crew and I are staying longer. We'll make up for any lost customers."

"That's not the point." Glancing at the ceiling, I lowered my voice. The walls in the Victorian weren't particularly well insulated. "That isn't the point."

She crossed her arms. "Well, I don't see what the point is, then."

I struggled to calm down. "If you won't take down the video, would you at least remove the Wits' End and Doyle tags? That way, people searching for us won't find death vortexes."

"Then how will people find my video? People are interested in Doyle after everything that's happened here. They're looking for explanations."

"Calling it a death vortex isn't doing Doyle any favors. The town depends on tourism."

Her smile turned infuriatingly smug. "Trust me, that won't be a problem."

"But it obviously is if people are canceling their reservations."

She rolled her eyes. "Fine. I'll take the Wits' End tag off the video. Happy?"

No, but I'd take what I could get. "Thank you."

She stomped up the stairs.

Shaking my head, I double checked the front door was locked, and I walked into the kitchen.

Arsen wasn't there.

Bailey raised his head from his dog bed and whuffed a gentle greeting.

I bent to pet the beagle. "At least I can count on you."

I straightened.

At the sink's open window, a gray, alien face stared in at me.

I yelped, leaping backwards and crashing into the kitchen table. "Arsen!"

Bailey leapt to his feet and howled.

The face at the window vanished.

And so had my perfect lemon curd! That was my only jar for tomorrow's breakfast!

Arsen charged from the parlor. "What? What's happened?"

Swearing, I lurched away from the table and to the porch door. "That alien stole my curd!"

"What?"

I fumbled the lock, then charged onto the lit porch. "Come back here, you bastard!"

"Susan, wait!"

The garden was empty, the roses swaying gently in the breeze. I grasped the porch railing and used it to swing over the steps and onto the lawn.

Arsen joined me, and we turned, scanning the yard.

No one in the gazebo. No one on the lawn. No one hiding in the roses.

At least, no one that I could see.

Rose petals skittered across the green lawn. A neighbor's wind chime tinkled.

I stared into the blank, night sky. It seemed to return my gaze, impassive, unyielding.

I shuddered.

"What happened?" Arsen said. "What alien?"

"There was something at the window." It must have been the same alien that Clare had seen. How many aliens could be running around Doyle?

Not that I believed in aliens.

Not really.

"I didn't see anything," he said.

"You weren't here." How could he expect to see the alien when he hadn't even been in the kitchen? I could hear the doubt in his voice, and I was starting to understand how Clare felt. "It stole my lemon curd!"

"Why would an alien take your lemon curd?"

That... was a mystery. But whatever the reason, that stupid alien would pay.

CHAPTER 10

Mahir, toast hanging from his mouth, poked his head into the kitchen. The cameraman removed the toast. "Um, there's someone knocking at your front door."

I frowned. Why would anyone knock? I unlocked it every morning. "Thanks." Smelling trouble, I walked through the foyer and opened the door.

Mrs. Steinberg stood on the porch. Swathed in enough black scarves for a depressed fortune teller, the elderly woman glowered. "Good morning, Susan."

"Mrs. Steinberg?" I stepped away from the door.

She stumped into the foyer, her wooden cane making divots in the faux-Persian carpet.

"What brings you to Wits' End?" I smoothed my green, flowered blouse. She'd never just dropped by for a visit. She and Gran had been friends, but I think she saw me more as a minion.

She sniffed, an action that rippled through her small frame and too-big black dress. "Your grandmother's coffee cake?"

"Yes. Would you like some?"

"That's not why I'm here." Her gaze traveled from my sensible shoes to my hair, twisted in a chignon.

"What can I do for you?" I asked.

She plowed through her black handbag. "You're treading in dangerous waters, young Susan."

Oh.

That.

Mrs. Steinberg's hobby was delivering cryptic hints and dire warnings, but no real information. But how had she found out I was helping Clare? I still hadn't figured out how to break the news to Clare that I had to quit.

Bailey trotted into the room, his collar jingling.

"Well?" she asked, stooping to pet the beagle. "Cat got your tongue?"

Bailey sneezed.

"No offense, young Bailey," she said.

Grumbling, the beagle laid down on the carpet and lowered his head to his paws.

"I suppose you heard about the alien at my window last night," I said.

She pointed at me with her e-cigarette, which was thankfully, unlit. "Alien at your window?"

"He stole my lemon curd." And I was still annoyed. True, I could make more. But stealing was wrong. "I want it back."

"Lemon curd?" Her face tightened. "Who cares about lemon curd?"

"It was Gran's recipe."

She sighed. "I know you miss her. I do too. But this is no time for lemon curd thieves."

"It was an alien curd thief," I said.

"Why would aliens be interested in you?"

I stiffened. Why *wouldn't* I be interesting to aliens? After all, I had a fake UFO in my roof. "Maybe because I've started chasing them on Clare's behalf."

"Clare Fitzgerald? Is she seeing them too?"

Dammit. I wasn't supposed to say anything. "Client confidentiality," I said belatedly.

"In other words, yes." She shook herself. "I'm afraid you won't be able to do much about the alien problem. I'm talking about murder."

Mrs. Steinberg's *other* hobby was warning me off murder investigations. She must have assumed I'd stick my nose into the colonel's death. "I don't think you have anything to worry about."

"A good man's dead. I warned him about being too predictable, but he didn't take me seriously."

"Predictable?"

"The digitalis in his juice cup!" She thumped the rug with her cane for emphasis, and I jumped a little.

"It was in his juice?" That explained a lot. Even I'd gotten used to seeing the colonel wandering his yard with his morning thermos-thing of green juice.

"There's more going on than meets the eye. For your own good, you need to stay out of this."

"I am. I mean, I told the sheriff I would." Was Mrs. Steinberg using reverse psychology too? "Though I think she may have wanted my help—"

"She doesn't."

"Have you spoken to her? If you know something about the colonel's death, you should talk to her."

"I know more than I want to," she said darkly, "and more than you should."

"So, there is more to his death than simple murder. Is that why Agent Manaj is here?"

She started. "Manaj? When—?"

Danella backed from the dining area. "...charming guest house, and vortex free." She winked. "Though it may have a ghost or two. Perhaps their happy influence is why the inn's famed roses bloom all year?"

Mrs. Steinberg stiffened. "You."

Danella froze, then swiveled to face us. "And here's the innkeeper, Ms. Susan Witsend."

"Don't you film me," Mrs. Steinberg said.

"I couldn't if I wanted to." Bob lowered his camera. "Sorry, I've got a technical difficulty here." He tapped the camera with one finger. The red light above the lens blinked out.

"Are you kidding?" Danella said. "Since when?"

"Since five seconds ago," he said, fiddling with the controls. "Just give me a minute to figure this out."

Danella huffed and turned to smile at me. "I want you to know, Susan, that I heard what you had to say last night. I've decided to film an episode about how safe and delightful Wits' End really is."

"Thanks," I said, feeling like a jerk. She hadn't meant to cause problems, and she was trying to fix them. "Wow. I really appreciate that."

"Of course," she said, "I haven't checked your private quarters for vortexes. Would you like me to?"

Mrs. Steinberg snorted.

"Um, no," I said. "That's okay."

"Suit yourself." She headed for the stairs. "Let's take it from the top." She climbed the carpeted stairs.

Bob trailed behind and muttered over his camera.

"Fool," Mrs. Steinberg growled.

"You can't possibly think I should have let her check my bedroom for vortexes."

"Not you. Her!" She pointed up the stairs with her black cane.

"You watch her online show?"

"I don't waste time online. It's packed with vipers."

"Then you know her... personally?" Because Danella hadn't acted as if she'd recognized Mrs. Steinberg. In fact, she'd completely ignored the old lady, and that didn't seem in character.

"That woman's dangerous, Susan. Get her out of Wits' End as soon as possible. And remove that FBI agent!"

"How?" And how did she know Manaj?

She pivoted and marched out the front door, the thuds of her cane echoing on the porch steps.

My insides quivered. *Danella, dangerous? Weird.* Danella wasn't a Doyleite. What did Mrs. Steinberg know about her that I didn't?

The phone rang, and I wrenched the receiver from its cradle. "Wits' End, this is Susan speaking. How can I help you?"

"Hi, I'd like to make a reservation?"

At last! Someone coming rather than going. I made the reservation in our old-fashioned book and hung up.

The front door creaked open. Marion Fitzgerald sidled into the foyer, her eyes reddened. "Was that Mrs. Steinberg I saw leaving?"

"Yes, she stopped by to say hello."

My neighbor's tanned brow creased. "That doesn't seem like Mrs. Steinberg."

There was a lot of uncharacteristic behavior going around. "She and my grandmother were old friends."

She came to stand in front of the scarred reception desk. "Hm." Her expression turned calculating, putting me on guard.

Then I felt guilty about that too. She might be a gossip. She might be anti-roof-UFO. But she was also a new widow. "Marion, I'm so sorry for—"

She raised her hand. "Please don't say it. I know you mean well, but I can't take any more sympathy, or I'll crack into pieces. You don't want to see me crack." Her voice was hoarse from crying. "I'm an ugly crier, and this is important." She looked away, but not before I saw her mouth tremble.

Bailey trotted to Marion and leaned against the leg of her cream slacks. She knelt to scratch the beagle.

"Sor— Okay," I said quietly. "What can I do for you?"

She nodded approvingly. "I want you to help me save Clare."

My breath caught in surprise. "How?"

"Evict that psychic." She rasped and stood.

I blinked. "Excuse me?"

The older woman scraped back a wisp of her frosted hair. "She's been harassing us. Me. And her living right next door makes it all too easy."

"If she's harassing you, you should speak to the sheriff." Because Danella and her team were paid up through the end of the week. Unless they set something on fire, I couldn't evict them.

"Do you think I haven't? She says as long as my daughter keeps inviting her over, there's nothing I can do."

"Your dau– Clare?"

"What other daughter do I have?"

Technically, Clare was her stepdaughter. I couldn't imagine either of my parents dropping the "step" part of the equation. Clare hadn't. "I can't imagine how difficult it must be for you both."

"The sheriff told me my husband was murdered," she said, her voice dull. "I don't know how to tell Clare. My husband always knew how to handle her. I don't." She slumped, one manicured finger trailing across the edge of the desk. "Clare didn't used to be this way."

"What way?"

"Withdrawn. Selfish. Distracted." She looked up, her light green eyes snapping with frustration. "It's like... she's going through puberty all over again."

"People grieve in all sorts of ways," I said carefully.

"That's not it. I mean, of course she's grieving, but before."

"Before?"

"When this UFO business started." She shook herself. "You're right. It's not fair to blame the medium, even if she is delusional. What do you know about her?"

"Only what I've read on the internet," I said. "Sorry." It was one thing for the sheriff to ask about my guests. But I couldn't gossip to Marion, even if she was going through something awful.

"But she's living here. You must have noticed something."

"She likes pancakes." I leaned one hip against the wooden desk.

"Everyone likes pancakes!"

"I know. I'm sorry. I wasn't trying to be flippant. I'm just not comfortable discussing a guest."

She stepped closer and lowered her voice. "But she's not a normal guest! I think my husband knew her."

"You mean, because of the séances?"

"No. Not from now. From before. But Ted wouldn't talk about her. It's like he was ashamed." She blinked rapidly, tears swimming in her eyes. "You don't think they could have been having an affair?"

I couldn't imagine the colonel in a romantic clinch under any circumstances. "I doubt that's—"

She wiped at one eye. "You don't understand. I could always tell when he was lying. He learned it in the military. You'd ask him one question, and he'd answer another, but make it seem like he was answering yours. Like the time I asked him about Area 51. He said, 'Well, there weren't little green men running around, if that's what you're asking.'"

"What—?"

"But what if they were gray men? Or what if they were lying on autopsy tables instead of running free? See?"

Had the colonel been more tied up in UFO phenomenon than I'd believed? What were the odds that someone who'd worked at Area 51 had a daughter abducted by aliens? Unless him working at Area 51 had put the bug in Clare's brain.

"I guess I do see." I scratched my hand, and a patch of dry skin flaked off and dropped to the carpet. Embarrassed, I put my hands behind my back.

"What do you think's been happening to Clare?" I asked.

"I *thought* she was just going through something. She and Emmery are talking about getting married. It's stirred up questions about her birth mother. She's— she died when Clare was young. But my husband thought there was more to Clare's lapses and missing time than relationship stress. So, he was relieved when she moved in with us. I thought he'd figured out what was bothering her. He was so... agitated that night. Like he was about to go into battle."

Behind my back, my hands gripped together more tightly. "What night?"

"The night before he..." She swallowed and looked toward the shelf full of UFO souvenirs. Her mouth trembled. "...before he died. But he let them go ahead with that damned séance, so I guess I was wrong."

The sheriff needed to know about this. And I needed to know more. "Has Clare said anything about, um, me?"

She glanced at the brass ceiling lamp. "She and Emmery told me they'd asked you to look into the UFO side of things," she said in a low voice. "I've got to tell you, I don't believe in any of it. But your investigation seemed to ease Clare's mind."

"In that case, would you mind if I took a look around your house?" Okay. I would quit the investigation later today for sure. After I talked to Clare.

"I'll do anything to help Clare." She hesitated. "Do you really think poking around my house will make a difference?"

"I hope it will."

She nodded. "Then let's do this. She doesn't listen to me anymore. Maybe she'll listen to you."

I grabbed the EMF meter, a notebook, and pen, and we walked to her house next door.

"So, are you and Arsen going to tie the knot anytime soon?" she asked casually.

"Not if my parents have anything to do with it," I muttered.

"What? Your parents don't approve? But Arsen's the hottest bachelor in town. He's wealthy. He's handsome. And he's no philanderer."

My face heated. "No, that's not... They don't disapprove. They don't know about him." And then I remembered I was talking to the town gossip, and my face heated. "My parents and I don't talk much."

"That's a shame."

I paused in the living area. Take-out wrappers and plates lay discarded on the coffee table.

Marion drew a hand through her short hair. "Sorry about the mess. My husband was the neat freak in our family. I just haven't had the energy to deal with much of anything."

"Please don't apologize," I said quickly. "It's nothing."

"The day he died, Ted was so tense, I easily believed he'd had a heart attack."

"Brought on by Danella? Or by the séance?"

"I don't know." She rubbed her bottom lip. "He was an extremely private man. Some would say paranoid. He wasn't one to share his thoughts and feelings. We never demanded much of each other, but we understood each other. I guess in my own way, I'm a private person too."

I choked back a laugh. *She* was private? The town gossip? Did Marion actually believe that? But we told all sorts of lies to ourselves to get through the day. I told myself I was in control... I swallowed.

She looked out a plaid-curtained window and gripped the sill. "Maybe we should have talked more. And now it's too late."

I shifted my weight. "Would you like me to go?"

"No." She turned to face me. "No, let's get this over with."

I switched on the EMF detector, and the plastic device screeched.

"What's that?"

"This just checks for unusual electricity spikes. May I?"

She slumped onto the plaid couch. "Go ahead."

Watching the meter, I ran the EMF detector along the wooden walls. The meter didn't budge.

"Though I doubt you'll find anything," she said. "My husband was meticulous about keeping the house in order, inside and out."

She was right. I didn't find any odd electrical spikes in the living room. "The kitchen?" I asked.

She motioned toward the doorway. "Go ahead."

I walked into the kitchen. Its tile counters were cluttered with dirty dishes and crumbs. "I suppose you heard he was killed with foxglove," I said.

"Foxglove?" She came to stand in the doorway. "No. The papers said it was digitalis."

My breathing quickened. Did she really not know digitalis came from foxglove? "Did the colonel make his own green juice?"

"Yes, in his blender."

I scanned the counter. "I don't see it."

"Oh," she said, "the police took it."

So much for that. Opening the refrigerator, I peered into the vegetable box. It was empty. "Did the police take anything from your refrigerator?"

"The night's dinner leftovers and all of my husband's greens."

"How did he store his greens?"

"Washed and bundled in plastic bags. Is this part of your UFO investigation?"

It *was* possible the murder was connected to what was going on with Clare. If that was the case, I'd be negligent not to explore it. "I'm not sure." Could the killer have added foxglove leaves to a bundle of greens? If the colonel had pre-washed them, he might not have looked too closely at what was going into his blender.

Marion braced one shoulder against the doorframe. "The police think the killer added digitalis to his vegetables, don't they?"

"I don't know," I lied. "But if someone had added it to the greens, he might not have noticed. Digitalis is, er, leafy."

"But practically *everyone* was here that morning. An entire TV crew! Plus that idiot, Rufus."

"Emmery's father?"

She flushed. "I shouldn't have called him that. If Clare hears of it—"

"She won't from me. But I noticed Rufus and your husband arguing."

She crossed her arms over her pale blouse and lowered her head. "They were always arguing."

There was another possibility – that no one had added the digitalis to the colonel's greens that morning. Maybe they'd been added the night before. "And Clare? How did she get along with her father?"

"Clare would never harm her father," she said fiercely. "Never. Clare and I may have never really understood each other, but she loved her father."

I thought of my own controlling mother. Our relationship was still... fraught.

I couldn't abandon Clare. Not now. Not when there were so many unanswered questions.

"The two were so alike in many ways," she continued. "I just worry..."

"About what?"

"Clare told me you came to her house last night, and there was an incident. But she wouldn't give me any details. What happened?"

If Clare hadn't given her stepmother details, I couldn't either. "She was fine when we left her," I said. But was Clare really okay? Was she the dangerous one? Or was Clare in danger?

I remembered the face at my window and shuddered.

CHAPTER 11

Movements spasmodic, Clare paced in front of the cabin window. Her reflection wavered in its black reflection. "You came back."

"Of course we came back." I gulped her coffee, which was delicious, my lightweight jacket rustling.

Arsen shot me a warning look from his perch on Clare's blue sofa.

The jerk alien who'd stolen my lemon curd had done me one favor. He'd provided me evidence that there *was* a jerk alien.

Arsen couldn't deny that evidence. He'd agreed to continue our investigation. But we'd also agreed we wouldn't tell Clare about my own "visitation." Missing lemon curd aside, I had no real proof, and we worried about the effect on her.

"We're going to set up in that stand of trees over there." I pointed with the blue enamel mug to the curtained window and realized the gesture was – *ha* – pointless. All I could see was my own reflection. "We'll flash the light three times when we get to the spot, so you know where we are." I didn't want her to mistake us for aliens.

"Thanks." Her voice trembled. "Thanks."

"What time is Emmery getting back?" Arsen asked.

"I'm not sure," she said. "Late. He's working another double shift since Deputy March died. He's doing his job and March's in evidence. At least he'll be safer in the evidence room."

I rubbed my hands. They were so dry, they itched. The skin around my fingers was white and cracked. "He should be." I grimaced at my hands.

"What's wrong?" Clare asked.

"I ran out of lotion and keep forgetting to buy more. My skin is Death Valley dry."

"I've got some good stuff. I'll get it for you." She vanished into the hallway.

"Nice job," Arsen said in a low voice. He beelined for the rustic desk and rummaged through the papers there.

Mug to my lips, I sucked in my breath and choked on a mouthful of coffee. "What are you–?"

"Do you trust her?" he whispered.

I coughed. "No," I admitted and drank more to ease my throat.

"Then we need to know more."

I finished the mug as he riffled her desk.

This felt like a betrayal. But he was right. We needed to know. Edging toward the door, I listened for her return.

Clare's footsteps sounded in the hall.

"Is that you, Clare?" I said loudly.

Arsen stepped away from the desk.

She handed me a squat glass jar. "It's from Ground."

"I love her scrub," I said. "I didn't know she made lotion too."

"It's new. Jayce makes the best stuff, and it's all organic. I wish I'd had this when we were living in the high desert."

"You and your family moved around a lot?" Guiltily, I rubbed a generous dab of lotion into my hands. It smelled like coffee, the best scent in the world next to chocolate and Arsen.

"Yeah, I was a military brat. My favorite place was Colorado Springs, but boy was the air dry."

"And Area 51?" I asked.

Her gaze slipped sideways. "We never actually lived there."

"But I heard your father worked there?" I said.

"He couldn't talk about it."

I nodded. It was only recently the military even admitted the base existed.

"We should get set up," Arsen said.

I returned her jar of lotion. "Thanks."

We walked outside, and I pulled my flashlight from my jacket pocket.

Arsen placed his hand on mine. "Let your eyes adjust. It'll be better this way."

That's what *he* said. I stumbled behind Arsen to a stand of pines with a clear view of the small cabin.

I blinked my flashlight three times. Clare turned her cabin's living room light off and on in response.

"Interesting that she's so cagey about Area 51, since she thinks she's the victim of alien abductions."

"Yeah. I wondered if she believed there was a connection between Area 51 and her experiences. But she didn't bring it up." I squatted on a thick pine root and rubbed my hands, but the lotion had absorbed quickly. I was going to need to stop by Ground and buy a jar.

He sat close beside me, his body radiating warmth.

"I'm glad you're here," I said, "even if you're skeptical."

He grasped my hand. "I'm skeptical of Clare, not you. Never you." He kissed me lightly, and my blood zinged.

Arsen peered through his night-vision binoculars and lowered them to his chest.

Knees nearly to my chin, I shifted on the pine root. It made a lousy bench. For all my planning pride, I hadn't considered bringing lawn chairs.

"What do you expect to find out here?" he asked.

"I'm not sure. But her father was murdered. And I know what I saw. That lemon curd was taken. Something's going on."

"Clare's paranoia started before her father's death."

"It makes me wonder if his death and her missing time are connected."

"I guess," he said slowly, "there are three possibilities. One, Clare's problems and her father's death aren't connected."

"And what are the odds of that?"

"Low. Two, whoever is harassing Clare also killed her father."

"A much higher probability," I said. "But what's the goal?"

"And three..."

"What?"

"Well, there is the possibility that nothing is happening to Clare. Or that whatever is happening is in her own mind."

"No," I said. "The proof is in the lemon curd. If Clare's nuts, so am I."

"But. If Clare's crazy, then we don't really know what she's capable of."

I stilled. "Patricide? She'd have to be..." Oh. Right. Crazy.

Was she insane? My parents and I were at odds, but to kill your father... I shivered.

He looped an arm over my shoulders. "Cold?"

"Not anymore." I pressed closer to him. Even through his thick jacket, I felt the hard lines of his muscular frame.

We sat in companionable silence and waited for something to happen.

An hour went by.

Two.

I should have been bored. But Arsen was here, and a strange contentment stole through me. We just were. Here. In the now. The books were right. It really *was* only the moment that mattered, and I started noticing more and more.

I abandoned the tree root and leaned against a sugar pine. Its heady vanilla scent twined around me. The trunk was broad and comforting, and I imagined I could feel it breathing, the movement of its sap drawing inward as the mountainside cooled. Being present was awesome!

I rubbed my hand. Ick. The sap was sticky.

Arsen remained a still and silent shadow, perched on the tree root.

An owl hooted.

I craned my neck, searching the branches for the bird. A break appeared in the clouds. A waning gibbous moon flooded the forest with light.

White flashed above me.

I drew back, tensing.

"What?" Arsen whispered.

I rubbed my eyes. Had I imagined it?

There. Again. A flash of white.

I smiled. *An owl.*

"Just an owl," I murmured.

The owl dove through the air, its wings adjusting, and landed on a higher branch.

I blinked. Higher? It must have been an optical illusion, because I'd swear it had dived. Diving meant down.

I moved deeper into the trees, trying to get a better look.

"Susan?" Arsen whispered. "Where are you going?"

A branch cracked.

The owl's head turned, tracking my movements. Our gazes met.

I froze, trapped in its golden eyes.

Time stopped. The bird's eyes were fathomless pools, drawing me closer. My feet seemed to rise off—

"What are you doing here?"

I gasped and staggered backwards.

A man in a blue parka and plaid hunting cap glared at me. "Well? Answer my question."

"We're friends of Clare's," I stammered.

"Who's we?"

Arsen emerged from the darkness. "Susan and I." He slung his arm over my shoulder, steadying me. "What are you doing here?"

"I live here," the man said. "What's your excuse?"

"Clare knows we're here. We're watching for night birds." Arsen pointed upward. "Clare told us she'd been seeing a white owl, but we didn't quite believe her. They're unusual in the Sierras."

The man looked up. "Well, I'll be damned." He adjusted his hat. "I've never seen one in these parts. That's a beautiful animal."

I started to speak, but my tongue felt thick in my mouth. Weariness hit me like a hammer, and I yawned.

Arsen frowned. "We're sorry if we bothered you."

"This the first time you've been out here?" the man asked.

"Yes," Arsen said, "this is our first time birdwatching at Clare's."

"I guess I should have figured. You two aren't using flashlights. Those others must be idiots."

"Others?" Arsen said.

"I've been seeing lights around Clare's place," he said. "Now I understand why. Birdwatchers. Though if you're looking for owls, I'd think you wouldn't wave around a flashlight."

"When did you see these lights?" Arsen asked.

"Last night, briefly. But there've been other times."

There was a loud flapping, and the man looked up. "Oh, well. I guess it's gone hunting." He peered into the sky. The clouds drifted further apart, and the forest lightened. "Going to be a nice night after all. You two take care."

"You too," Arsen said.

We watched the man vanish into the pines.

"Maybe this wasn't a waste after all," Arsen muttered.

I swayed and shook myself.

"Are you all right?" he asked.

"I think all this dark and quiet is putting me to sleep." I slurred and scrubbed my hands across my face. "It's like I've hypnotized myself." *Sinking into the owl's eyes? Ridiculous.*

"You said Clare's only bothered on cloudy nights?"

"According to the log she gave us."

"Well, it's clearing up. I say we call it a night."

I yawned, glad he was driving. "Fine by me." We walked toward the cabin. I flashed my light three times again to let Clare know we were leaving.

There was no response. She was probably asleep.

A car crunched up the drive, its headlights blinding. The twin lights expanded, roaring, monstrous.

I flinched, shielding my eyes.

Arsen grasped me more tightly, halting. I buried my face in his parka.

"You okay?" he asked.

I looked up and shook my head. Those headlights... "I think my eyes adjusted too well to the darkness."

Emmery's blue SUV glided to a halt. The passenger window whirred down. "Arsen? Susan? What are you two doing here?"

"A stakeout," Arsen said. "Didn't Clare tell you?"

"She told me Susan was going to be here." Emmery's handsome face darkened. "She didn't mention you."

"I wasn't going to let Susan sit in the forest alone," Arsen said.

"No, of course not." He flushed. "Clare's not—" He clamped his jaw tight. "Sorry. Long night. Thanks for stopping by." He gunned the engine, pebbles pinging off the SUV's undercarriage.

Arsen waved away the dust billowing in the car's wake. "He's not a happy man."

I rubbed my eyes. "Glah."

"I know. Clare's father was murdered, and he's working long hours. Little wonder Emmery's tense. You really are a better person than me, Sue."

"Mmph." I was pretty sure that wasn't true, but I was too tired to argue.

We strolled toward the cabin. Emmery emerged from his SUV and strode up the stairs, slamming the door as he went inside.

Arsen opened the passenger door of his Jeep Commander. Normally, helping me inside is just a courtesy. But I felt wobbly after our long night and was grateful for his strong arm as I stepped up.

A flutter of white caught my eye. I balanced for a moment on the car's ledge.

The white owl perched on the peak of the cabin roof and stared down at me. And then its face contorted, growing longer, its eyes bigger. The feathers melted into its body. Its wings distended, long and gray and grasping.

A wave of cold fear flushed my body. I gasped and dove into the SUV.

"Susan?"

Arsen! He was out there with the alien. I couldn't leave him defenseless.

My heart was exploding in my chest. I grabbed the stun gun wedged between the seats, turned.

The alien stood at the open car door.

"Arsen!" I whimpered. What had it done with Arsen?

The creature reached for me, its narrow fingers stretching.

I pulled the trigger.

The weapon jerked in my hand. It *whumped*, and something dark flew out. The alien vanished.

Arsen.

I scrambled out of the Jeep and skidded off the Jeep's metal ledge. My feet hit the ground hard, jarring me.

"Susan?" Arsen stood in the driveway, his arms pinioned to his sides.

I gasped. "We've got to get out of here."

"Yeah," he said, caustic. "That would be nice."

I looked at him in surprise.

His hazel eyes blazed. He wobbled. Tilted. Fell. Fell the fall of a tree in the forest, not putting his hands out to brace himself.

"Arsen!" Time slowed again. I reached for him. My fingertips brushed the rough netting.

He hit the gravel with a heavy thud.

"Susan?" He glared through the net encasing him. "What the hell?"

Aghast, I stared at the weapon in my hand.

I'd net gunned Arsen.

CHAPTER 12

Damn, damn, damn! Sleepless, I squeezed my eyes shut and rolled over in my bed. How had I mistaken Arsen for an alien? It was inexplicable.

Crazy.

My breath tightened.

No. I wasn't crazy. There had to be a rational explanation that did not include me losing my mind. Had I been drugged? Was there something wrong with the coffee she'd served?

Was Clare crazy?

Was I?

Had my mind been playing tricks after hearing Clare's story? The business with the owl I could chalk up to being-in-the-present-giddiness. The books had warned about that.

But the alien at my window was something else – I had missing lemon curd as proof. Now I felt even more sympathy for Clare. I'd *swear* I'd seen an alien last night. I wouldn't swear it to Arsen though. Normally, getting net gunned would be the sort of thing he'd laugh off. But I guess ex-military types are especially touchy about being shot with their own weapons.

And why did my hands smell like musty parsnips?

Dragging myself from bed, my eyes gritty, I got to work.

But I yawned through breakfast, unable to meet the gaze of the FBI agent. She left after waffles for parts unknown.

Then I stumbled through the online reservations, fumbled through the Wednesday cleaning. And when I'd accomplished the bare minimum, I staggered into the kitchen, slumped at the table, and rejiggered my day planner. Did I need to wash the windows today? Why? There was time tomorrow.

Dixie ambled into the kitchen and poured a cup of coffee. "What's wrong?" She set the mug on the butcher block counter.

"Nothing."

"You look like hell." Dixie folded her arms over her black tank and leaned against the kitchen counter.

"Thanks."

"What's wrong?"

"Alien encounters."

"Cool."

The afternoon sun streamed through the curtained window behind her. It gleamed irritatingly off the linoleum floor.

"Not cool," I snapped. "Scary and exhausting."

"No, it's not."

"Is too! And how would you know? You weren't there."

"Contrary to the movies, most people get a sense of peace from alien encounters." Her eyes narrowed. "And where were you?"

Exhaustion was my only real excuse for asking Dixie's opinion on the Clare situation. I was supposed to be keeping quiet. But I knew Dixie wouldn't blab, and she was the real UFO expert. So, I told her about last night's adventure, omitting the bit about the net gun.

Dixie cocked her head. "You saw an owl?"

"It was more than an— Forget the owl." My hands shook slightly as I raised my own mug to my lips. My muscles were rubbery from pushing the heavy vacuum and scrubbing out showers. "What do you think of Clare's experience? Her lost time–"

"I didn't hear about any lost time."

"She goes to bed, wakes up to a nightmare, then finds herself somewhere else."

"Where?" she asked.

"Usually outside."

Dixie picked up her mug and gulped coffee. "You've never been precise when it comes to UFO phenomena." She brandished the mug.

"I'm precise! It's why I use this." I brandished my planner.

"A day planner isn't very living-in-the-now."

"I use a planner so I *can* live in the now," I said. "And I have a log."

"Lost time refers to losing time when you appear to be fully conscious. You're awake, and then suddenly time has passed. What you're describing sounds like something else. I dunno, maybe it was a drug trip or something, but not lost time. I mean, by your definition, every time we wake up from a nap, we've lost time."

"Okay."

"You lose time every time you go to sleep at night."

"Okay, okay," I grumped. "I get it. But what about the owls?"

"That makes it even more likely something non-UFO is happening. The face of an owl looks a lot like the face of a big-eyed alien. I mean, owls have feathers and are a lot smaller, but if you're whacked out – does Clare do drugs?"

"No! I mean, I don't know." And I certainly didn't do drugs... aside from a battery of herbs I took for anti-anxiety. But those didn't count. I'd carefully checked for all possible side effects and contraindications.

"You didn't ask her?" she asked, incredulous.

"It seemed rude. Her father was an Air Force colonel!"

"So?" Dixie rolled her eyes. "You are so naive."

I hesitated. "Have you ever...?"

"I'm not going to mess with my brain. I *need* my brain." Dixie grinned. "My liver is another matter. You?"

"No. Same reason." I didn't like the idea of giving up control.

"Find out what Clare's been taking."

"And if she hasn't been taking anything?"

Dixie shrugged. "She's hired a psychic and now you to deal with her problems." She put the last word in air quotes. "It seems like overkill. Maybe she's just an attention seeker."

And what *was* Danella doing for Clare at this point? "Clare said something else. She said she tried some light hypnosis."

Dixie shook her head. "Bad idea."

"I thought so too."

"But I'll bet you didn't think why."

"I'll bite. Why do you think it's a bad idea?"

"When you watch a movie or TV, your subconscious doesn't understand it's not real. For the subconscious it *is* real. It becomes a memory. These false memories can become part of a recovered hypnotic memory. Take the case of the Hills in 1964. They saw a UFO and were disturbed enough to see a hypnotherapist. In hypnosis, Barney Hill recalled an alien with big eyes wrapping partway around its head. But ten days earlier, a popular TV program had aired a show with an alien just like Barney described. Barney Hill probably wasn't lying, but his memory was."

I nodded. I remembered reading about the Hill abduction but hadn't heard about the false memory. Dixie really was the expert.

She grabbed my planner and tore a page from the notes section.

"Hey!" I said, indignant.

Dixie scribbled on the page and returned it to me. "Ask Clare these questions. If the answer is no, something's not right with her experiences."

I studied the page. "But I saw an alien at the window too. He stole my lemon curd."

"Really?" Dixie lowered her voice. "Lemon curd?"

I nodded.

She looked around the kitchen. "You know what that means?"

Breathless, I leaned closer. "No, what?"

"It means you're as daffy as Clare. What would an alien do with lemon curd?"

"I don't know why he took it," I said stubbornly, "but he did."

"How do you know it was a he?"

"Well, I... I didn't see... It was just a face in the kitchen window."

She snorted. "You're imagining things."

I propped my head on my fist. But it *did* take my lemon curd. It had happened. "Thanks." *For nothing.*

"No problem. Let me know how it goes with your investigation, will ya?"

"Sure," I said, surprised. Dixie had never seemed all that interested in what I was doing before.

"Because if you get sent to the funny farm, I get Wits' End." Dixie bounded out the kitchen door.

"No, you don't," I called after her. "All the people I owe money get it." The roofer. The plumber. The furnace guy…

Tallying up debts in my head, I retreated to my sitting room for a nap. Bailey curled up beside me on the black velvet couch, and I closed my eyes.

My phone rang on the coffee table, jerking me to sitting.

The room was draped in cobwebby darkness. I swayed, disoriented, on the couch. The phone rang again.

Yawning, I answered without checking the number. "Hello? This is Susan at Wits' End." I wiped my chin.

It was damp. *Ick.* Drool.

"Susan." Clare whispered, her voice taut as an electric wire. "Help me."

I stood and banged my shin on the coffee table. "What's wrong?" I winced.

"Someone tried to kill me."

I snapped to attention. "Where are you? Are you in a safe place?"

"I'm at the circus. Emmery's not answering—" She sobbed, a quick, pained sound. "Please come."

"Have you called the police?"

"Just come. They'll know where at the ticket booth."

"They—?"

She hung up.

Hands shaking, I called back.

"This number is unavailable or not in service," a pleasant, mechanized voice said.

Swearing, I hung up, grabbed my purse and keys.

Bailey whined and thumped his tail on the floor.

"It's okay," I said. "I'll be back soon."

I pelted down the mountain highway in my Crosstrek until I reached a dirt track. Slowing, I bumped along it to a makeshift parking lot dotted with oaks. Colorful circus tents clustered in the nearby field.

I swallowed. There'd been a UFO festival here last September – a festival where a man had been killed. I didn't really believe in ghosts, but if bad mojo was a thing, this field had it.

"Why did it have to be here?" I muttered. But it was the perfect spot for a circus. The vineyard on the nearby hill owned the property and rented it out for events.

Without much hope, I called Clare.

No answer.

I called Arsen. It's what I should have done from the start, but Clare's panic had been contagious.

"Hey," he said cautiously. "How are you feeling?"

"Fine." I glanced at the clock. "Why wouldn't I be?"

"Last night you shot me with a net gun."

"Only because I thought…" I'd thought it was a stun gun, and he was an alien. I winced. "I'm sorry. Again. Look, I got a call from Clare that she's in trouble. She's at the circus. I've come to get her."

"I'm in Bear Valley," he said. "It will take me forty minutes to get to you."

"Hopefully I'll be back at Wits' End by then."

"Susan–"

"It's okay," I said. "It's a circus." What can happen at a circus?

"Be careful."

"I will. Thanks." We said our goodbyes and hung up.

I stepped from the car. Hitching my purse over my shoulder, I hiked through the tall grass to the ticket stand.

A woman in thick green eyeshadow and a blue lamé turban eyed me. "The circus is free. Entering the tents requires tickets. How many do you want?"

"I'm, uh, here to meet Clare Fitzgerald?"

She stared at me for a long moment. "Oh." The woman pointed. "Second tent past the tattooed man."

"Thanks," I said, uneasy. If the ticket taker knew about Clare, then Clare probably wasn't alone. She was likely all right. So why was my heart thumping unevenly, clammy sweat slicking my neck?

A teen in a baseball cap brushed past. Out of the corner of my eye, I saw an arm reach into my purse. I jerked backwards, clutching my bag, and looked around wildly. The teen had vanished around a corner. Heart banging, I searched my bag. My wallet was still there. I exhaled slowly and zipped it up. I'd swore I'd seen a hand reach into the bag, but I was seeing a lot of things these days. Aliens. Owls. What was a disembodied arm in the grand scheme of things?

Agent Manaj strode past in her black outfit. I raised my hand to wave then dropped it to my side. The FBI agent could be an ally. Or she could make Clare really uncomfortable when we found her. And I *would* find her. But what was Manaj doing here?

Pensive, I walked past carnie games, past teenagers eating cotton candy, past a calliope bleating a doleful circus tune. The circus wasn't exactly packed. But it was only a Wednesday night.

The little man who'd given me the circus flyer emerged from a tent and stepped on my foot. "Whoops."

I winced, curling my toes. "Excuse me, do you know where—?"

"No time, no time." He tipped his top hat and walked on.

"Never mind then," I muttered.

Quickening my pace, I hurried onward. The paths between the tents grew narrower, gloomier. I passed fewer and fewer people. Finally, I found the tent, a cloth painting on its side of a tattooed man. It stood at the bleeding edge of the circus, and then, empty fields.

Confused, I circled the tent. At its rear, a low, temporary fence formed a barrier in the dirt. Beyond it was darkness.

I peered into the shadows. The silhouettes of tents rose on the other side of the fence. I guessed these were the private residences of the circus workers.

I edged around a break in the fence and stubbed my toe on a rock. Muffling a curse, I dug into my purse for my flashlight. My shoulders collapsed. I'd left it on the kitchen table.

"Great."

I walked on, trying to let my eyes adjust, and passed a dark and silent tent.

Beyond it stood another. Light streamed from a break in its canvas. The wind flapped the thick cloth, making a hollow sound.

Swallowing, I edged to the lit tent. "Hello?"

No one answered.

I knocked on the canvas. "Hello?"

A woman wrenched the canvas entry aside. Her face was covered in makeup of dizzying, fantastic, black and white designs. "Yes?" she asked, her voice shockingly deep.

"I'm Susan Witsend. I'm looking for Clare. Clare Fitzgerald."

She looked me up and down and sneered. My capris and blouse must have seemed pedestrian compared to her outfit: a sequined leotard, flesh-colored tights and matching slippers. She turned and dropped the tent flap.

Had that been an invitation or dismissal? I pushed the fabric aside and walked into the tent.

I stopped short and stifled a gasp.

The tent glittered like Ali Baba's cave - a wash of color and light. Lanterns of colored glass hung from the ceiling. Carpets covered the floor. Three daybeds piled with pillows in shimmering fabrics stood against the tent walls.

Clare sat on one of the daybeds. She leapt to her feet. "You came." A swollen, red bruise marked her temple.

Oh, no. Heart thumping, I hurried to her and grasped her upper arms. "Are you all right? What happened?"

"I came here with Emmery. Somehow, we got separated."

"You said you were attacked."

She gulped and nodded. "I was looking for Emmery. Someone grabbed me from behind and began dragging me away from the tents. I thought— I thought they were going to kill me. His hands were over my mouth and nose and eyes. I couldn't breathe, couldn't scream, couldn't do anything."

"How did you get away?" I asked, aghast.

"I struggled. He got angry and banged my head on a... a bench I think. And then I heard the Wyrd Systers, and he let me go."

"The Wyrd...?"

The woman who'd answered my knock bowed. "The Wyrd Systers. I am but one."

"Did you see who attacked her?" I asked.

"Alas," she boomed, "no. We found your friend and brought her back here to recover."

"Clare," I said, "this is serious. Why didn't you call the police?"

"I saw the owl again. It's here. It's following me." She grasped my wrist, her voice shrill. "They'll think I'm crazy, but it's real, and Emmery's gone. He wouldn't leave me. I know something's happened to him. What if they have him?"

The Wyrd Syster rolled her eyes.

I bristled. Sure, Clare sounded hysterical. But if Clare was crazy, so was I.

Was I? I clutched my purse, then shook myself. Didn't matter. We lunatics needed to stick together.

"We need to call the sheriff," I said. "If Emmery's missing—"

Emmery thrust aside the canvas flap and strode into the tent. "Clare! I've been worried sick." He pulled her into his arms.

I looked discreetly away.

Two women identical to the first Wyrd Syster glided into the tent. They nodded to their sister.

"Are you all right?" he asked. "What happened to your head?"

"This?" Clare plucked at her hair, pulling it forward to cover the bruise. "It's nothing. I fell."

"Clare," I said, "that's—"

"Honestly, Susan, it's no big deal," she said rapidly. "All that's been hurt is my pride."

"As long as you're sure," I said uncertainly. I'd brushed off the net gun incident to Arsen, claiming tricks of the light and exhaustion. If I couldn't admit the truth to him, I couldn't blame Clare for holding back with Emmery. But I'd been making a lot of excuses for Clare lately. And for my own behavior.

"I was looking all over for you," she said to Emmery. "What happened?"

"I turned around and you were gone," he said. "You weren't answering your phone. I've been looking all over for you. And then… It doesn't matter. What's Susan doing here?"

"I ran into her, and she agreed to help me look for you." She turned to me, her gaze pleading.

"Yeah," I said, ignoring the little voice shrieking in my head that it was time to come clean. "I thought I'd check out the circus when it wasn't too busy."

He shook his head and winced, rubbing the back of his skull. "Thank God you're all right. Someone cracked me on the head. I thought— Never mind what I thought."

"You were attacked?" I asked.

He gave an embarrassed laugh. "Someone stole my wallet. It's humiliating, me being a cop and all."

My jaw tightened. An attack on Emmery – to get him out of the way and get to Clare? "Someone tried to pick my pocket earlier. When did this happen?"

"Not long after I noticed Clare and I had separated. Hey," he said defensively, "I looked for the guy, but he's long gone."

I shook my head. This was serious – a planned attack. We had to start telling each other the truth. "Clare–"

"Let's go home." She grabbed Emmery's hand. "I want to get out of here."

He kissed her lightly on the forehead. "Sure, babe." He eyed me. "Maybe we should walk you out too, Susan? With everything that's going on..." He eyed the Wyrd Systers.

"Yeah," I said, drawing out the word. "I guess I've seen everything I wanted to."

We thanked the Wyrd Systers and walked through the tents to the lonely parking lot.

"Clare, there's something I want to ask you," I said, remembering Dixie's two questions.

"What?" She shot me a nervous look.

"These alien experiences you've been having, you said they started a few months ago. But do you remember anything similar happening when you were younger?"

She paused beside a cotton candy stand. "No. Nothing like that. Why?"

"Sometimes people who experience UFOs start young," I lied. Actually, they nearly always started young. I'd checked up on Dixie's two questions. On to question number two: "What about your father? Did he ever experience anything similar to what you have?"

Her mouth slackened. "My father?" She looked away, her lips crimping inward. Clare blinked rapidly.

"Her father's death is still a little raw," Emmery said. "Come on, let's go." He tugged her forward.

We walked on.

"My father's experiences," she said quietly. "Do you mean at Area 51?"

"I don't—" Did I? "Anything you can think of."

"He never talked about aliens, and he thought my experiences were all in my head." She swallowed jerkily. "We fought that morning, before he... He wanted me to see a psychiatrist."

Emmery stiffened.

"I was so... angry at him," she whispered.

"What happened wasn't your fault," Emmery said.

"I know," she said. "I know. But... Let's not talk about it anymore. Let's talk about anything else." And Clare kept up a lively and irritating chatter on our walk back to the parking lot.

But the person I was really irritated with was myself.

Emmery had been attacked, Clare's father murdered, my lemon curd stolen.

Okay, the lemon curd wasn't that big of a deal in the grand scheme of life. But it was real evidence that something was going on.

And yet... Clare had answered "no" to Dixie's two questions. Clare didn't fit the pattern of UFO abductees. I shoved my clenched hands into my pockets. What *was* going on?

CHAPTER 13

Dixie's jaw compressed. "There are no such things as interdimensional aliens. You're turning this into something supernatural. UFO phenomena has to be studied using the scientific method!" Thursday morning sunlight streamed through the stained glass above the transom. The colored light streaked her olive tank top.

"Please." Danella rolled her eyes. The psychic looked like she'd just strolled out of Haight-Ashbury. Low-slung jeans. A red and blue peasant top. Mandala beads around her neck and big silver rings on her fingers.

"What *science* is behind UFOs?" Danella asked. "Science is a rigorous process of testing and replicating results. You can't replicate results with something that's here today, gone in an instant."

"You can try." Dixie jammed her hands on the hips of her cargo shorts.

The honeymooners pretended to examine the alien bobble heads on the shelf in the foyer.

Agent Manaj studied the debaters unabashedly. Bailey leaned against the FBI agent's ankle. I hoped she didn't notice the fur he'd left on her black suit trousers.

"Scientists think there may be other dimensions," I offered, trying to make peace. On any other day, the argument would have seemed delightfully eccentric. Now I just worried the insanity was catching. And I really wanted to talk to Dixie about Clare's answers to her two questions.

Bailey whuffed and sat on the FBI agent's foot.

"That's not what she's talking about," Dixie said. "The idea of aliens using interdimensional travel, like worm holes, to bypass the limitations on lightspeed or greater-than-lightspeed travel just makes sense. You could move from one point in the galaxy to the next almost instantaneously." She rubbed the back of her head. "It would also explain why the spaceships stored at Area 51 don't have living quarters. But she's talking about—"

"Aliens from other dimensions," Danella said.

"Which is nuts," Dixie said.

"We don't know there are spaceships at Area 51." I glanced at the FBI agent.

Of course, I'd read about the infamous scientist who claimed to have worked on the ships. He said our government had been attempting to reverse-engineer alien technology. What UFOlogist hadn't? But it was one man's word against the silence of the US government. And if the colonel had known about spaceships at Area 51, he hadn't talked. But *had* he known something? Was that why Manaj was interested in his murder?

"The fact is," Danella said, "there's a long history of interdimensional abductions."

"*UFO* abductions," Dixie said.

The beagle's head swiveled between the two women.

"For example," Danella said, "look at the witch trials from the middle ages. The witch hunter's bible, the *Malleus Maleficarum*, details signs of people practicing witchcraft. These signs are the same as those of people reporting abductions."

Manaj smoothed her sleek, ebony bun. "She's not wrong."

Dixie made an exasperated noise. "What does that have to do with different dimensions?"

The honeymooning couple edged closer.

"Marks on bodies," Danella said, "the mysterious deaths of farm animals, nighttime flights, meetings in circles in the woods. All these things are associated both with medieval witchcraft and with today's alien abductions."

Nighttime flights? I worried my bottom lip and thought of Clare's description of being taken. She'd said she'd felt like she was flying. And there had been that moment in the woods, when I'd felt like *my* toes had lifted off the ground.

But they hadn't, of course. I'd been tired and in the present and definitely not crazy.

Danella flipped her graying ponytail over one shoulder. "The small gray aliens described by abductees strongly resemble medieval descriptions of fairies," she continued. "The tall, gray aliens strongly resemble medieval descriptions of the devil."

"Which is it?" Dixie asked. "Small or tall?"

"Lucifer is associated with the brightest star in the sky," Danella continued more loudly. "Is it coincidence alien abductees claim to see lights in the sky?"

"No, because UFOs come from the *sky*," Dixie said. "Through our atmosphere. From outer space. They're not interdimensional."

Danella shook her head. "Dixie, interdimensional travel is much more plausible than spaceships. Everyone knows lightspeed is impossible."

Agent Manaj frowned.

"Maybe not," Dixie sputtered. "But even if they are traveling interdimensionally, that doesn't mean the aliens are from fairyland. It means they're from another planet. They simply understand a level of physics that enables interdimensional travel."

"Occam's Razor," the psychic said. "The simplest answer is the correct one. Interdimensional travel means interdimensional aliens."

"Wow," I said. "Instead of me giving the next UFO lecture, maybe you two should hold a debate."

Dixie glared at me.

"I don't have anything to prove." Danella stalked up the stairs.

"Neither do I." Dixie turned to storm out.

"Wait," I said.

Dixie blew out an exasperated breath. "What?"

I glanced at the FBI agent. Maybe now wasn't the time to talk about Clare. Besides, I really already knew what her "no" answers meant.

I handed Dixie a bucket. "Room three's ready for cleaning."

She scowled and stomped up the carpeted stairs.

The honeymooners drifted outside.

"Sadly," Manaj said, "I *do* have something to prove, and the day is wasting."

"I saw you at the circus last night," I blurted.

She paused beside the front door. "What were you doing there?" she countered.

"Oh, you know." I hunched my shoulders. "I understand there was an assault."

"An assault?" she asked, looking interested.

"A police officer was mugged. His wallet was stolen."

"Oh? Who?"

"Emmery Berghoff." I angled my head toward the colonel and Marion's cabin.

"Interesting." She drifted out the door.

Well. That hadn't been helpful.

I sat behind the desk and busied myself with my myriad of housekeeping chores that don't involve actual housekeeping. Renewing chamber of commerce dues. Paying bills. Paying bills. Paying bills.

The two cameramen trotted down the steps, followed by the psychic.

I shoved back my chair, rumpling the Persian rug, and stood. "Oh, hey, Danella?"

"There's no problem with our staying longer, is there?" She strolled to the desk, her mandala beads rattling against her peasant top.

"No, it's fine. You can stay."

"Then I hope this isn't about my argument with your assistant."

"Who?" I asked. "Oh. She's my cousin, and no. I was just wondering how people got onto your show?" It still seemed odd Clare had gotten Danella here so quickly and seamlessly.

Danella blinked at me. "My show? Why? You're already on it."

"I mean, what's the process? In case anyone asks me."

"We're exclusively online, so we're more streamlined. That means our process, as you call it, is fairly quick. Usually they contact my producer, who vets the requests. If any look promising, she'll interview the person and take a look around the site. And if that works out, we'll book the show."

I slipped my hands into my pockets. "How long does that take?"

"We've already booked the next season."

"So," I said, "about a year?"

"Yes, why? Don't tell me you want me to return to Wits' End for your ghosts?"

"No," I said. "I was surprised, that's all. It seemed to go more quickly for Clare."

"Oh." She glanced at the front door, where her cameramen lingered. "You two can wait outside," she said to them.

Cameras on their shoulders, the men tromped onto the porch.

Bailey shook himself, collar jingling, and followed them out the front door.

"This is our last show of the season," Danella said. "And the guests who'd been lined up – owners of a haunted house in Victorville – fell through. My producer thought Doyle would make a good spot. There's been a lot going on here."

An odd chill clenched my heart. Was Doyle getting... weirder? Lately, the happenings in Doyle seemed less oddball and more ominous. Disappearances. Reappearances. And now the colonel's murder, a colonel who'd worked at Area 51. It was enough to turn me into a conspiracy theorist.

Cameraman Bob poked his head through the open door. "Hey, Susan. Your, um, tire is flat."

"My tire?" I hurried to the door and onto the front porch. I pushed open the screen door.

My Crosstrek sat at an odd angle in the driveway. The other cameraman, Mahir, squatted beside a sagging tire. Its rubber pooled on the gravel.

I bit back a curse. "Oh... no." Sometimes, being polite and professional felt inadequate to a good swearword.

Beside Mahir, Bailey looked up at me, his doggy face morose.

A freaking flat. Just what I needed. I sighed. "Thanks for letting me know."

"I can change it for you," Mahir said.

"We don't have time for that," Danella said. "Sorry, but we're on a strict schedule."

"Are you headed to Clare's?" I asked.

"Where else? Let's go, boys."

The three clambered into the TRUE MEDIUM van and drove off.

I had a spare tire, but that would just get me to the mechanic's. So, I pulled my phone from my pocket and called the garage.

They promised to send someone over with a new tire. There was no nonsense about towing or me waiting in the garage while they worked. I knew the mechanic and he knew me, and he'd get it handled. It was one of the nice things about small town life in Doyle.

My stomach tightened. And then there were the disappearances...

My gaze darted around the yard. I hurried inside the Victorian and got to work cleaning rooms.

An hour later, Kano, the mechanic, shouted up the stairs. "Susan? I'm done."

My hair pulled back in a kerchief, I hurried down to the foyer. "Thanks. What do I owe you?"

The elderly Asian man handed me an oil-smeared invoice.

"I'll get my checkbook," I said.

He trailed after me to the desk.

"Susan, someone slashed that tire."

I froze, my hand on the desk's drawer pull. "Slashed?"

"Yep. I think you should make a police report."

"Police report?" I stammered. "But it can't have anything to do with the colonel."

His gray brows rose. "The colonel? I'm talking about these damned kids. Someone tagged my shop last week with graffiti. The local teens are getting out of control." His laugh was uneasy. "Unless you think aliens did it."

I stared.

"I was joking," he said.

"Oh." I smiled, sickened. "Right." The tire *could* have been random vandalism. But after the flipped switches in my fuse box, it didn't seem likely.

Someone was targeting… me.

He shook his head. "Doyle is changing, and not for the better. I'm thinking of retiring to Nevada. No state tax there. They don't have the alien problem we do either."

"Isn't Nevada sort of famous for UFOs?" I asked, tentative, because I wasn't in the habit of contradicting my elders.

He tapped the side of his head. "But not for abductions, and that's all I care about." He looked up, as if he could see through the roof. "Strange lights in the sky. Aliens on Main Street—"

"What aliens on Main Street?"

"Haven't you heard?" He hitched up his oily black slacks. "Mrs. Kettlebaum saw an alien crawling up the wall of Antoine's bar Tuesday night. She said he looked like a big, gray spider."

"That's a– Really?" Mrs. Kettlebaum wasn't a drinker, and she wasn't stupid or crazy. I sagged against the desk. Clare and I weren't alone. That didn't make me feel better. "When was this?"

"Last night, around eleven I think. It's in the paper."

"It is?"

He chuckled. "If you're going to run a UFO B&B, you've got to keep up on these things." His expression turned grim. "Or get out like the others."

"What others?"

"The Henderson family is moving. Wife saw something in the sky the other night, and that was it. She's convinced her kids are going to be stolen. I pity the alien who nabs Andrew. That boy's a horror. But aren't you helping out Clare with her little alien problem?"

I blinked. "Where did you hear that?"

"One-armed Frank told me."

"One-armed... How did he hear that?"

He shrugged. "No idea. So, is it true?"

"Ah, I really can't say." *One-armed Frank?* I barely knew the man. Had Dixie blabbed? Had Arsen?

"Gotcha. Top secret stuff. Mum's the word." He watched me expectantly.

"Oh! Your check. Right." I paid him and saw him out. Then I hurried upstairs to room seven, where Dixie was vacuuming.

"Dixie, did you hear that Mrs. Kettlebaum saw an alien on Antoine's Bar?"

"Duh. It's in the paper."

"Why didn't you—?"

"You're in my vacuum path." She nudged my foot with the vacuum.

"One-armed Frank told Kano that I'm investigating Clare's alien problem."

"And?" She shifted a chair.

"Did you tell anyone?"

"Do you think I want people to know my cousin is chasing aliens with Clare Fitzgerald? The same woman who hired a *psychic?*"

"So... that's a no?"

"That's a no."

Hmph. Fat chance I'd tell her about any more alien experiences.

I jogged downstairs and to the kitchen. My laptop computer screen glowed gently on the round table. I sat and surfed the *Doyle Times* website.

DOYLE, CALIFORNIA – A report of an alien, gray-skinned creature crawling up the side of a local bar has locals puzzled.

According to the description provided by the witness, the alien appeared tall and slender, with oddly short arms and legs, was bipedal, with gray skin and no body hair. Its head and feet seemed oversized. Witnesses claim the creature crawled up the side of Antoine's Bar at a "supernatural speed."

Doyle Sheriff Donna McCourt said her office investigated the sighting but was unable to find any corroborating evidence. "People do and see all sorts of things outside Antoine's Bar," she said. "I don't intend to jump to any conclusions. Neither should the public."

Anyone who has had a similar sighting should email Tom Tarrant at the Doyle Times.

I shifted on the chair. *Weird.* Really *weird.*

I printed out a copy of the article for my investigation binder. Then, because B&Bs don't run themselves, I drove to the grocery store for tomorrow's breakfast. Wits' End had a reputation to maintain, and that included fresh fruit on the table.

Arms loaded with groceries, I returned home later than I'd expected. I put the groceries away and hopefully checked my schedule. But I had nothing going on. No investigations. No cleaning. No chores.

I wandered upstairs. Dixie had finished her cleaning and departed, and not a creature was stirring. The old Victorian was empty.

At loose ends, I wandered into the side yard. "Bailey?" I called. "Want to go for a walk?"

He did not come bounding around the corner of the Victorian. I must have missed him sleeping inside. I returned to the kitchen and strolled into my sitting room. "Bailey?"

He wasn't in his dog bed.

I frowned at my open bedroom door. If he'd decided to make my bed his, we were going to have words.

I strode into my bedroom.

No beagle lay on the neatly made bed.

"Bailey?" I skimmed through the downstairs rooms. No dog. I jogged upstairs. "Bailey?"

I hurried to the end of the upstairs hallway and onto the exterior landing. Bracing my hands on the rough wooden railing, I gazed into the backyard. Where was Bailey? Gran had trained him well. He knew not to leave the yard without me or Dixie...

Dixie. Of course.

Relieved, I pulled my phone from my capris and called my cousin.

She answered after five rings. "What?"

"Is Bailey with you?"

"Why would he be with me? Wait, you mean he's not with you?"

My breath hitched. "You don't think he could have accidentally gotten locked inside one of the rooms?"

"No." She hesitated. "Maybe. Oh, damn. I'm sorry, Susan. If I locked him inside—"

"It's fine." I returned inside and pulled the master key card from my back pocket. "It's not like he'll eat the upholstery."

"Call me and let me know when you find the little guy, will you?"

"Sure. It's no biggie. I'm sure he's fine."

But my stomach churned as I went from room to room, looking for the dog.

He wasn't in any of them.

Okay. Logic. Maybe he was asleep somewhere outside, and I'd just missed spotting him. I returned to the yard and checked all the usual places. The gazebo. The spot he'd hollowed out beneath a rose bush. My grandmother's spirit house from Thailand.

He wasn't at any of them.

I swallowed, mouth dry. What if he had run off? What if Bailey had gotten hit by a car? What if he was lost?

I called Arsen.

"Susan." His voice was a warm rumble. "I was just thinking about you."

"I can't find Bailey."

"He's lost?"

"No!" My voice shook. "I mean, yes, I guess so. But he—"

"Never leaves the yard without you or Dixie. Could he be with Dixie?"

"I called her, and she doesn't have him. I've checked all the rooms, even the guest rooms in case he got locked inside. He's nowhere."

"He's somewhere, don't worry. His contact info is on his collar. Call the pound and let them know he's missing. I'll be right over to help you search."

"Thanks."

He said goodbye, and we hung up. I called the pound. A very judge-y woman who seemed to think I'd been reckless with my dog snarled at me. But I hadn't been reckless, had I? I loved Bailey, and I knew his patterns. He was an old dog, set in his ways, and he wouldn't leave the yard!

I stared sightlessly into a pink rosebush and blinked back tears. "I'm sorry, Gran," I whispered. "If you're listening, please help me find him."

Arsen's monster Jeep pulled into my drive ten minutes later. "Sorry it took me so long," he said. "I wanted to get my game finder." He brandished a device that looked like a high-tech hose nozzle.

"Game?"

"Infrared heat detector for finding downed animals. He could be hidden behind a bush somewhere, sleeping."

Sleeping. Right. Breath tight, I followed Arsen as he scanned the rose bushes. A heat detector. Of *course* he'd have a heat detector. But today I was grateful for his security gear. At least we were doing *something*.

"So," he said, "do you want to talk about the other night?"

"The other night?"

"When you attacked me with my own net gun."

"Oh. That other night." I exhaled slowly. "I thought…" How do you tell your boyfriend you only assaulted him because you thought he was from Mars?

"Thought what?" He swept the lattice beneath the kitchen porch.

I swallowed. "Look, I know this is going to sound crazy."

Arsen knelt beside the steps leading up to the kitchen porch. He extended the detector to the right and frowned.

My hands fluttered. "But a lot of weird things have been happening," I continued. "I mean, you know about the lemon curd."

"Yeah, and I'm on it. The only guy who poaches food from your kitchen is me."

"Ha ha. Yeah. Well, the thing is, I thought—"

Reaching between two rose bushes, he wrenched open the lattice door to the crawlspace. "I got something." He crawled inside.

"What? Is it Bailey?"

Arsen grunted. There was a thud, and he swore. "He's here!"

"Oh, thank God." My shoulders collapsed with relief. But what had the beagle been doing beneath the house?

My brain froze. Hold on. Bailey hadn't closed that lattice door behind him. He couldn't have.

Arsen emerged carrying a limp Bailey beneath one muscular arm.

I stepped backward, my knees wobbling. "Bailey. Is he–?"

"He's breathing, but he's unconscious."

"Oh my God."

He jogged to his Jeep. I leapt into the passenger seat, and he gently laid Bailey on my lap.

"Hurry," I said.

Arsen drove as fast as he could, and not half fast enough for me. We screeched into the vet's parking lot, and Arsen took the dog from me. Before I could unbuckle my seatbelt, he was racing across the lot to the vet's office.

We waited. And waited. Thirty minutes ticked by. An hour.

I paced the linoleum floor. "Someone did something to him." I wiped my eye.

"He had a strong pulse," Arsen said. "And he's in good hands. Bailey will be fine."

"Who would hurt an innocent dog?"

"It looked to me like he was drugged."

"Or poisoned?" The foxglove. Was it toxic to pets? But Bailey wasn't a plant eater, and that foxglove had been there for years. Could the killer have fed it to him too? I clenched my hands. "I've got to get that plant out of the garden. He's never eaten the flowers before, but what was I thinking? It's poisonous to humans. It's got to be poisonous to dogs."

"He'll be fine."

I rounded on him. "What if he isn't?"

"He'll be fine," he repeated. "I'm more worried about you."

"Me?" I said. "I'm fine. I mean, I'm worried about Bailey—"

"I meant the net gun attack."

"I wouldn't call it an attack. I wish you'd stop calling it an attack. It was an accident."

"Why'd you shoot me?"

A plump woman clutching a dachshund edged away. Her chair's legs squeak, squeak, squeaked against the linoleum.

Tell him. Just tell him. I crossed and uncrossed my arms. "I thought I saw an alien," I blurted.

The dachshund owner stood and hurried from the office. The bell over the door jangled.

Arsen's face smoothed. "An alien."

My legs wobbled. He thought I was crazy. But why wouldn't he? "Arsen—"

The vet emerged from the back room. He pushed his glasses up his nose. "Bailey's going to be fine."

"Thank you." Sagging with relief, I wrung the man's hand. "Thank you. What's wrong with him? What happened?"

"Um." He rubbed the back of his head. "How do you get on with your neighbors?"

"My neighbors?" I ran my hands through my hair. "Fine. Why?"

"Because someone drugged your dog."

CHAPTER 14

Bailey sat at my feet and panted happily. His tail thumped the kitchen floor. Muddy paw prints splattered the linoleum. A tiny bandage marred his neck where the vet had inserted a tracking chip. After the dognapping, Arsen and I had agreed the tracker was for the best.

I wiped his paws, dirty from digging in the garden. But I wasn't going to scold him, even if he did bury a bone in my daffodils.

Dixie paced the kitchen and scowled. "When I find out who hurt Bailey, I'll do something I *won't* regret." A frame of late-afternoon sunlight streamed through the window and brightened her bare shoulder.

"Get in line." Arsen looked up from the newspaper.

"What was he drugged with?" she asked.

"They're still doing tests," I said. But at least it wasn't foxglove. The vet had ruled that out. I really needed to pull that up.

"Who would do that to a dog?" Dixie raised her arms and dropped them helplessly. "Bailey's harmless. He doesn't even bark much."

My stomach writhed with guilt. Because this wasn't about Bailey. The trick with the lights, slashing my tires... This was about me. "Someone doesn't want me helping Clare." I rose and examined the dishes piled in the sink.

"Fine," Dixie said. "Then *I'll* help Clare."

The kitchen door swung open. Sheriff McCourt stormed inside. She whipped off her hat and ruffled her blond hair. "What did you do?"

I slid a plate into the dishwasher. "Did the vet tell you about Bailey?" Because I hadn't. That said, I knew she kept tabs on me. After all, I *was* her confidential informant. It warmed my heart to think her concern extended to Bailey.

"What does your dog have to do with anything?" Her curls quivered with annoyance. "You've been poking around in my murder again, haven't you? Do I have to arrest you for interfering in an investigation?"

"I haven't!" I said, clutching a plate. "But I have been helping Clare with something else."

"Helping her with what?"

"A UFO thing. It's nothing." And since even One-armed Frank knew about it, it didn't matter if I told the sheriff.

The sheriff's cornflower eyes narrowed. "Don't tell me you're getting into the interdimensional alien act too?"

"No such thing," Dixie said.

"*Something's* going on," I said.

"Oh," the sheriff said, "so you're seeing little green men too?"

My mouth puckered.

The sheriff folded her arms over her khaki shirt. "Say it isn't so."

"There was something at my window the other night," I said.

"Not an alien," the sheriff growled.

"It had big black eyes—"

"Not an alien!"

"And gray skin—"

She threw her hat on the table. A line encircled her Shirley-Temple curls, where her hat had rested.

With one finger, Arsen slid her hat away from him and towards the sheriff.

"There are no such things as aliens," she snarled.

"Fine," I said. "Someone in an alien mask stole my lemon curd. And Clare's been seeing it too. And if something isn't up, then what's Manaj doing here?"

The sheriff froze. "Manaj? Agent Manaj is here? Staying at Wit's End?"

"Yeah." I nodded. "Didn't you know?" I'd thought they were working together.

McCourt swore long and colorfully. She blew out her breath. "I'll deal with her later. Now, how exactly have you been investigating this... alien?"

I pulled open the kitchen drawer and drew out my tabbed binder. "Don't worry. I've got it all organized. So, if this needs to go to court, we'll have an accurate record."

She rolled her eyes.

I turned the pages. "My own observations, photos, dates, moon phases, weather patterns – Clare's experiences always seem to happen on cloudy nights. And you know how much rain we got last spring. I mean, I'm glad we're out of the drought, but enough is enough—"

She snatched the binder from my hands and flipped through it. "Huh. That's actually..." She looked up. "I'd like to take this, if you don't mind."

Of *course* she did. Very carefully, I did not smile.

"I'll make you a copy." Dixie held out her hands.

With a show of reluctance, the sheriff gave her the binder.

Dixie trotted from the kitchen. "And you have hat head," she called as the swinging door closed.

"Clare's visitations started months ago," I said. "Do you think the murder of Clare's father could be connected?"

McCourt ruffled her hair. "I think you should stop thinking about the colonel."

"It's hard not to when he lived right next door," I said. "Worse, the foxglove might have come from my garden. I'm digging it all up tomorrow."

"No," she said, "you're not."

"But Bailey—"

"I don't want you disturbing that garden until I'm sure my deputies are done with it." She eyed me. "You're lucky you've got no motive. Otherwise, I might think you were a suspect."

Oh, please. The sheriff knew perfectly well I was one of the good guys. This was just a little game she played, pretending we weren't working together.

"It's commonly believed the colonel worked at Area 51," Arsen said. "If someone was trying to scare Clare, using aliens as a theme makes a sick sort of sense."

The sheriff's brows sketched upward. "Commonly believed?"

Arsen raised his hands in a defensive gesture. "Hey, I'm just repeating the local gossip. I can neither confirm nor deny."

"Mrs. Fitzgerald did sort of confirm it to me," I said.

"What were you doing talking to Mrs. Fitzgerald?" she asked.

My face heated. "Just, um, neighbor stuff. And what about that alien spotted on Antoine's Bar?"

The sheriff's jaw clenched. Carefully, she picked up her broad-brimmed hat and replaced it on her head. "The next person who says the word *alien* is getting handcuffs. Am I clear?"

We nodded silently.

Dixie walked into the kitchen and handed the sheriff a sheaf of papers.

Sheriff McCourt glanced at it. "Is Manaj in?"

"I saw her run upstairs fifteen minutes ago," Arsen said.

"What room?" the sheriff barked.

"Er," I said, "seven."

She winced and strode from the kitchen.

Arsen and Dixie visibly relaxed. I did not. What was she going to say to Manaj? And room seven... That was where the sheriff's ex had died last year. It must bring back all sorts of bad memories.

That first chaotic investigation was how we'd bonded. I had weirdly fond memories of it.

Dixie turned to me. "What do you need?"

"Huh? I was hoping to track down Mrs. Steinberg today," I admitted. "She knows—"

Dixie cut me off with a hand gesture. "Say no more. I'll stay here and manage Wits' End. And I won't let Bailey out of my sight."

"And I'll install those video cameras we talked about," Arsen said.

Slowly, I nodded. "Thanks." Cameras felt a little too Big Brother to me. But whoever was responsible might hurt a guest. They'd already hurt a helpless dog.

I fled, grateful I'd escaped having to elaborate on my owl-to-alien confession.

Arsen hadn't brought it up on our ride home from the vet's today.

He actually hadn't said much of anything.

A chill touched my left shoulder, and I shrugged it away.

Stop thinking about the future. The future didn't exist. "Live in the now," I mumbled beneath my breath.

Since Manaj and the sheriff hadn't emerged, and I hadn't heard any gunshots upstairs, I hopped into my Crosstrek. I *could* walk to town. But there were lonely stretches of road between Wits' End and Main Street. Today, the car felt safer.

I parked in the lot behind Lenore Bonheim's bookshop and walked the three blocks to Town Hall. Brick with a domed cupola, it was a historic landmark. It was also where Mrs. Steinberg worked.

Climbing the concrete steps, I passed through high, wooden doors to a circular hall. I smiled at the young woman behind the polished, oak help desk.

"Hi," I said, "I'm here to see Mrs. Steinberg."

The clerk adjusted her round-rimmed glasses. "Mrs. Who?"

"Steinberg. She works in records."

She frowned and tapped at a computer keyboard. "Doesn't sound familiar, but... No, I'm sorry. I don't see a Mrs. Steinberg on here. Do you know her first name?"

As far as I was concerned, it was *Mrs.* "No. Did she retire?"

"She'll never retire," a man said behind me, and my shoulders drew inward.

Tom Tarrant, local reporter for the *Doyle Times* grinned. "Hi, Sue." He gazed at me with you-can-trust-me blue eyes. And I had. Right until he pulled the rug out from under me.

"Tom." My mouth flattened into a straight line. Tom had once taken me on a "date." All he'd wanted was to pump me for info on a murder I'd accidentally gotten involved in.

No one likes being a sucker.

"You're looking for old lady Steinberg?" he asked.

"*Mrs.* Steinberg," I said.

"She's here, in the basement."

The woman behind the counter shook her head. "But she's not—"

"You know they've been having trouble updating the computer system, Gail," Tom said.

The clerk frowned. "That is true."

"You must have seen her around," I said to her. "She wears black dresses. Looks about a hundred? Smokes e-cigs on the lawn?"

Her face cleared. "Oh, her!" She frowned again. "She works here? Shouldn't she be retired?"

Tom sighed. "I'll show you the way."

"That's okay," I said, "I really don't—"

But he was already hustling me past the help desk and down a curving staircase that spiraled through the marble floor. "Rough news about your neighbor," he said. "I hear you were there when it happened."

And there it was. The real reason he was "helping" me. Though in fairness, I'd been doing some covert snooping of my own.

"I don't know anything," I said, "and I've got no comment."

"How can you have no comment if you don't know anything? You must know something."

"About an accidental death?"

"If it was an accident, why were deputies nosing around your garden the other day?"

I widened my eyes. "Were they?" Did he really think I'd betray the sheriff's confidence? She was obviously keeping the news it was murder from the press for good reason.

"Come on. Give a guy a break. I'm a hardworking reporter in a dying industry. They've even got me podcasting now in a desperation play. Podcasting!"

"I hear podcasting is really taking off. So, did you get any responses to your article asking about other alien sightings?"

"Oh yeah." He frowned. "Too many."

"Is that possible?"

He stopped on the stairs and turned to me. "My editor's told me to knock off the UFO stuff. In print, anyway. He doesn't seem to care about my podcast, largely because no one listens to it. I don't think *he* even listens to it," he muttered.

"Seriously? But Doyle's all about UFOs. It's the foundation of our tourism industry." Once Dixie learned the newspaper had put the kibosh on UFO articles, she'd be sure conspiracies were afoot.

We walked down a long hallway. The overhead florescent lights flickered and pinged in a defeated way.

"The mayor and the sheriff paid an unexpected visit to the newspaper yesterday afternoon," he said. "When they left the editor's office, I got the word. No more UFOs."

"But why?"

"He said it's because they're scaring people." He heaved a sigh. "My editor may be right. Doyle's getting tense. Haven't you noticed?"

I glanced sidelong at him. I had noticed, but I didn't say anything.

We stopped in front of a door with a pebbled glass window labeled RECORDS.

"Here it is," he said. "Records. Sure you don't have anything for me on the murder?"

"Who said it was murder?"

"A guy's got to try." He winked. "I'll see you around."

Not if I see you first.

I knocked on the door and walked inside. A pasty-faced young man looked up from his desk. "Can I help you?" His eyes bulged slightly, as if he'd spent too much time underground.

"I'm looking for Mrs. Steinberg."

"Who?"

Seriously? "Old lady. Black dress. E-cigs."

"Oh. Her. She's at lunch."

"Do you know when she'll be back?"

"Nope."

"Thanks." I left Town Hall and emerged, blinking, in the hot summer sunlight.

I could stake out Town Hall, but I decided to stake out Ground instead. There was coffee at Ground. And noise and people. And I wouldn't have to wonder about what Arsen was thinking about my confession.

I walked down Main.

A familiar figure in a black dress craned her neck at Antoine's whitewashed, wood plank walls.

My pace quickened. "Mrs. Steinberg!" I waved.

She puffed an e-cigarette and ignored me.

"Mrs. Steinberg." Huffing, I jogged to the old woman. "Hi."

"Susan. Did you just come from Town Hall?"

A cowboy edged through the batwing doors. He tipped his hat to us and strode past.

"I did," I said. "It's a funny thing, you're not in their computer system—"

"And I won't be," she growled. "Not if I have anything to say about it. Young people don't understand the value of privacy anymore."

"But you work there."

"Your point?"

Was pointless. "What were you looking at?" I studied the bar. Where exactly *had* the alien been spotted?

"Nothing, apparently."

"Oh." I looked away, disappointed.

"Is that all?"

"Um, no. What can you tell me about Clare Fitzgerald?"

She blew a smoke ring. "A better question is, *why* should I tell you anything about Clare?"

"Because she's in trouble. And now whoever's been targeting her seems to be targeting me."

"I warned you not to get involved."

"But I am involved."

"Where's your young man? I'd have thought he'd be keeping a closer eye on you."

My insides twisted. I'd been a coward not to stay and talk things over with Arsen. If I had, I wouldn't be standing here worrying about it now. "He's installing security cameras at Wits' End."

"Is he now?" She eyed me. "Maybe he's not as dunderheaded as he appears."

"He's really not." Oh. That was kind of insulting to Arsen. "I mean–"

She chuckled. "I know what you meant. So. Clare." She gazed at the porch above us, shading our section of the raised sidewalk. "There's money of course. The colonel was smart and careful. If Clare dies, her half of the money goes to her stepmother."

"To Marion? But, wouldn't it go to Clare's heirs?"

Her brow pinched with annoyance. "Yes. Like I said, to Marion. Clare has no other heirs."

"Really? Sorry, I just didn't think they got along that well."

Mrs. Steinberg shrugged. "The mother-daughter relationship can be complicated."

Tell me about it. Arsen thought I was joking when I said my mother terrified me. I tugged at the collar of my blouse.

"So," I said, "I guess Mrs. Fitzgerald got the other half of the colonel's estate?"

"Guessing is dangerous work." She blew a smoke ring. "But yes."

"I heard Mrs. Fitzgerald manages Clare's share for five years after the colonel's death."

"An unusual arrangement," she said. "But yes, I might have read that too."

"And if something happens to Clare?"

"Like murder?"

"Or insanity?" I asked.

The Perkins family's station wagon sped past, suitcases piled on the roof. A horn blared, and I flinched.

"I suppose the lawyers would step in then," she said. "Someone would be appointed to manage the estate."

"Like Mrs. Fitzgerald?"

"Possibly."

"Anything else?" I asked.

"I work in records. Do you expect me to know the details of Clare's personal life?"

"Um, no. Well. Thanks."

"Take care, young Susan."

I sighed. "I know, there's more going on than meets the eye."

"More than you can ever know." She ambled toward the domed town hall.

I crossed the street and walked back toward my car. So, Marion Fitzgerald inherited. Well, the spouse was always the prime suspect. And if Clare went around the bend, then she might keep control of the entire package.

A man shouted.

I looked up and stopped short.

Lenore and a scruffy, bearded man in a stained raincoat stood in front of her bookshop.

The man raised his arms, looming over the slender shop owner. "He was in on it, don't you see?"

Lenore replied in a voice too low for me to hear.

Tourists turned on the street to stare. They quickly moved on, ducking their heads, averting their gazes.

I forced my legs to move. "Hi, Lenore!"

The man turned, and my steps faltered. He was one of the Returned, Winston Green, and a surge of pity squeezed my chest. The homecoming of the Disappeared/Reappeared had been tainted by fear and suspicion. Many, like Winston, had been damaged by an experience they could neither remember nor explain. But none of them had been violent.

So far.

I approached warily.

"You!" He stared at me and took a step backward. "You're in on it too."

I stumbled to a halt. If he really thought I was a threat, was I helping by being here or making things worse?

"No," Lenore said, "she's not. She only lived near the colonel. That's all."

Winston stretched a shaking hand toward me. His nails were dark with grime. "She has a UFO in her roof. And he was part of the Area 51 coverup." In a quick movement, he gripped Lenore's arm, and I bit back a startled gasp.

"They're coming back," he hissed. "They're coming back for all of us. That cloud. The aliens. You need to run. Run!"

"Winston." I spoke quietly, my stomach writhing.

Our gazes met.

"It's been ages since we've talked," I continued, and my voice was even.

His gaze shifted. He shook his head.

"How've you been?" I asked.

"I'm…" He looked up. His eyes widened. Winston released Lenore as if she were acid. He ran his hand down the front of his raincoat. "Not so good, I guess."

"Want to grab a cup of coffee?" I asked.

He rubbed his head. "No. It's not clear. None of it's clear anymore. I shouldn't. I'm sorry."

"How's your mom?" I asked. *Stay calm. Act like everything's normal.*

"She's good. Real good. She worries about me."

"We all worry about people we love," I said.

"Yeah. Yeah." He glanced at Lenore. "Sorry. I shouldn't have grabbed you. I just get so…" He shook his head. "I get angry. It's wrong. I need to control it. I'm sorry."

"It's all right," she said. "I've got tea in the bookstore, if you'd like a cup."

He smiled bitterly. "That's kind of you."

The little man from the circus appeared at Lenore's elbow. He tipped his top hat. "Are you the proprietor—?"

Winston reared back. "You. You're one of them!" Knocking Lenore aside, he tore down the sidewalk, his raincoat flapping.

"Goodness," the man said. "Is he all right?"

"No," I said. "He's not." Were any of us?

CHAPTER 15

I leaned against Lenore's high counter and sipped a cup of herbal tea. Its minty scent mingled with book smell. Footsteps silent on the thin, gray carpet, a handful of customers browsed the shelves.

Lenore put down the phone. "Connor will call Winston's mother. They'll take care of him." She flushed. "I meant help him."

"It's okay," I said. Connor was her boyfriend and worked at the Doyle sheriff's station. "I knew what you meant." Even if it had sounded sort of ominous.

"How are you doing?" Lenore fiddled with the cuff of her ivory blouse.

I opened my mouth to tell her about the slashed tire. But suddenly, I'd had enough of dwelling on the past and worrying about the future. I could be more present right now. I could enjoy a conversation with someone I liked and respected. "One of my guests is a psychic. She has an interesting explanation for witchcraft."

Lenore cocked her head, her blond hair cascading past her slim shoulders. "Oh?"

"She said witches back in the day were really experiencing UFO abductions – or interdimensional abductions – when they thought they were flying. I have to admit, she made a compelling case." My ears grew impossibly hot. *This* was my light conversation? Was I looking for some tell that she was a witch?

She blew on her tea. "How so?"

"The night flights, the animal deaths, the circles in the woods..." I blundered on. "They're similar to the experiences of abductees. I mean, the floating, cattle mutilations, and, well, circles in the woods."

"You know, that's not the only explanation."

"What's the other? Hallucinations?"

"Sort of. Some believe that the flights were hallucinated, through the use of flying ointments."

"Flying ointments?"

Her cheeks pinked. "Sorry. I guess the feminist in me doesn't like to think medieval witches were all victims. I want to believe at least some really were trying to work magic. Ever since I took over Mike's rare book business, I guess I've gotten a little obsessed." She leaned across the desk. "He specialized in the occult," she whispered.

"Really? Did he have anything on UFOs?"

She laughed. "Sorry, no."

"How's that side of the business going?"

"Good. I've learned a ton about rare books. And I have to admit, the subject matter is fascinating. Do you know *occult* actually means *secret?* People think it's something dark, but it's really about the exploration of the unknown. And let's face it, there's a lot about this world that we don't know."

I grimaced. That was for sure. And just because she'd been homeschooled and sold occult books didn't make her a witch. But it did make her a bit of an outsider. For some people, I guessed that was enough.

"Well," I said, "thanks for the tea. I'll see you around."

She studied a blank greeting card. "Let me know if you need anything, will you?"

I slid my new Eckart Tolle book into my purse and glanced at her. "Um, sure." What would I need? And why did I get the feeling that Lenore had been changing the subject? But changing it from what?

Bemused, I left the bookstore and rounded the corner to my Crosstrek. The pint-sized SUV had gotten good and hot in the shade-free parking lot. I drove home with only my fingertips touching the wheel.

I pulled into my driveway and stepped from the car. An alpine breeze played with my hair, and I stopped to stretch. Somewhere on the Victorian, a window slammed.

I walked across the lawn and around the corner of the B&B, towards the kitchen entrance.

Danella, in bell-bottom jeans and a red blouse knotted at her waist, stood on the lawn and stared at her bare feet. A large, tie-dyed bag was slung over one of her shoulders.

"Hi, Danella."

She raised her head and frowned. "Have you seen these?"

"Seen what?" I ambled closer.

She pointed at a ring of mushrooms in the lawn.

"Huh. Bummer." I guess I'd have to pull them out, though the ring seemed kind of charming. But Gran had never let weeds of any sort mar her lawn, and I wasn't about to break that tradition.

"Bummer?" A bead of sweat trickled down her neck. "Don't you know what this means?"

"That I've got a mushroom infestation?" I should ask Arsen if these were edible.

"It's another sign." Her knuckles whitened on the strap of her bag. "And it's in your yard."

"Oh." Lenore was right. There was a lot about this world we didn't understand. But I wasn't going to get scared by mushrooms. There were other things to be scared of.

She gazed at the blue sky. "They're sending me a message. I just wish they would be clearer." She shook herself. "I'll have to talk to Clare about this. She'll want to know." She strode around the corner and to the rear of the B&B. Her footsteps sounded on the exterior stairs.

Dixie pushed open the kitchen door.

Bailey galloped onto the porch, his ears flapping and collar jangling. More cautiously, he made his way down the three steps to the lawn and trotted to me.

"Is she gone?" Dixie asked from the porch steps.

I bent to pet the beagle. "Yep."

She came to stare at the ring. "Well, I guess if you can't get a crop circle, this will have to do."

"Very funny. Want to help me pull them?"

"Not really. Learn anything?"

"If Clare dies," I said, "her stepmother gets her half of the estate. That's in addition to the half she already got from the death of the colonel. And if Clare goes nuts, then she keeps control of it."

"You think Clare's in danger."

I pushed a wisp of hair off my face and swayed lightly on my feet. "What's been happening to her doesn't quite fit the UFO literature. It definitely doesn't fit Doyle."

Dixie nodded. "You're learning. In Doyle's past, there was no messing around with repeat alien visitations. People were just taken." She snapped her fingers. "Like that."

"We don't know for sure if they were taken. They just disappeared and reappeared weeks or months or years later." Like Winston Green. I hugged myself.

Dixie made a face. "Are you kidding me? An entire pub—"

"I know, I know."

"And an alien crawling up Antoine's Bar is a first too."

"That had to have been a prank or a drunk, right?" I glanced uneasily toward the Victorian. The sunlight glinted off the UFO in its red roof.

Dixie jammed her fists in her cargo shorts and rocked on her heels.

"What do *you* think's going on?" I asked.

"The fact is, the pattern *has* changed," she said slowly. "Everyone who went missing came back. That never happened before. And now... Maybe it's changing again. I'm not picking up any weird radio signals or anything. But I have been tracking the police scanner. Calls to the sheriff's department have doubled in the last week. It's not normal. Something's happening."

I squeezed my arms tighter. "That might explain why McCourt asked the *Doyle Times* to stop reporting UFO stories."

She straightened. "Are you kidding me? They're trying to hide the truth again? Because it went so well the last time."

"The last time?"

"The disappearance of the Bell and Thistle pub! The government did a masterful job making the rest of the world think it was a hoax. But keeping people in ignorance just causes more panic. I *knew* there was a conspiracy. McCourt has to be in on it. No wonder Manaj is back. She's checking up on the sheriff."

In spite of the sweltering heat, an icicle slipped down my spine. Sheriff McCourt was one of the white hats. She wouldn't conspire to hide the truth.

"I don't know if I'd call this a conspiracy," I said. "It sounds like people are panicking. The sheriff just doesn't want the *Times* to fuel the fire."

"Oh, come on. An entire pub disappeared with everyone in it and the people reappeared months later. This is huge news! Did you see it on any of the major networks? The mainstream media should have been camped out on your lawn. Instead, it's just the UFO nutters who tracked down the story and come to Doyle."

"In fairness, some might call you a UFO nutter."

She planted her fists on her hips. "I'm an investigator. The difference, as you well know, is skepticism."

"And it's not like anyone from the government's been keeping us from talking."

She paced the lawn, her boots sinking into the thick grass. "That's the genius of it all. How do you hide the biggest story in human history? You let people like One-armed Frank tell it."

"I heard his cows went missing."

"Yeah, he won't shut up about it. Which is exactly my point. No one who counts is listening. No one believes us. No one ever will believe us. And I'm heading home."

"Um, where's Arsen?" I tugged the collar of my blouse away from my neck.

"He said he'd be back at three-thirty. He was missing a part for those cameras."

I checked my watch. Three-thirty-two. "Thanks. And thanks for staying with Bailey."

"You're welcome." She strode to the front of the yard and vanished through the low, front gate.

Bailey sniffed a rose bush.

"Come on, Bailey. Let's go back inside."

He ignored me, which was sort of par for the course.

Heaving a sigh, I walked to the dog. "Bail—"

A footprint marked the loose earth in the flower bed. Nearby, a foxglove sat stripped of its leaves.

My heart gave an ugly lurch. This wasn't the same stripped foxglove as before.

Digging a quarter from my pocket, I dropped it next to the footprint and took a photo. I'd probably seen the sheriff use the quarter trick at some time, to give a print perspective. Or maybe I'd seen it on TV. But the way things were appearing and disappearing, I wanted a record.

"Hey, Susan." Arsen strode around the corner of the Victorian, and I straightened. "I'm almost done with the cameras." He stopped short. "What's wrong?"

"Why do you think something's wrong?" My voice came out high and shrill, but I kept talking anyway. "It's not like I'm crazy."

"I know you're not."

He did? After that half-baked outburst? But the tension in my shoulders trickled away. "Sorry. I— I found something." I pointed to the print.

He came to squat beside it. "Small. Looks like a woman's shoe. Not much tread on its sole."

"It could be one of my tennis shoes."

"No, you're a size eight. That's a six."

He knew my shoe size? It was a strange detail to notice. I hoped he didn't think he'd have to track me some day. "And you can tell just by looking at it?"

Arsen pointed to a small, round circle in the dirt. A faint number six was in its center.

"Oh." Heat warmed my face. "Danella was out here earlier."

"She's a ten. Dixie's a five."

"Okay, it's getting a little weird that you know all our shoe sizes."

He rose. "This is a fresh print. It's not from anyone in your B&B." He stared across the fence at the colonel's shingled house.

"I don't suppose you know what Mrs. Fitzgerald's shoe size is?" I asked, glum.

"No." His bronzed brow furrowed. "I don't know Clare's either, though I should, with everything that's been happening."

"I'm starting to think Mrs. Fitzgerald isn't the easygoing gossip she appears to be." I told him what I'd learned from Mrs. Steinberg.

"There's one way to find out if it was her or Clare," he said. "We check their shoes."

We walked to the street, around the fence, and to the colonel's A-frame.

No one answered our knock.

We waited a bit, then walked down the front steps.

"Her car's in the drive," I said, pointing at the vintage Mercedes.

"She could have walked somewhere."

"Yeah." But I shifted, uneasy.

There was a high-pitched noise. A fluttering sound, like the flapping of wings, came from the back yard.

"That sounds like wild turkeys," Arsen said.

We walked around the side of the house.

I froze, a chill spreading through my core.

A flock of turkeys marched in a circle, heads bobbing, spindly legs lifting in odd precision.

In the center of their circle lay Marion Fitzgerald.

CHAPTER 16

I stared, the blood turning arctic in my veins.

The turkeys continued their eerie circling. My thoughts orbited as uselessly as the birds. *Do something. Help her. Do* something.

But Marion was dead, her eyes half-closed and staring. A white crust had formed around her mouth. A tumbler lay on the lawn beside her curled hand. The back of her tunic and slacks were darkened with dew.

Sickened, I pressed one hand to my mouth. Marion. Marion the gossip. Marion who had lost her husband and loved her stepdaughter.

Possibly to death.

"She's gone," Arsen said quietly. "Let's not disturb the body."

I pulled out my phone.

"I'll call the sheriff," he said, not noticing my movement. His eyes, like mine, were transfixed by the sight of the parading birds.

I swallowed and turned on my phone's video recorder. I wasn't filming the scene for the sheriff. I was doing it for myself, to confirm this was happening. This was real.

"Yes," Arsen was saying. "All right." Phone to his ear, he moved into the circle of birds.

They scattered up the hillside in a flurry of flapping wings and affronted gobbles.

Arsen knelt and pressed his fingers to Marion's throat. After a long moment, he shook his head. Still speaking into the phone, he carefully backed away along the same path he'd taken.

The turkeys peered at us from the low bushes.

There was a perfectly reasonable explanation for the birds' behavior. But I was damned if I knew what it was. I shivered and turned off the video recorder.

Arsen pocketed his phone. "They'll be here soon. I need to wait here and make sure no one disturbs the body. Susan, you don't have to stay. You can go inside."

I slipped my hand into his. "I'm not leaving." I knew this wasn't his first dead body. I knew he'd seen worse. But this was different.

Lightly, he squeezed my hand. "How are you doing?"

I leaned against him. "They were neighbors." I didn't have to say more.

Arsen understood. He always understood.

We waited in silence until the sheriff came. Then we stood aside for her small army of deputies.

Manaj came to stand on my B&B's kitchen porch. She was dressed in black yoga pants and a matching tank.

I guessed this was her Men-in-Black casual wear.

The agent watched the activity, her arms folded. Ignoring Manaj, the sheriff crouched beside the body.

Sheriff McCourt looked up. "Hernandez!"

A nearby deputy stopped unwinding crime scene tape.

"Take Mr. Holiday's statement." The sheriff rose and walked to me. "This way, Witsend."

She walked to the end of the Fitzgerald's driveway, and I followed.

"Why did you come here?" Sheriff McCourt pushed up her hat brim.

I glanced at Arsen, by the foot of the A-frame's stairs. He spoke earnestly to the deputy, who I knew was a friend of his. "There was a footprint," I repeated. "Near some foxglove in my garden that you told me not to disturb, and I didn't disturb it. But someone had cut more foxglove leaves. The person who'd left the footprint, we guessed." I stepped sideways and brushed against a rose bush. It plucked at my blouse, and I yanked away.

"That doesn't explain why you came here instead of calling me."

"It looked like a woman's footprint." I rubbed my arm, where the rose bush had plucked at it.

"And?"

"And Mrs. Fitzgerald is a woman."

The veins bulged above her uniform collar "So you were investigating."

"No. Well, maybe a little. We just wanted to make sure she was all right."

"The only reason I'm not arresting you for interfering in an investigation is because I've got enough on my hands with this body."

Sure. Right. We both knew she wasn't going to arrest me. I was her inside gal. But I nodded like I believed it. If she wanted to put on a show for her deputies, that was fine by me.

"Why are you winking at me?" she asked.

"Am I? Something must be in my eyes." *Wink, wink.*

"Bah. It looks like she's been out there all night. I thought Clare Fitzgerald was living with her stepmother? Why didn't she report her missing?"

"Clare's not staying here anymore. She said…" I trailed off, feeling like a narc. Is there UFO investigator-client privilege?

"She said what?"

"She said it was Marion's house, and she didn't feel comfortable staying there."

"Huh. I suppose it's a good thing you found her when you did. Hold on." Sheriff McCourt walked to the body, squatted and photographed the bottoms of Marion's shoes. The sheriff returned to me. "Show me this footprint."

I led her into my garden and pointed at the shoe print beside the clipped foxglove. She compared the photo on her phone to the print. "Could be Marion Fitzgerald's."

Still ignoring the FBI agent on the porch, McCourt dropped a quarter to the ground beside the footprint.

We were totally in sync, a fact I would have taken more pride in if Marion hadn't been killed.

The sheriff snapped another picture. "Don't touch anything. I'll send some techs over to take a look at it."

"There's also this." I pulled up the video I'd taken and handed her my phone.

"What the—?" She cursed. "Well. At least you got video of Arsen checking the body and backing away. That will be useful in a trial. I'll need this video."

"I'll email it to you now."

On my kitchen porch, Agent Manaj coughed loudly and folded her bare arms.

McCourt returned my phone.

"Then I'd like you to delete it," she said.

My hands dropped to my sides. "Delete it?" *Delete evidence?* Had I heard right?

"You know how people will react to seeing that."

"I would never show anyone—"

"I don't want to take any chances."

I bit my bottom lip. "Those turkeys… it *was* weird."

"There's nothing weird about it. Turkeys are flocking birds. The leader probably started circling the body because it was nervous or curious, and the others followed. But people won't see that. They'll see a dead woman and apparently strange animal behavior and think aliens are involved."

The sheriff made sense. I was an alien agnostic, and after seeing those birds, *I* was ready to believe. But I was a little offended she thought I'd let someone leak that video. This wasn't my first rodeo.

"Okay." I sent her the email with the video. "Check to make sure you have it before I delete my copy."

She checked her own phone and nodded. "I've got it. Go ahead."

She watched while I deleted the video, then she checked my phone.

It was almost as if she didn't trust me.

"Good," she said. "And keep your mouth shut about this."

"I will. But what about Agent Manaj?" I nodded toward the porch.

"*Ms.* Manaj is on vacation. She's not involved in this."

"Oh." A rush of hot embarrassment on Manaj's behalf swept my chest and neck.

Bailey pushed through the kitchen door and past the FBI agent. The beagle barked and raced toward the sheriff.

I scooped him, wriggling, into my arms before he could harass her or dig up evidence.

Dig...

I frowned and stared at the flower bed. A few pieces of earth flecked the nearby lawn. "This isn't right."

"What's not right?" the sheriff asked.

"I caught Bailey digging here this morning. This footprint is right on top of the ground where I repaired the damage. It was put here after I refilled the hole. But you said Mrs. Fitzgerald's been dead all night."

She opened her mouth, snapped it shut. "I said that's what it looked like. We'll have to wait to hear what the coroner says. And by *we*, I mean me."

"But—"

"Stay out of this, Susan."

"But—"

"Out!"

Really, she was taking this faux sheriff/civilian antagonism a little far.

I climbed the porch steps.

"Tell me everything," Manaj said.

"Um, the sheriff told me not to tell anyone."

"I'm an FBI agent."

I wet my lips and glanced over my shoulder toward the deputies. "But... she said you were on vacation."

"When you're in the FBI, there's no such thing."

"Oh." Uncertain, I shifted the beagle in my arms.

"Do you want me to flash my badge?"

"No. I mean, I know who you are."

"Well?"

"Fine." I told her what I'd told the sheriff.

She nodded.

Since she didn't offer any insights, I left her on the porch and went inside.

Arsen joined me in the kitchen a few minutes later. We tried not to be obvious looking out the window at the deputies searching my garden. Connor climbed the hill behind the colonel's house, poking at the ground with a stick. He slipped, righted himself, looked around to make sure no one had seen.

Arsen coughed. "Susan, we should talk about the other night and that owl. I wanted to give you time, but it's been bugging me all day."

I jerked away from the butcher block counter. "Look, forget I said anything. I know it's crazy. I mean, I *know* it. And—"

"I believe you saw something."

I laughed shakily. "You do? Because Arsen, I'm not sure I believe me, and I was there. Plus, you didn't see what I did."

Arsen pulled me against his body and wrapped his arms around me. "I believe you."

Relief washed over me, and then a hollow sadness. *Poor Marion.* I laid my head against his muscular chest and listened to the steady thump of his heart.

"We'll figure this out," he said.

Poor Clare. "Clare." I jerked away from him. "She doesn't know."

"Let the sheriff tell her."

"Right." *Right.* The sheriff had told me to keep my mouth shut. I could keep my mouth shut. We stood beside the kitchen window, drinking coffee and speaking in low voices.

The deputies left.

A new guest checked in.

Life went on.

But not for Marion Fitzgerald.

CHAPTER 17

Friday's were normally busy at Wits' End. In spite of the recent cancellations, today was no exception. Danella's new video seemed to have worked.

I scrubbed room five's clawfoot bathtub in a better mood than tub scrubbing warranted. Maybe it was the new ylang-ylang scented cleaner that made the bathroom smell like a spa. Maybe it was me trying to be in the present.

Or maybe I was just really, really good at denial.

Two of my neighbors had been murdered. A killer had been right next door. Bailey had been drugged, and...

I took a deep breath. Bailey was fine. My guests were fine. I was alive, here, now, in a Victorian bathroom that smelled like tropical flowers.

The phone rang in the rear pocket of my khakis. Sitting back on my heels, I peeled off my purple gloves. I pulled out the phone and checked the number.

Sheriff McCourt.

"Hi, Sheriff. What—"

"It's out."

"What's out?"

"That damned video!"

"You mean, the turkeys?"

"What other video could I be talking about?" she asked.

There was a leak in the sheriff's department? If her own deputies couldn't be trusted, no wonder she relied on me. I sucked in my breath. Unless she thought... "I didn't—"

"I know you didn't," she growled. "I saw you delete the video. I checked your phone."

"Then who leaked it?"

"Did you tell anyone about those birds?"

"No."

"Not even that cousin of yours?"

"No one," I said. Except for Agent Manaj. But she wouldn't leak a turkey video. Would she? She was a federal agent. And how could she? I'd deleted it from my phone before we'd talked. Unless she had some secret, Men-in-Black tech that could rip videos off my phone before I deleted them... I cleared my throat. "And I'm sure Arsen didn't either."

"That's what he says." There was a long silence. "I uploaded it to my private computer at the sheriff's department."

"Someone hacked you?"

"It looks that way."

"An inside job?"

"Or an outside one."

Uh, oh. Now I understood why the sheriff was asking about Dixie. My cousin was notoriously loose when it came to other people's data, and she knew how to hack.

Worse, the sheriff knew she knew how to hack.

I forced myself to breathe. "But isn't an inside job more likely? I mean, who else would have known about that video?"

"It would have been easier from the inside." She exhaled heavily. "Our tech guy is looking into it. I don't know why I— I just wanted to give you a heads' up. You're named as the source."

Maybe she didn't suspect Dixie. Maybe she really did just want to warn me. After all, she knew she could trust me.

I hunched my shoulders to my ears. I'd kind of betrayed that trust. "Oh. Um. Agent Manaj might have known about the video."

"Might have?" she growled.

"Well. You know. She was there. And she sort of insisted I tell her what happened."

"I told you not to tell anyone!"

"And I told her that. But she was very persuasive. Th—"

She hung up.

I winced. All right. Maybe I deserved that.

And even though I knew what was in the video, I searched the internet for 'Susan Witsend Turkeys.'

My video was at the top of the page: *More evidence of UFO activity in Doyle?*

I squeezed the phone, my palms growing damp. "Uh oh." That was exactly what the sheriff had been afraid of.

I read the description.

Video taken by Susan Witsend of a dead body being circled by turkeys in Doyle, CA.

The video already had... I gaped at the red number below the video. Half a million views?

Unable to stop myself, I pressed play. It was all there. The circling birds. The corpse. Arsen, scattering the birds to take Marion Fitzgerald's pulse, shaking his head. Backing carefully away. And then it ended.

But how were a dead body and a flock of turkeys evidence of UFOs? I mean, yes, the video was weird. Disturbing. Super creepy. But alien?

I sat on the rim of the clawfoot tub and searched the web using the terms *UFOs* and *animal behavior*. There wasn't much online, and I felt ridiculously relieved.

Then I felt guilty about that. Both Clare's parents were dead. The video was evidence of murder, not UFOs.

I called Clare.

"Hello?" Her voice was a raspy whisper.

"Clare, it's Susan. I'm so sorry about Marion." I paused. "What can I do?"

"It's my fault, isn't it?"

"No." But what if it was her fault? What if Clare was the killer? I squashed that thought. "The only person at fault is the person who killed Marion."

"Killed her? Sheriff McCourt told us it looked like suicide."

"Did she?" I paused. That couldn't be right. "I must have misunderstood. Forget what I said."

"She sounded like... The sheriff didn't come out and say it, but suicide... I think she thinks my stepmother killed my father."

It was all too possible. But there was that footprint...

"Do you know something?" she asked. "You discovered her body. I saw the video."

Urgh. What had compelled me to film the scene? "Turkeys are flocking birds—"

"That's what the sheriff said. She called me this morning."

And she hadn't told Clare that it was murder? I rubbed my forehead. *But why?* Had the coroner determined Mrs. Fitzgerald died yesterday morning and not the night before? "Are you alone?" I asked.

"No, Emmery's here."

I relaxed slightly. "Good. Can I come over later?"

"I think... Maybe it's not such a good idea right now."

"All right," I said, worried. "I'll call you later."

"Okay. Bye."

"Bye." I hung up.

Dixie, in cargo shorts and a tank, appeared in the bathroom door. She brandished a phone. "Holy crap. This video! It says you took it. Why didn't you tell me?"

"The sheriff confiscated the video and swore me to silence."

"But I'm your cousin! This is... evidence!"

"And then someone hacked into the sheriff's computer and posted the video online."

"How did you...? She called *you*." Dixie fell silent. "She thinks I hacked her computer, doesn't she?"

"No." I hoped not. "How could you? You didn't even know about the video." I swallowed. "Could you have gotten it? Hacked into her computer, I mean?"

Her gaze shifted sideways. "Maybe."

"I don't think she was really calling about you," I said. "She's worried about a UFO panic. That's why she asked me – well, why she confiscated the video. That, and because it was evidence."

Dixie shook herself. "Do you need to go to the store or anything?"

"Not really, why?"

"Not really? Then there's something? Because I can stay here today and watch Bailey."

I narrowed my eyes. Dixie was only helpful when she wanted something. "Why?"

She studied the embossed ceiling tiles. "I just think it's better if I stay here. Your internet connection and computer are so last century."

"Stay here, where you can't be accused of hacking anyone?"

She nodded.

That horse had already fled the barn, but I pretended to accept her explanation. "Okay. Lenore texted me that a book I'd asked about is in. I wouldn't mind going to pick it up. Let me just finish up in here."

"What book?"

"Danella's."

"Whatever." She pivoted on her hiking boots and stomped from the room. A door slammed.

Weird. But I'd long given up trying to understand the ways of Dixie.

I finished cleaning the bathroom, doublechecked I'd removed all the cleaning supplies, changed, and walked into town. The streets felt oddly deserted. It was a Friday in May, and there were a handful of tourists. But those were the only people on the street. I didn't recognize a single person from Doyle.

At the bookstore, I waited in line. When I reached the front, Lenore handed me a thick hardback with Danella's smiling face on the cover. "I ordered it for the colonel," she said, "but you may as well have it." Her gray-blue eyes widened. "Wait, you're not just buying it because I asked you to, are you? Because I can send it back." She reached for the book.

"No, I want it." I handed her my credit card and glanced at the line extending behind me. "Busy today."

"Mm."

Declining a bag, I wandered to Ground and walked through its red-paned door.

Heads swiveled toward me. After a painful moment, gazes returned to laptops, to paper coffee cups, to muted conversations.

I walked to the counter. The only sound was the whir of the espresso machine.

Jayce's smile was perfunctory. "Hi, Susan. What can I get for you?"

"My usual. Oh, plus a jar of your coffee hand lotion."

She made a face. "Sorry, I'm out. But I'll brew up a new batch for you."

"Thanks!"

She rang up my coffee, then smoothed her hands on her green apron. "So," she said, not looking up from the register. "I heard you found Mrs. Fitzgerald yesterday."

"Where did you—?" Oh. The video. I handed her some cash. "You saw the video."

"Everyone saw the video."

I glanced over my shoulder. A pall seemed to hang over her funky coffeeshop. "Is that why things are so quiet here?"

"That and my speakers aren't working. It's probably the speakers. I hope it's the speakers. Oh, who am I kidding? This morning, a customer asked me if the aliens had taken out my sound system. I told her no, but I don't think she believed me. How are things at Wits' End?"

"Oh, you know," I said. "At Wits' End, the strange and unusual are a feature, not a bug."

She returned my change. "Let me get your coffee."

I waited by the cash register. The skin on the back of my neck prickled. I turned.

Winston Green stood about eight inches behind me. "You found her." He wore the same soiled raincoat. It smelled even more pungent than when I'd encountered him days ago.

I arched away, my back touching the counter. "Her?"

"Mrs. Fitzgerald." His gaze burned through my skin. "She knew the truth. That's why they killed her. You need to be careful."

"I will. Thanks."

"You don't understand. The sheriff knows."

"The sheriff doesn't know who k— Who's responsible for Marion."

"She knows." His voice rose. "You need to stay away from her. It isn't safe."

Heads popped up to stare.

Pity, not fear. My grip tightened on the hardback. "I hear what you're saying," I said quietly. "I'll be careful. Thanks for thinking about me."

A bell jingled above the door.

"The owls are everywhere," he hissed. "They're coming for me. I might not be able to stop them if they come for you again."

"Again?"

He pointed at my chest. "Don't think they're not coming for you. You can't trust them." He walked to a table. "Or you. Or you."

I stared, stricken. I'd made this worse. And I had no idea how to make it better.

Winston dropped into a squat. Grabbing his head, he made an odd, moaning sound. "They're coming. I can't stop them. They're going to take me again and they're coming they're coming they're coming."

Arsen strode to him. "Hey, buddy. It's me, Arsen. You're in Ground. You're safe."

"Not safe." Winston rocked on his heels. "There's nowhere safe. They know where you are."

"Look for red," Arsen said. "Do you see the color red?"

Winston looked up. He pressed his eyes shut and blew out a breath. When he opened them, his voice was steadier. "I see a red door. A red painting."

"You're in Ground," Arsen said. "And you're with friends. You're safe."

Jayce hurried around the counter and said something to Arsen. He nodded.

"Let's grab a table and talk, Winston." Arsen maneuvered Winston to a corner table, away from most of the customers.

Jayce returned to the register and handed me a paper coffee cup. "Have I mentioned how amazing your boyfriend is?" she whispered.

My throat squeezed. Love for Arsen mingled with guilt at my own failure. I'd thought I'd been calming Winston down, but I'd only set him off.

I put a lid on the cup. "He kind of is amazing, isn't he?" Arsen didn't wear a uniform anymore. And last week I'd caught him and Dixie testing how many marshmallows they could jam into their mouths at once. But when the chips were down, he was always there, my lodestar.

"I called Winston's mother," Jayce said. "She should be here soon."

"You're pretty quick thinking yourself."

She sighed. "Not really. This isn't the first time I've had to call her." She looked around at the silent customers. Tension vibrated through the brick room. "We've got to put an end to this," she muttered.

I nodded. Winston was a symptom, not the cause of Doyle's problems. "I'm sure the sheriff is trying."

Jayce blinked. "What?"

"But when people are convinced there's an imminent invasion – and let's face it, with all those disappearances… Well, the only surprise is that we haven't had a riot."

"Oh," she said. "Right. The sheriff's, um, great."

Ten minutes later, a worn-looking woman entered the coffeeshop. She trudged to Winston's table and said something to Arsen. The men rose, and she led Winston from the café.

Arsen walked to my chair and laid a hand on my shoulder. "You okay?"

I captured his hand with my own. "I'm fine. You were really great with Winston."

He shrugged. "Dixie told me you went to the bookstore."

"Yeah, I should return to Wits' End."

"I'll walk with you."

We were quiet on our walk home. I was thinking about Winston, and I guessed Arsen was too. We strolled down the driveway, our feet crunching on the gravel.

I roused myself. "Thanks for putting up those cameras. I didn't really get a chance to thank you yesterday."

"You didn't have to." He paused on the porch steps. "The sheriff asked me if I'd told Dixie about the video."

"She asked me the same thing." I shifted my weight. "But neither of us did, and Dixie didn't steal it, so she's okay."

"Are you sure about that?"

I rested my hand on the screen door. "Am I sure she didn't hack the sheriff's computer? She told me she didn't. So, yes. The sheriff says she's got a techie on it. He or she will figure out how the video was stolen, and Dixie will be cleared."

Right?

He rubbed his chin with his knuckles. "I'm going to talk to Connor, see what he can tell me."

"You don't think Dixie's a serious suspect?"

"The sheriff isn't going to want this to be an inside job."

"But she's not going to ignore the truth," I said.

"People ignore the truth all the time."

But not the sheriff. She might not be Dixie's biggest fan, but she was honest. I opened my mouth to tell him so, then thought better of it. There was no sense arguing.

"Are you staying in for the rest of the day?" he asked.

"I didn't have any plans," I said, stiffening. He wanted me to stay away from Clare, but he was too polite to say so.

"Okay, I'll come by later." He kissed my cheek. "I love you."

Stunned, I watched his muscular form stride down the drive. He loved me? He'd said it casually, as if he'd said it every day. But he hadn't. This was the first.

Arsen walked around the corner of the picket fence and vanished behind a tree.

I pulled open the screen door and walked inside. The foyer looked the same. Fake Persian rug. Scuffed desk. Light from the stained-glass transom sliding across the shelves filled with souvenirs. But nothing was the same.

I stopped beside the reception desk and dragged my finger across its smooth surface. My stomach clenched. If Arsen had meant the declaration to be a big deal, he would have stuck around. But he'd had things to do.

So did I.

Things were spinning out of control, and Jayce was right. We needed to stop the panic before it started. Any one of my guests could have seen me take that video or heard the sheriff and I discussing it.

And Danella's bedroom window overlooked the garden.

I jogged up the stairs.

Dixie was closing the door to Danella's room. "Hey, I just finished here."

"There's something I, er, forgot to check." I edged past her.

"Don't you trust me?"

"Implicitly." I walked inside.

Danella's suitcase was open, clothes spilling from the bag.

"I didn't do that," Dixie said. "I don't mess with guests' stuff."

"I know." I looked over my shoulder at her. "You can go on to the next room. I just want to air this one out."

"Whatever." Dixie left, closing the door.

I jerked open the window and gazed into the colonel's neat yard. From this vantage, Danella would have been able to see Mrs. Fitzgerald's body. But had she been in her room? I hadn't been tracking the psychic's movements, but maybe I should have been.

Muscles jumping, I cracked the door so I could hear anyone coming. I hurried to her desk. A blue folder lay upon it. I flipped through it. The folder was filled with articles on Doyle, but nothing on Clare's case.

I rummaged through Danella's blue-plastic suitcase. Something was off about the woman. She'd come to help Clare too quickly, and she was staying way too long. Reality TV shows made money because their production was quick. It took hours or days, not weeks, to produce a show. Danella's show might be online only, but the same had to be true. And Danella and her crew had been here a week now.

I glanced at the closed door. There was more to this story than a simple reality show.

But if there was incriminating evidence in her suitcase, I didn't find it. I opened a smaller matching case. A faded photo of a smiling toddler was clipped in its lid. Frowning, I tugged the picture free. I'd seen this girl before, at the colonel's house.

It was a photo of Clare.

"What are you doing in my room?"

I whirled.

Danella stood in the doorway.

CHAPTER 18

Danella stepped into her room. She slammed the door behind her. The floral-print curtains fluttered at the open window. "I said, what are you doing in here?" She flung her long braid over one shoulder of her red top.

I didn't bother looking for escape or excuses. One thing I'd learned from Dixie is the best defense is a strong offense. I raised the photo in my hand and stepped away from the suitcases. "This is Clare."

Her face reddened. "You have—"

"What are you doing with her baby picture?" I asked. "And don't tell me this is part of your research. Your research files are over there, on the desk. This was clipped in your suitcase, like something personal. Private."

She snatched the photo from my hands. "Private is right."

"What is she to you?"

"It's none of your business."

I turned to the door. "Then I'll ask Clare."

"No!" She grasped my arm. Her nails dug into my flesh.

"Let go."

To my surprise, she did. She stepped backward, toward the bed. "Please don't tell Clare." Her eyes pooled with tears.

"Danella, your presence here is strange. You didn't follow the usual procedure for your show. You've stayed way too long. And now the photo. What's really going on?"

"Nothing. Can't I stay in a charming B&B?"

"There have been two mur— deaths next door, and you're connected to the victims. The sheriff—"

"Don't tell the sheriff!"

"That you're stalking Clare, a woman who's being haunted by alien visitations? Visitations you may be responsible for?"

She dropped onto the edge of the bed, rumpling the quilt. "That she's my daughter."

I stared. I hadn't been expecting that. "What?"

"Clare." She looked up, expression fierce. "You didn't think *that* woman was her real mother, did you?"

I took an involuntary step backward. *That woman?* Could Danella have gotten rid of *that* woman to clear the way for herself? "Why doesn't Clare know?"

She shook her head. "I haven't had a chance to tell her."

"So, you're lying to her." My voice hardened. She was manipulating Clare, just like whoever was playing those tricks on her. *Had* Danella set the whole thing up?

"It's not that simple."

My teeth ground together. How many times had I heard that from my own parents? "Then simplify."

"Clare hasn't seen me since she was a little girl. She thinks I'm dead. And now with everything going on… How am I supposed to tell her the truth?"

"You'll need to figure something out. Because if you don't tell her, I will."

"You don't understand."

"Then help me understand."

She exhaled shakily and clutched her hands together. "I was never good enough." With her thumb, she kneaded the skin on her other hand. "Ted and I never should have married. I was wrong to leave, I know, but I was young, and he was so rigid. So many rules and ways of doing things… I felt like I was being smothered–"

"One day."

"What?"

"You have one day to tell her. Then I will." Shaken, I swiveled on my heels and strode from the room. I raced down the carpeted steps. *Danella* felt smothered? What about Clare? How could she have left her daughter?

I stopped short on the stairs. The colonel must have recognized Danella. Was that why he'd been so set on tossing her out of his house? More slowly, I walked downstairs to the foyer.

Dixie slipped off the reception desk. "What did she say?"

"You knew Danella was on her way to her room? Thanks for the warning." I stalked through the foyer.

Dixie trotted behind me. "Hey, you didn't tell me you'd be snooping."

"But you figured it out." I pushed open the kitchen door.

Bailey looked up from his dog bed, his tail thumping the linoleum.

"So," Dixie persisted, "what did she say?"

"She said she's Clare's mother. That's why she and her team got here so quickly when Clare applied to be in the show."

"Did you believe her?"

"I–" I hesitated. It was like something out of a soap opera. So why *had* I believed her? "I don't know."

"Did she say where she's been all this time?"

"No."

"Did she say why she left?"

"She said she was young. She wasn't good enough. The colonel was too rigid and smothering–"

Dixie gave a harsh laugh. "You must have sympathized."

"I did not," I said hotly. "She's manipulating Clare, tricking her. She hasn't told Clare she's her mother. And Danella may be behind everything that's been going on. I don't care what her reason is, there's no excuse. And two people are dead!"

Bailey whined, and Dixie bent to scratch the beagle.

"We don't know if Clare's aliens have anything to do with the murders," she said.

I grabbed a mug from its hook beneath the wooden shelf. "But we can't rule it out."

Dixie straightened and braced her hands behind her on the butcher block counter. "I wonder if you're—"

"If I'm what?" I slammed down the mug. The day was too warm to drink tea.

She shook her head. "Never mind. I should get going."

My cell phone rang.

Dixie waited while I answered it.

"This is Susan, at Wits' End."

On the other end of the line, Lenore Bonheim laughed lightly. "You sound tense. That kind of day?"

I made a rueful face. "I guess. What's up?"

"Hey, that book you ordered on Area 51 came in today. I'm sorry, I should have told you when you were here earlier, but I spaced. Do you want me to deliver it?"

I'd originally ordered the book because I thought I might like to sell it at Wits' End. But now I wanted to learn more about the colonel's old workplace.

I checked my open planner on the table. Today's arriving guests had already checked in. My afternoon was free. "No, that's all right. I'll come by and pick it up myself."

"Okay, I'll see you when I see you." She hung up.

"Want me to take Bailey for a while?" Dixie asked.

"Yeah, that'd be great. I'm just going to the bookstore. I'll come by your trailer afterward and pick him up."

She slipped the leash off the clip by the door, and Bailey bounded to his feet. Dixie and Bailey ambled out the kitchen door.

Grabbing my purse, I left the B&B. I speed-walked, trying to burn off the anger heating my veins.

Why was I steamed? This was good news, if Danella was telling the truth. It meant Clare hadn't lost all her parents.

But how could the colonel have done that to his daughter? Was it kinder to tell Clare her mother was dead and not that she'd abandoned the family? But Clare was an adult now. Continuing the fable was wrong. Another lie. Another manipulation.

An airplane droned overhead. Involuntarily, I looked up. Clouds shaped like flying saucers drifted above the mountains.

No wonder Clare was a mess. The most important people in her life had been lying to her. How could she know what was true? Had Marion Fitzgerald known about Danella? She must have.

Ten minutes later, I walked into the bookstore. Aside from Lenore, behind the high counter, it was empty.

She looked up and smiled. "Ten percent discount on that book since I made you come here twice in one day."

"Don't worry about it," I said. "I needed the exercise."

She slid the book across the counter. "Everything okay at Wits' End?" The overhead fan rippled the fabric of her ivory blouse.

"Wits' End is fine. It's my neighbors I'm worried about."

Her pale brow furrowed. "I heard Mrs. Fitzgerald's death was suicide. Did she show any signs—?"

"No," I said quickly and dug in my purse for my wallet.

"She didn't seem the type to kill herself."

"I guess you never really know what's going on in people's heads."

"But you have good instincts, Susan. Do you think they're right, that it was really suicide?"

What I *thought* was that the sheriff was going to arrest me if I blabbed. "There are a lot of strange things going on in Doyle."

She winced. "I saw that video you shot. It was… unnerving."

"Turkeys are flocking birds," I parroted. "The leader started circling to see what was wrong with Mrs. Fitzgerald. The others followed."

"I'm sure you're right." She looked away, pursing her lips.

"I wish I'd never taken that video," I muttered. "The sheriff's afraid it may send Doyle over the edge."

"How?"

"You saw Winston. He's not the only person who's been pushed too far. I was in your sister's coffeeshop earlier, and the atmosphere was tense."

"But Doyle's always been odd, because of… you know."

"And people have been able to pretend it wasn't," I said, frustrated. "Then all those people came back, and we kept pretending. But now things are happening again, and people are scared. It feels like the town is under threat. I'm just afraid I'm making things worse."

"How?"

I'd said too much. Everyone seemed to know about my work for Clare, but it didn't seem right to blab. "Wits' End," I lied. "Is a UFO-themed B&B really appropriate right now?"

"It's not like you can change it on a whim."

"No."

"Sometimes, the best way to deal with your fears is to laugh at them. Wits'

End gives us that. It pokes fun at the whole UFO mythology. Maybe that UFO in your roof doesn't let us forget. But it reminds us that we're still here, and life is kind of ridiculous."

I handed her my credit card. "I hope you're right."

"I am right. How's Clare doing?"

A horn blared outside. We glanced out the bookstore's front window. Was I imagining that I was hearing more horns lately? That people's nerves were fraying?

"Clare?" I asked. "I wish I knew. I can't imagine losing both parents like that."

"You haven't seen her then? She hasn't fired you, has she?"

"Hold on. You know I'm conducting a UFO investigation for her? How?"

She pinked. "Arsen told Connor. Connor told me."

"It's true I'm—"

"Leave us be," a woman shouted, and our heads turned toward the noise.

"Out. Out!" Outside Lenore's front window, Mrs. Steinberg flailed her cane.

A purple fedora sped past the bottom of the window frame.

"And don't come back!" the elderly woman shouted.

Lenore and I shot puzzled looks at each other. We hurried toward the front of the bookstore.

Mrs. Steinberg banged open the door, jangling the bell. She flounced inside. "Of all the nerve. That horrible man."

"Man?" I asked. "What man?" Only a child or an extremely short person could have been wearing that purple hat.

Oh. "Was that the man from the circus?" I asked.

Lenore's lips pressed together. She gave a tiny, disapproving shake of her head.

I frowned. Prejudice against the height challenged was unkind, but allowances had to be made. After all, Mrs. Steinberg was of a different generation.

"He surprised me, that's all." The old lady smoothed her black dress. "Well? You said you had something for me?"

"Right," Lenore said. "Your book." She hurried behind the counter and rung me up. "We should grab coffee sometime, Susan."

"That sounds great. Give me a call." Gripping the hardback, I exited the bookstore and hesitated on the sidewalk.

The man in the purple fedora stood at the corner of Antoine's bar. His gaze met mine. He ducked around the corner of the wood-slat building.

I peered at the old-west building housing Antoine's Bar. Had he been trying to avoid my notice?

No, I hadn't imagined it. Was the man from the circus… spying on Lenore?

CHAPTER 19

I glanced at the bookstore.

Why would someone from the circus watch a bookstore or Lenore?

Or me?

Answer: he wouldn't. And whatever was going on with him, it had nothing to do with me or the murders.

But instead of turning toward Wits' End, I walked in the opposite direction. I paused in front of a shop selling motorcycle tees and gazed at the polished window.

In its reflection, the little man from the circus hurried along the raised sidewalk opposite.

I pivoted.

The sidewalk was empty. I stared at the ice cream shop across the street. Had he ducked inside?

My scalp prickled, as if I was being watched.

I walked on and stopped in front of Ground's signboard. Head bent, I pretended to study its specials. I looked out of the corner of my eyes. In the mirror made by Ground's red-paned windows, a purple fedora bobbed down the sidewalk.

I turned my head and scanned the deserted street. What the…?

A hot breeze tossed the hanging vines in their planters.

Where had he gone?

Shaking myself, I walked into Ground and inhaled the soothing scent of coffee. I ordered a drink at the wooden counter.

Jayce raised a brow. "Another? Don't tell me you're turning into a java addict?"

"It's been a weird day. And make it iced."

She braced her elbows on the counter. "Oh? What's going on?"

"I think I'm… It's crazy."

"I adore crazy." She grinned impishly. "Tell me. Tell me tell me tell me."

"I think I'm being followed. By a little man from the circus. He followed me from Lenore's."

She blinked and straightened. "Huh?"

"I know. It's bonkers. I'm bonkers. My neighbors have… died. Their daughter is going through something awful. And I've seen the alien that was on Antoine's, and no, it's probably not an alien at all, but it stole my lemon curd."

Her brows sketched upward. "Lemon curd?"

"I know. I know! What's with the curd? What's the connection? Missing cows. Aliens on Antoine's. It has to be connected, right?"

Her mouth made a moue of polite confusion. "So... let's go back to you being followed."

"I'll bet he's out there now."

She turned toward the window.

"Don't look!"

She whipped her head back to look at me.

"He's amazingly stealthy," I said.

"I'm just going to go to the end of the counter, and I'll casually check the window. Okay?"

Doubtful, I shuffled my feet. "It can't hurt, I guess."

She returned a few minutes later with my iced drink. "There's an extremely short man in a purple fedora sitting on the bench across the street."

"Whoa. You saw him?" Because I was starting to wonder if I'd dreamed the whole thing.

"I can be stealthy too." She leaned closer. "Look, if you want to lose this guy, I've got a back door."

"Jayce, you're a lifesaver. Thanks!"

She ushered me through a blue, stripey curtain, and into a narrow kitchen. Jayce opened the rear, metal door.

I stepped into the alley and looked around.

"Now go home," she said, "lock your doors, and call that hunky boyfriend of yours." She laughed and shut the door, leaving me alone in the alley.

It was good advice.

But what would Arsen, security consultant, ex-military, and general troublemaker do?

He'd turn the tables.

I walked down the alley and around the corner. Carefully, I peered around the brick building. The little man sat on the bench and swung his feet.

After thirty minutes, he checked his phone.

Another boring thirty minutes went by. His fidgeting increased. He swung his legs. He shifted his weight. His arms went along the back of the bench and dropped to his lap.

I was doing pretty much the same thing, minus the bench work. My coffee was long gone. I needed a bathroom.

Finally, he hopped from the bench and crossed the street, walked into Ground. Five minutes later he emerged. His movements were stiff and jerky as he strode, arms pumping, down Main Street.

I followed.

He didn't look over his shoulder, which made my job easy. The man continued over the humpbacked, stone bridge. He strode past wine tasting rooms and restaurants, until Main Street petered out at a ramshackle barn in a weedy field. He turned left, taking a side road, and then stopped beside a beat-up white Toyota.

One of the Wyrd Systers sat on its roof, another on its hood, and a third leaned out the open window.

They seemed to argue about something, the little man gesturing vehemently. Then they all got into the car and drove off.

Huh.

I rubbed the back of my neck. Had I learned anything?

Not really.

Bladder threatening to burst, I hurried to Dixie's trailer. I used her teeny-tiny bathroom, collected Bailey, and walked home.

I didn't tell her about the little man. The story was too bizarre, even for Dixie.

In the kitchen, I unhooked Bailey from his leash. He pawed at the kitchen door and shot me a pleading look.

"Fine," I said. "You can go out, but no digging and don't talk to strangers. You know what happened last time." I opened the door.

He bounded past me, ears flying.

Smiling, I walked inside my private sitting room and dropped my purse on the coffee table. My phone rang inside it, and I excavated the device.

Arsen's name flashed on the screen.

"Hey," I said, stomach fluttering.

"Hey back. Where are you?"

"Home. Are you still planning on stopping by?"

"I thought I'd take you and Bailey to dinner. Say, seven?"

I checked my watch. It was five-thirty, and I was a sweaty mess. "Perfect. I'll see you then."

I walked into my bedroom and stopped short.

On the center of my smooth, blue coverlet lay a white feather.

Hands trembling, I picked it up. The feather was long, and the white glowed with perfection. Unnatural perfection.

The feather hadn't just dropped onto my bed.

Someone had been in my private quarters. Someone had gotten past Arsen's new locks.

The bedroom tilted. I grabbed the headboard for support, the air squeezing from my lungs. I had to get out of here.

I turned and hurried toward the door.

Brutal hands grasped my shoulders and thrust me into the open closet. I fell, grabbing helplessly. A fistful of summer dresses came down, hangers clattering. My knee hit the floor. Pain rocketed up my leg.

The closet door banged shut behind me, plunging me into darkness.

CHAPTER 20

Blinded, I clawed my way to standing, ripping more maxi dresses from their hangers. They tumbled to the carpeted floor.

A door slammed. Outside, Bailey howled.

"Bailey!" I staggered from the bedroom closet and raced through my rooms to the porch. The kitchen's screen door banged shut behind me. Wildly, I looked around.

The beagle stood inside the picket fence and barked his head off.

The steel band around my chest released. Relieved, I dropped to my knees and hugged the dog. "You're okay," I said.

He licked my face.

"Yeah," I said, half-laughing, "I'm okay too."

I stood and scanned the street past my fence.

My neighbor, Mr. Berghoff, ambled toward us smoking a cigar.

Breathing hard, Bailey and I walked around the fence to the street and waited.

Rufus Berghoff stopped in front of me. "Hello, Susan," he said between puffs of his cigar. His balding head glistened in the afternoon sun.

"There was an intruder." I gasped. "In Wits' End. Did you see anyone?"

He yanked the cigar from his mouth. "What? Are you all right?"

"I'm fine." And I wondered about that. A year ago, getting shoved into a closet would have left me a shaking wreck. But I shoved the thought of my new, steely coolness away. Well, mostly cool. My heart was still pounding.

"Have you called the sheriff?" he asked.

"Not yet. I will. But if you didn't see anyone…" I studied the end of the court. Whoever it had been could have cut through the colonel's yard. Heck, he could have rampaged through the yard of the stoners across the street. Dunk and Finn never would have noticed.

He shook his head. "I wish Emmery had become a botanist, like he'd planned, rather than a deputy. I thought Doyle would be a nice, quiet change for him from big city policing. I thought it would be a place where he could—

" He bit off the words. "But this town isn't what it used to be."

It used to be that people would go missing and no one would talk about it. Now it was all we could talk about, and aliens were popping up everywhere. Antoine's Bar. My porch. Stealing my lemon curd. My fists clenched. What *would* an alien want with lemon curd?

Smoke coiled lazily from the remains of his cigar. "I had my beefs with Fitzgerald, but I can't believe he's gone – him and Marion."

"Have you talked to Clare?" I asked.

He snorted. "I'm the last person she wants to see."

"I doubt that's true. You're Emmery's father."

"Isn't it?" His wry smile collapsed. "I was at the colonel's earlier, to talk to Emmery. Clare practically threw me out of the house. I don't blame her, she knows how her father felt about me, and she's hurting. But I worry about her, about Clare and my son."

"So do I." I rubbed my damp hands on the thighs of my capris. Was Clare target or killer? "Both her parents are gone. I can't imagine what she's going through."

"It's more than that." He studied the smoldering end of cigar.

"If you're worried about her safety, so am I. But she's got Emmery watching her."

"That's what concerns me."

I scrunched my brow. "You don't think Emmery would hurt her?"

"No," he said explosively. "God, no. I hear she hired you to investigate the aliens after she brought that psychic in."

"Oh." Why was I surprised? One-armed Frank knew I was investigating. Why wouldn't Emmery's father?

"Don't two investigators seem like overkill?"

"I don't know what's normal in this situation."

"Neither do I," he said slowly. "In fact, under other circumstances, I'd think her reaction was almost natural."

"Other circumstances?"

He hesitated. "Clare's mother, her birth mother, was… unstable."

"You knew her?" I asked, taken aback.

He bent and ground out the stub of the cigar on the pavement. "I never met the woman. It all happened in another town."

"What happened?"

"The colonel traveled a lot for work," he said, "he wasn't home much. I think he blamed himself."

Bailey leaned, a comforting weight, against my leg.

"For her leaving?" I asked.

"She didn't leave." He studied the ragged end of his cigar. "He had her committed to an asylum."

My jaw sagged. "An asylum?" Okay. Okay. Just because every escaped-mental-patient-murderer movie was now running through my head didn't mean Danella was a threat.

"I heard she died there." He looked past me. "Tragic, really."

I gripped the picket fence with one hand. *Died?* Then who was staying in room five?

"They say insanity skips a generation," he continued scrutinizing the frayed cigar. "But I'm not so sure it did." He met my gaze. "I'm worried about Emmery. He's drawn to people who need help. It's why he got into policing. But I think he might have bitten off more than he can chew with Clare. I've told him, but he won't listen to me."

Maybe Clare really was in the middle of a breakdown. And if Emmery knew her history, it explained his protectiveness. If she was mentally disturbed… I lowered my voice to a whisper. "You said the colonel's wife died? How do you know for sure?"

"Am I sure she's dead?" His brown eyes widened slightly. "You think she might be the one behind this? That she found the colonel and his wife?"

"Is it possible?"

"I don't know." He tossed the cigar butt into my Mr. Lincoln rosebush.

My eyes narrowed. Okay, the cigar was probably biodegradable, but that wasn't cool.

"The colonel told me she was dead," he continued. "He remarried. If she wasn't dead, or he hadn't gotten a divorce, he wouldn't have married Marion. One thing I'll say about the colonel, he was a straight-up guy."

"Do you know the name of the asylum?"

"Even if I did, I'm sure patient records are confidential."

"But death records shouldn't be. What was his wife's name?"

"Hm." He looked at the darkening sky. "Darla? No. Danielle! That was it. Danielle."

A name that was a lot like Danella.

I swallowed, mouth dry. If she was the long-lost wife, I could see why she hadn't mentioned the asylum. *If* she was the real Danielle and not an imposter. "Do you know what town she was in when she was institutionalized?"

"It wasn't something the colonel talked about much."

But it had happened when Clare was three. Her mother probably would have been taken to a facility near the colonel's home.

He hesitated. "I've told the sheriff about the mother. Emmery isn't happy about it, but…" He looked away and his mouth compressed. "He's my son."

"Does Clare know about her mother?"

"I don't know. I didn't tell her."

Pensive, I brought Bailey inside and locked the door behind us. I glanced up the green staircase. What good was locking doors if the danger was on the inside? But whoever had attacked me, had run outside.

Danella *could* have run outside through the kitchen and returned inside through the front door.

Bailey's stomach growled.

I snapped my fingers. "The cameras."

Hurrying to my laptop on the kitchen table, I opened the security camera program. It showed four black squares. I clicked the library tab, like Arsen had shown me.

Nothing happened.

What was I doing wrong? "Stupid technology."

I called my friend, Sheriff McCourt.

"What now?" she rapped out.

"Someone broke into my house and shoved me inside a closet." I fussed with the computer program. "I have security cameras, but they're all black."

"You mean you didn't turn them on?"

Whoops. "Was I supposed to?" I thought they were motion activated or something.

"Since you sound more irritated than scared, I'm guessing whoever broke in is gone."

"Yeah, but—"

"Did you get a look at the guy? If you tell me it was a bug-eyed alien—"

"It wasn't," I said. "At least, I don't think it was. I didn't see him. He was behind me."

"He?"

"Fine. It *could* have been a she or a gender-neutral alien from Alpha-Centauri."

There was a long silence.

"I'm joking," I said.

"Look, I can't get over there right now. Give me an hour."

"Fine. Th—"

She hung up.

"Thanks," I said to the dial tone.

Blood pressure rising, I futzed around with the program for another thirty minutes.

I cursed, which didn't help, and gave up. I made sure the doors to the kitchen were deadbolted, and I showered and changed. Then I went back to the computer and messed around some more.

Bailey watched worriedly from his dog bed.

"Gagh." I pounded the kitchen table hard enough to bounce the laptop. "What is wrong with this thing?"

The porch door rattled. "Susan?" Arsen called. "Are you okay?"

I knocked back my chair and let him inside. Behind him, twilight streaked the western sky.

"You're early." I was so glad he was early.

He kissed me deeply, and my knees wobbled.

"I missed you," he said when we broke apart. "Why'd you bolt the door?" I told him about my intruder.

His face went white, then red. His jaw clenched. He scanned me, then nodded and picked up my laptop. Cradling it in one arm, his fingers sped across the keyboard.

I frowned. Not even a *thank-God-you're-all-right?* I mean, I *was* all right. But there are certain boyfriendly expectations that were not being met here.

"Damn." He set the computer on the kitchen counter and strode onto the porch.

Bailey and I looked at each other, then followed him outside.

Arsen balanced one foot on a porch railing. Gripping the roof ledge, he ripped a piece of black tape off the camera and swore. "Did you call the cops?"

"Sheriff McCourt should be here soon."

"Then I'll leave the rest of the cameras for her to print. Susan, this wasn't a casual break-in."

I folded my arms.

"What's wrong?" Arsen said.

"It's nothing. Never mind." I was being unreasonable. "There's just… a lot going on. It's more than the break-in." There were disappearing cows and disappearing lemon curd and aliens on Antoine's… something was going on. And for the first time in a long time, it felt like more than my planner could handle.

"Is this about your parents?"

"My parents?"

"Look, Dixie explained everything. I won't push anymore."

A wave of heat washed from my chest to my scalp. "*Dixie* explained? You went to Dixie?"

"Well, you weren't telling me what was going on." He hopped down, landing agilely on the porch.

"You never asked," I said. "You just assumed. Just like you're assuming I'm fine when someone broke into my house and shoved me in a closet!"

"I'm sorry I talked to Dixie about your parents. But I didn't think you were okay today. I thought you were handling it, and I didn't want to push."

"Then what *do* you want to do?" I demanded.

"I want to break the arms and legs of whoever did this. I want to throw you on a bed and make sure you're not hurt. But the police are on their way, and—"

A sheriff's department SUV crunched to a halt in my gravel drive. Its headlights dimmed.

I blew out my breath, mollified.

Deputy Connor Hernandez stepped from the car. "Hey, Arsen. Susan."

I smiled wanly. "Hi, Connor. Any luck finding those cows?" Even though I liked Connor, I swallowed an irrational disappointment. The sheriff and I had a certain relationship. Why hadn't she come herself?

There was only one possible reason. She must have been really busy. I knit my bottom lip. I hoped she was all right.

Connor ran his hand along the top of his curling, dark hair. "The herd's gone AWOL. One-armed Frank is camped out at the station, demanding we arrest the aliens responsible."

A light flashed on in the second floor of the Victorian.

"Wait," I said. "How does he know which aliens are responsible?"

"He doesn't. I mean there aren't aliens. He saw lights in the sky from the circus, and…" The deputy laughed shortly. "You wouldn't believe the calls we've been getting. People are seeing aliens everywhere."

"Really?" I adjusted my collar. More sightings? What was going on? "Where?"

"Um, the sheriff said you had some trouble out here?"

"A break-in." Arsen gripped Connor's hand. "Susan surprised the intruder. They put tape on my video cameras to cover their tracks."

Connor winced. "Did you take the tape off them all?"

"Just this one," Arsen said.

"Maybe we'll get lucky," Connor said, "and find some prints."

We didn't get lucky.

CHAPTER 21

The next morning, I poured over my agenda at the kitchen table.

Across from me, Dixie hunched over a plate of scrambled eggs. A rivulet of sweat trickled down her bare arm.

I was still annoyed she'd told Arsen about my fraught relationship with my parents. *I* should have been the one to explain things. And I wasn't sure I'd like Dixie's interpretation of my family life.

Arsen leaned against the butcher block counter, a mug of coffee in his hand. The ceiling fan ruffled his whiskey-colored hair, but the air was hot, oppressive.

At least I'd made up with Arsen (rather spectacularly) last night. And he'd assured himself I was not covered in hidden bruises.

He still didn't really get it about my parents, but how could he? He'd been raised by two adoring aunts who'd basically let him run wild.

And my parents…

Tentacles of anxiety wriggled through my chest. I paused, took a breath, and highlighted my shopping days in yellow for the week ahead. Determinedly, I forced the shadow away.

My parents had controlled everything. What I wore. What I ate. How much I ate. Who I was friends with. My every gesture, every word, was scrutinized, dissected, critiqued. My only moments of freedom had been summers in Doyle with Gran. I'd been so brainwashed I'd gone along with the career path they'd chosen for me. And then Gran had died and left me Wits' End.

I shut my planner and looked toward the kitchen window and the mountains beyond.

The logical thing to do – the expected thing to do – had been to sell the B&B. If it hadn't been for Dixie, storming down to San Francisco one wild night, demanding to know whether I was going to upend her life or not, I would have.

I'm not sure even Dixie knew she'd saved me.

So, I guess I couldn't be mad at her now.

"All planned out?" She slathered a new batch of lemon curd on a poppyseed scone.

I glanced at the white owl feather, lying on a wooden shelf above the counter. The shadow crept closer.

"No," I said. "I mean, yes, my work here is planned. But I haven't been as organized with Clare's investigation."

"What are you talking about?" Arsen raised his mug in my direction. "You had that whole UFO investigation SOP."

"That means standard operating procedures," Dixie said.

"Thanks," I said dryly, and pulled the investigation binder closer. "The problem is, not much of what's been happening has been standard." I'd written down every alien sighting and owl sightings and all Clare's odd experiences. But what did they add up to? A big fat nothing.

"I dunno." A strap of her green tank slid down her shoulder, and she hitched it up. "Weird visions are pretty standard in the UFO literature."

"But it's more than that," I said. "Obviously, there's something non-paranormal going on here."

"The murders," Arsen said darkly.

"They've got to be tied to whatever's happening to Clare," I said.

"I don't know if they've *got* to," Arsen said, "but what are the odds they're not?"

"Let's say Danella's behind it all, Clare's so-called abductions, everything." I grabbed the cow-shaped pepper shaker and set it in front of me. "She, of all people, had the easiest access to these rooms in Wits' End."

"She had the opportunity to kill the Fitzgeralds," Dixie finished.

"But why gaslight Clare?" Arsen asked.

My mouth flattened. I had an answer for that – to more easily control her, to make Clare turn to her when their true relationship was revealed. But I didn't say anything. The answer was too close to my own family experience.

But maybe I shouldn't look at this through my own, dark and twisted lens. "I need to find out her shooting schedule. We know when Clare had her experiences. If I can cross-reference those against Danella's location, maybe I can rule her out. Or in."

"There's another possibility," Arsen said.

I set the cow saltshaker beside the pepper. "Clare. She could be faking the entire thing. Danella let her into Wits' End the night someone messed with my fuse box. She claimed she didn't let her inside yesterday, but who knows?"

"Or Clare could be genuinely insane," Arsen said. "She might have killed her parents."

"Yeah," I said, not liking that solution, because then what had *I* seen? But I hadn't imagined my missing lemon curd.

Reaching across the table, Dixie grabbed the pepper and shook it over her eggs. "What about Emmery's dad, Rufus?" Dixie asked. "He and the colonel were always going at it. Maybe he killed the colonel, Mrs. Fitzgerald figured it out, and so he killed her too?"

"He had means and opportunity." A slight chill shivered my skin. *Everyone* had means. The foxglove in my garden was open to everyone. "But why make Clare think she's under alien attack?"

"But could he have been the one who broke into your room yesterday?" Dixie asked.

"Maybe," I said slowly. "When I went outside, I saw him on the street, walking toward me. He could have run out there and just turned around, acted like he was just walking home. But..." I scrunched my forehead, thinking.

"But what?" Arsen asked.

"His cigar was smoked nearly to the end," I said. "And I didn't smell cigar smoke in my rooms. Unless he kept a mostly smoked, unlit cigar in his pocket, I don't see how he could have done it. And his motive seems a little weak. He'd been mad at the colonel for years. Why kill him now?"

"There's one more suspect." Arsen folded his muscular arms over his logo'd golf shirt. "Emmery."

"He studied botany," I said, "so he should have known about foxglove being poisonous. It's not exactly uncommon knowledge. But what's the motive? He loves Clare. Besides, he's the one who pushed to get us involved."

"To get *you* involved," Arsen said.

"Same difference," I said.

Dixie stretched. "I vote for the lemon-curd-stealing alien."

"Not funny," I said. Not after my own owl incident. "And I'm not the only one who's seen the alien. The sheriff's worried the town's going to go over the edge." My hand tightened on my pen. I was already jittery, and that scared me.

Dixie raised a brow. "If you ask me, Doyle went over the edge long ago. Disappearances, witches—"

"Will you cut that out?" I tugged down the hem of my loose, blue blouse. "Lenore and her sisters are not witches."

"They kind of are," Arsen said.

I collapsed back in my chair. "Oh, come on. Not you too." *Witches. As if.* "Jayce just calls her lotions and scrubs magic as a marketing gimmick."

"I think the sheriff's got a point about the town though," Arsen said. "Janet closed her t-shirt shop yesterday. Said she was taking a vacation. But the timing's wrong. We're getting into the high season for tourism, and she looked scared."

I ran my thumb along the planner's spine. "You think she left because of the murders?"

"She was asking me about your turkey video," Arsen said.

I slumped in my chair. Taking that video had been the worst impulse ever. And I'd thought I was being so organized and practical!

A scream cracked the air and raised the hair on my arms.

Bailey leapt from his dog bed and howled.

Arsen, Dixie and I shot to our feet and scrambled for the porch door. We raced into the sunny side yard. I scanned the garden, the rose blossoms still wet with dew. My gaze raked the nearby hill, dotted with pines.

I rocked slightly on my heels, my stomach rolling. "That scream *did* come from this direction, didn't it?"

"I'll check the backyard," Arsen said. "Dixie, you take the street. Susan, take the side." He jogged toward the gazebo.

Dixie ran in the opposite direction. I stood alone in the side yard, which was obviously empty.

Bailey whuffed by my ankle.

"Okay." I bent to pet him. "I'm not alone. You're here."

Collar jingling, he trotted to the spirit house.

Lacking any better ideas, I followed, my footsteps leaden.

He squeezed between two rose bushes and stopped beside the picket fence. Unable and unwilling to fit between the roses, I stopped behind him.

On the other side of the fence, Clare lay motionless on the lawn. Her eyes stared at the hard, blue sky.

CHAPTER 22

The sheriff threw her hat on my kitchen table. "Why does it always have to be you?" Sweat stained the armpits of her button-up khaki shirt.

"It does seem strange," I admitted and pushed aside the short, blue curtain. I peered worriedly out the kitchen window.

Two EMTs loaded Clare into the back of an ambulance. Arsen stood to one side, talking to Connor.

"Do you know if Clare's going to be okay?" I asked her.

"I'm a sheriff, not a medic."

"But the EMTs didn't say anything to you?"

"Who's running this interrogation?" she snarled.

Interrogation? Why was *I* being interrogated? I thought we were a little beyond that at this point.

Dixie snorted. "You can't be serious. You think Susan's a suspect?"

The sheriff rounded on her. "When I want your opinion, I'll drag you down to the station in handcuffs."

Dixie raised her hands in a pacifying gesture and backed from the kitchen.

"Dixie's right though," I said. "You know I'm no suspect. I'm as baffled as you. Though Clare has been acting erratically—"

"How do you know how she's been acting?" Sheriff McCourt backhanded sweat from her brow.

"Because of the UFO investigation I've been conducting on her behalf. Remember?"

The sheriff's eyes bulged. "Still? I thought I told you to knock that off."

Please. We both knew what she'd really meant. My UFO investigation was integral to her murder inquiry. "I don't think you did," I said. "You took a copy of my notes, remember? Were you able to figure out if Danella was filming on the dates Clare had her experiences?"

"Why would I—? No!"

Bummer. I'd just have to do it myself. "That's okay. I'll let you know what I turn up."

"No. Do not turn anything up. Do you hear me? Clare's obviously disturbed."

"I'd be disturbed if aliens were stalking me. And one did steal my lemon curd."

She closed her eyes and pinched the bridge of her nose. "Your investigation has gone far enough." The phone rang on her utility belt. She checked the number, frowned, answered. "Hello, Ms. Mayor." She glanced at me. "I don't think that's—" Her face purpled. "She's not an expert!" The sheriff grimaced. "No, ma'am... Yes, ma'am... Th—"

Jerking the phone from her ear, she stared at it disgustedly then jammed it into her belt loop.

"Everything okay?"

"Everything's fine." She clawed her hands through her damp curls. "One lunatic's bad enough, but the whole town's going crazy. Doesn't anyone understand gas leak?"

"Is there a gas leak? Oh, you mean the story about what happened to the Disappeared. People understand it. They just don't believe it. But can you blame them? It's not very believable. People don't just disappear – an entire pub doesn't disappear – for months and then wander out of the woods without a scratch."

She glared.

"I didn't mean the pub wandered out of the woods," I said.

"I know what you meant," she ground out. "You are not a UFO expert."

"Well, I sort of am."

"No, you're not."

"I do run a UFO B&B, so... a little."

"Fine, *expert*. Then tell me how to stop a full-blown UFO panic, because that's what this town is headed for if people don't start seeing sense."

"Wait, is that what the mayor was calling about? She wants my advice?" Wow. Who knew my random UFO knowledge would actually come in handy?

Her nostrils flared. "Just... tell me."

I rubbed the back of my neck, thinking. "The only real American UFO panic I know of – by which I mean people running around in fear of their lives – occurred in 1938. That was when Orson Welles broadcast *War of the Worlds*. A lot of people tuned in late and thought it was real. In New Jersey, people jammed the highway, fleeing for their lives. A woman ran into a church screaming the end of the world was here and New York had been destroyed. But these days, a panic means lots of people uploading odd photos to social media. Like of that weird cloud last week. It's not like the Welles broadcast, when people flooded police stations with calls—"

"I'm being flooded with calls."

"Oh. Really?" That... wasn't good.

"What did Welles do to calm people down?"

"When the studio found out what was happening," I said, "he interrupted the broadcast. He reminded people it was fictional."

"Not helpful. That would require someone behind all this. As far as I can see, it's just a random collection of odd events. People are linking them together to create an imaginary conspiracy."

"Some of the things that have happened are connected," I reminded her. "What's happening to Clare is connected."

She tapped her chin. "Unless…"

"They're not connected?"

"Unless we had a scapegoat." She stared at me unpleasantly. "Someone involved in the UFO business we could blame. Someone who'd benefit from making Doyle look like it was on the verge of a UFO invasion."

"I don't know who…" My stomach sank to the soles of my tennis shoes. I swallowed, my mouth suddenly dry. "You think I'm behind this?"

"You're not smart enough. But you'll make a good fall guy."

"You think someone's trying to frame me?"

"No, you idiot. I'm trying to frame you."

"But… That would ruin Wits' End! No one would stay here if they thought I was a hoaxer. What about Dixie? What about Bailey?"

At my feet, the beagle whimpered.

"I wouldn't do it without your permission," she said.

"Well, thanks for that. And no, you don't have my permission."

"But it would solve a lot of problems."

Yeah. I tasted something sour at the back of my throat.

I guessed it would solve some problems.

"But it isn't true," I said weakly.

"It's a post-modern world. Truth is subjective."

"But it isn't." It wasn't. There had to be something real to hang onto, or how could anyone function?

A vehicle beeped, reversing, and I chanced another look out the window.

The ambulance backed from the colonel's driveway.

A sheriff's SUV screeched to a stop behind it, and the ambulance lurched to a halt. Emmery leapt from the car.

What was he doing? His SUV was blocking the ambulance.

Arsen and Connor ran to him.

Emmery shouted something.

"Oh, no," I said.

"What?" The sheriff pushed me aside, cursed, and charged out the kitchen door to my porch.

I jogged after her into the yard.

"This is your fault," Emmery shouted at Arsen.

"Move your SUV," Arsen said.

Emmery reddened. "You made it worse."

In a quick movement, Arsen shoved him aside and got into the squad car. He backed it from the driveway.

The ambulance reversed into the court and drove off.

Arsen stepped from the car. "Okay, let's calm—"

Emmery charged. Connor stepped between the two men. Emmery feinted and punched Arsen in the jaw.

I gasped and ran into the court. "Arsen!"

He staggered but didn't fall. Arsen rubbed his jaw.

Connor grabbed Emmery by the front of his uniform shirt and pushed him backward.

"He assaulted an officer," Emmery snarled.

"You were blocking Clare's ambulance," Connor said. "Let's all calm down. This is just a misunderstanding."

"He stole my car!"

"*My* car." The sheriff turned an unresisting Arsen and snapped cuffs on him. She pressed his chest against the black and white SUV.

My pulse pounded erratically. "What? That's totally unfair!"

"Not totally." Shoving Arsen toward Connor, she spun Emmery around and cuffed him too. "You both need to cool off."

A gray shadow, immune to the sweltering morning, chilled my shoulder. "But..." I sputtered, dizzy. "You can't arrest Arsen."

"Can't I?" she said.

"Sue," Arsen said, "it's okay. Call Nick Heathcliff."

"I will," I said. Nick was Arsen's lawyer. "Don't worry, I'll follow you to the station."

"No," he exploded. He blew out his breath. "No," he said in a quieter voice. "I'd rather you stay here. Please."

I bit my lip, but I nodded. "I'll call Nick."

Dixie came out onto the front porch. We watched while the sheriff and Deputy Hernandez drove the men away.

She clattered down the steps. "Whoa. I saw everything."

Hands shaking, I tried to call Nick, but I kept hitting the wrong damn buttons. This was a nightmare. Literally. I have nightmares of pushing the wrong buttons on phones. Was I dreaming?

Dixie gently took the phone from my hands. She touched Nick's name, handed me the phone.

"Hey, Susan," the lawyer said easily. "What's up?"

"Arsen's been arrested."

"For what?"

"Pushing a cop, I think." My breath hitched. "There was also something about stealing a police car, but he didn't. He just moved it out of the way of an ambulance. It's crazy."

"Okay, slow down. Tell me what happened."

I explained again.

"All right. I'm headed to the station now. Don't worry, Susan. I'll get him out."

"Thanks."

He hung up.

Dixie shook her head. "The sheriff really doesn't like it when you steal police cars."

"It's not the same," I said shrilly. Dixie once, in a fit of youthful exuberance, had absconded with the sheriff's SUV. She'd paid dearly for that mistake. I just hoped Arsen wasn't in quite so much trouble. And none of that mattered. Arsen had been arrested. Arrested! I couldn't control this, couldn't help him, couldn't breathe.

Dixie grasped my shoulder. "It's okay."

"No," I choked out. "It's not okay."

"Focus," she said in a low voice.

I breathed slowly in and out. I could handle this. I could manage this.

"Emmery's an idiot," she said. "What was he thinking? His girlfriend was in that ambulance."

"He wasn't thinking," I said miserably. "He was freaked out and panicked." Like I was now. But the shadow's grip had begun to loosen. I could do this. Maybe I couldn't control everything, but I could control my own reactions.

"So, what now?" Dixie asked.

"Now?" I needed to think. I needed to get control.

I needed my planner.

CHAPTER 23

Stiffly, I hurried past the hanging spider plants on the porch. I let myself inside Wits' End.

Dixie trailed after me and let the screen doors bang shut. She glared at Manaj. The agent lounged in a black tank and workout slacks on the carpeted steps.

The FBI agent made a show of perusing a paperback about Roswell.

"What are you going to do?" Dixie asked me.

"Arsen doesn't want me at the police station." I strode past the front desk and into the kitchen. "I have to get organized." Sitting at the kitchen table, I opened my planner. In the notes section, I headlined three columns: *name, motive,* and *opportunity.*

The kitchen door swung open. Agent Manaj walked in, pulled out a chair, and sat opposite me at the table.

"Hey," Dixie said. "The kitchen is off limits to guests."

Manaj cocked a brow.

Dixie let out an exasperated huff and turned to me. "But what are you going to do?"

"Obviously," I said, "investigating Clare's little UFO problem isn't enough. I never should have let the sheriff derail me from the real investigation."

"I'll say," Manaj muttered.

Dixie scowled at her and plopped down beside me.

I listed names down the side of the paper. Danella, Clare, Rufus, and Emmery. The latter was obviously a jerk, even if he had gotten me involved.

"Motives?" Manaj asked.

"We're past motives," I said.

"If you'd been here earlier, you'd know," Dixie said.

"There were flying cows," I agreed.

Dixie's brows slashed downward. "And speaking of bovine excrement—"

"Were we speaking about that?" Manaj asked.

"What about Emmery's little stunt with the ambulance?" Dixie said.

"He's a jackass." My jaw hardened. But that wasn't fair. If Emmery was a jackass, so was I. Anyone could lose it when their loved ones were in danger.

"Jackass is good enough for me," Dixie said.

Manaj's head wobbled side to side. "Eh."

"And they all had the opportunity to poison the colonel." I ticked off the boxes. "They were all there that morning."

"What about Mrs. Fitzgerald?" Dixie shot a sidelong look at the FBI agent. "Who had the opportunity to kill her?"

I tapped my pen on the page. "That, I'm not so sure about."

"Really?" Manaj asked. "There's something you're not sure about?"

"You're not helping," Dixie said.

"It *would* be nice if I had more intel," I hinted to the agent.

Manaj snorted and opened her book.

"Fine." I flipped to the date in my planner. People were checking in today. I had grocery shopping to do. And a chimney sweep was arriving some time between ten and three. That probably meant four o'clock, but I had to be here. Unless Dixie...?

"I don't know why you're looking at me like that," my cousin said, "but whatever it is, I can't. You promised I could have today off, and there's something I've got to do at the circus."

"I wouldn't," Manaj muttered.

"What's wrong with the circus?" Dixie asked.

"Have you seen the clowns?" Manaj said from behind her book.

"I didn't realize the circus was still in town," I said, ignoring the agent.

"This is their last weekend," Dixie said. "And I've got business there. I'm sorry, but it's important."

"At the circus." Manaj narrowed her eyes. "The circus."

"I can have business at a circus," Dixie insisted.

I did seem to remember promising Dixie the day off. "I guess there's no reason to stick around here," I said slowly. "There's nothing either of us can do for Arsen right now. It's in Nick's hands. Have fun."

"At a circus?" Dixie sneered. "This is business. Important UFO business. My friend Janet made friends with the tattooed man, who knows—"

I raised my hand. "Ignorance is bliss."

Dixie left.

I stared at Manaj. "Why *are* you here? Because you don't seem to be doing much."

"I'm on vacation."

"Here? Now?"

She set her paperback on the table. "You know what I got when all those Disappeared returned to Doyle?"

"No."

"A public commendation and an office in the basement. The Bureau knows I had nothing to do with those people coming back. No one has any idea why they did return or where they were."

"You want closure?"

"Closure's a myth." Her eyes turned flinty. "I want to close this damn case." She stomped from the kitchen, the door swinging in her wake.

"Well, that wasn't helpful," I told Bailey.

Neither was my next move. I drowned myself in the three w's: work, worrying and waiting.

After my first half-dozen calls to Nick Heathcliff, the exasperated lawyer told me he'd phone when Arsen's legal status changed.

The chimney sweep arrived at five minutes to three, and the chimney was swept. As soon as I could get rid of him, I checked my phone. Nothing from Nick.

I couldn't do it. I couldn't be in the present when Arsen was in jail. I had to do something. The sheriff's station was out. So I drove to the hospital to check on Clare.

The county hospital is nicer than the ones you see on TV. Its main wing has plant-filled atriums, soft, natural lighting and soothing pastel tones.

But in my distracted state, I didn't go to the main wing. I walked into the bedlam of the ER. Half of Doyle seemed to be here. Patients slumped in chairs. Patients clutched their chests. Patients gasped at harried nurses explaining the difference between panic and heart attacks.

They could have just asked me.

I turned around and nearly knocked over a man in a white undershirt clutching his left arm.

"Whoops, sorry Mr. Parnassus. What happened? Are you having chest pains?"

The older man winced. "Thought I saw an alien behind my chimney and fell off the roof. It turned out to be a pigeon."

"Thank God you weren't killed."

"Stupid birds." He lowered his voice. "I think they're out to get me."

"The pigeons?"

"No, the aliens."

I looked around. How many of these people were here due to alien-related injuries?

A nurse I knew whizzed past.

"Robin," I said. "What's going on?"

She stopped short, poised on her toes for flight. "Alien invasion, looks like." She hurried onward.

I clutched my purse more tightly. The sheriff was right. Things were going from bad to worse.

Escaping the ER, I made my way to the main wing's moderately more peaceful front desk. I waited in a line that made a Mars mission look short. When I finally got to the front, an elderly volunteer beamed at me from behind a computer monitor. "How can I help you, dear?" She adjusted the reading glasses on her nose.

"I'm looking for Clare Fitzgerald's room."

"Let me check." She typed into her computer and frowned at the screen.

"She's in ICU. Are you family?"

"No."

"Then I don't think they're going to let you in, but I can call up, if you like."

"No. No thanks." If she was in intensive care, I shouldn't bother her. Not yet.

"Hi, Susan," a man said, and I started. Tom Tarrant glanced up from his computer tablet and flashed his wholesome grin.

I glared at the reporter. "Tom. What brings you here?"

"I could ask you the same thing." Beneath his black t-shirt, he shrugged his broad shoulders. "Did you hear my podcast?"

Oh, right. He had mentioned something about a podcast. "Sorry, no."

"It's a new thing. Maybe you'd like to be a guest some day? We could do a call in."

"No thanks," I said coldly, feeling the force of his football-player good looks. But I was impervious to his charm.

"Any comments on the recent rash of alien sightings?" he asked. "That's what we were talking about today."

This was where I should say something to defuse the alien panic. But I couldn't think of a damn thing. "I, er, don't think it's real."

His brows rose. "You don't think these injuries are real?"

"No. Obviously, they're real. I mean, I don't think there's an alien invasion. This seems like a panic over nothing."

"*Seems* like?"

"What else could it be?"

"This is Doyle," he said.

Yeah. That was tough to argue with.

"In that case," he continued, "any comments on Clare Fitzgerald? I heard you were the one to find her."

"Where did you–?" Urgh. A pox on small towns and well-connected reporters. "I hope she gets better soon."

"Was she being circled by any birds?"

"No," I said flatly.

"Anything else odd or unusual? Anything… alien?"

I crossed my arms. "Nope."

"So, what do you know about all this?"

My lips pressed together. "I know that this is a one-way street. You want information from me, but what do *I* get out of it? What do *you* know?"

"Look, something's up." He glanced around the crowded space, then took my elbow. Tom steered me to a nook filled with vending machines. "Check this out." He handed me his computer tablet.

I frowned at a photo of a medical chart. "I can't read this." The medical jargon was impossible.

"I know, it's a little unethical. But sometimes you need to bend the rules to get information."

Yeah. And the ethics. Heat raced to my face.

"But it's interesting." He took back the tablet. "When she was brought in today, Clare was doped to the gills. My contact said it's amazing she didn't collapse before this."

"Doped with what?"

"They're still trying to figure out what she took. It's not any of the usual suspects. But my contact said it's a mix of natural compounds."

"What she took? You mean, the doctors think she took it intentionally?"

"Word is," he said in a low voice, "there's insanity in the family."

No kidding. I rubbed my hands. They itched worse than ever. Had Jayce's lotion made them worse? "What do the drugs do?" I asked. "Aside from make her collapse, I mean."

"It's unclear. But they think the mix probably caused hallucinations, paranoia, the works."

"That explains a lot," I said slowly and stared at my palms.

"Does it? What's the scoop?"

"Huh? Nothing. Absolutely nothing. I just…" I made a helpless motion.

Tom tracked my gaze to the crowds milling in the hospital's high-ceilinged entry. He laughed harshly. "Maybe it's in the water, eh?"

"No, I don't think so… Thanks, Tom." I hurried from the hospital and checked my phone. There were no calls from Nick or Arsen. I clutched the plastic tight enough to pinch the skin on my palm. Why hadn't one of them called?

"Present moment," I whispered. "Present moment."

At a loss, I checked my planner.

Right. Shopping.

I drove to the grocery store, walked through the automatic doors, and stopped short. Lines stretched from the checkout stands deep into the aisles. People leaned on carts piled high with groceries.

Stunned, I walked down aisles of half-empty shelves.

An aproned stock boy snatched a bag of tortilla chips off the floor. His freckled face wrinkled in disgust.

"What's going on?" I asked.

"The end of the world." He looked harder at me. "Hey, you're that World's End chick. You know about these things."

"Wits' End," I corrected.

"What?"

"The B&B is Wits' End. And what things?"

"Aliens. What do you think? Is an invasion eminent?"

A zaftig blond woman halted her cart to listen.

"Um. No," I said. "No, an invasion is not *imm*inent. This is all a misunderstanding," I said more confidently.

"But what about the people who've disappeared?" the blonde asked.

"You mean, the Disappeared?" I said.

She shook her head. "No, the Hendersons. They're gone."

"I heard they moved," I said.

More shoppers crowded us.

"I heard they were taken," Martha Cohen said.

"I heard they were experimented on," said an older man.

"I heard a goat with two heads was born last night."

"And what about those missing cows?"

"Did you hear Tom's podcast?"

"Did you see those weird lights in the sky?"

"No," I said shrilly, "none of that happened. No one's been taken. It's all a misunderstanding."

"I heard the podcast," a teenage checker shouted, skimming groceries across her scanner. "That happened. Tom said nowhere was safe. It starts here, but they're going to take the entire USA."

"The weird lights are searchlights," I said. "From the circus." They had to believe that. I mean, it was just obvious.

"Then why were you investigating Clare Fitzgerald's lost time?" the blonde asked.

"Where did you hear about that?" I asked.

"So, it's true," someone shouted.

"No." My pulse fluttered rapidly. "I mean, yes. But–"

"And the turkeys?" the blonde asked.

"Turkeys are flocking birds," I said weakly.

"I heard that FBI agent is staying at her house again," someone muttered. "She's in on it."

"She's got a UFO in her roof!"

"I'm not," I said. "I'm not in on anything."

"Unless she's one of them." The stock boy fisted his hands and jammed them in his apron pockets.

The crowd bustled away, shooting me suspicious glances over their shoulders.

"There's no invasion!" I shouted to the departing crowd.

"You would say that." The stock boy tossed me the bag. "Your chips."

I clutched the bag to my chest and watched him hurry away.

I gulped. Had my UFO investigation fueled a full-blown panic?

CHAPTER 24

Hoarding? Panicked shoppers? My stomach cramped, and I pressed my hands to my blouse. I hadn't been responsible for the strange lights in the sky.

But I might have made things worse. This was awful. Terrible. Very, very bad. Unless Tom's stupid podcast really had said aliens were on their way.

Then it was his fault.

I jogged to my Crosstrek and drove toward Wits' End. In their driveways, neighbors piled luggage on cars glinting in the hot afternoon sun. Cars sped past going in the opposite direction. Knuckles tight on the wheel, I turned into the Wits' End driveway. I shut off the car. The ticking of its cooling metal felt like a countdown.

But the old Victorian was still standing. A margin of tension leaked from my shoulders. Home. I was home. I was in control. I could figure this out.

Hurrying into the high-ceilinged foyer, I strode behind the reception desk. I studied the shelf filled with UFO books. There had to be something here that had an answer. Haphazardly, I pulled out books, scanned for info on panics, dropped them on the nearby desk.

Bailey whined by my feet.

"Not now," I said, "this is serious."

I gathered the books and took them into the kitchen, dumped them on the round table. Frantically, I flipped through their pages. But there were no checklists, no guidelines, no SOPs for quelling a UFO panic. Neck corded, I opened my laptop computer and turned to Tom's podcast.

Welcome to the Doyle Alien Abduction Podcast, the place for alien aficionados and your antidote for audacious anecdotes. This is your host, Tom Tarrant. Today we're talking about the latest in UFO news from your favorite small Sierra town, Doyle, California.

Is local girl, Clare Fitzgerald, being haunted by aliens? Are aliens targeting the children of Air Force vets from Area 51? Susan Witsend, of California's only UFO-themed B&B, Wits' End and local UFO expert, is on the case...

I listened intently. His podcast was a little sensational, but he hadn't exactly declared an alien invasion. He'd talked a lot about me though, and Wits' End. So... no publicity is bad publicity?

I blew out my breath. It didn't matter. What mattered was my UFO investigation was feeding the panic.

And the only model for stopping a panic was the one the sheriff had suggested – finding a scapegoat.

I laid my head on the laminate table and whimpered. A shaft of sunlight slipped past the short, blue curtains above the sink and struck my eye. I winced, straightening.

It was on me.

I'd done this.

But if I stepped up and took responsibility for it all, called myself a hoaxer, it would be the end of Wits' End. I might even be run out of town.

Did people still do that? My head swam, my chest tightening.

But then what would I do? Become an accountant again? Who'd hire me? No one would trust a hoaxer with their bookkeeping. I couldn't ask my parents for help. My breath came in short gasps. I couldn't go back to that. I couldn't.

"Are you dead too?" Dixie prodded my shoulder.

I covered my head with my hands and groaned. "If only it was that simple. I thought you were at the circus?"

"My source was a bust. I never should have trusted a guy covered in that many tattoos. One was enough for me." She rubbed her lower back, wrinkling her tank. "It really hurt."

I sat up and closed my laptop. "So, you got bored?"

"UFO investigations will take you to all sorts of unsavory places. Can I help it I got stuck at a stupid circus? Besides, I had a bad feeling. I needed to get out of there." She took a step away from the kitchen table. "So, what's wrong now?"

"Doyle's starting to panic, really panic, and it's my fault."

"What is?"

I stood and motioned around the kitchen. "This! Everything!"

"You're responsible for everything," she said flatly. "That's a little arrogant."

I walked to the sink and gazed out the window. "You know what I mean."

Rufus exited the colonel's A-frame. Backpack under one arm, he turned and locked the door. Rufus waved to me, and I turned away. He was probably taking Clare's things to her in the hospital.

"Yeah," Dixie said. "I think I do know. You want to be responsible for everything, because that puts you in control."

"That's not true. I only ever wanted to be in control of myself."

"I met your parents. Remember?"

My face heated. How could I forget that awful night? Gran had died, and I'd learned I'd inherited Wits' End. Running it was impossible of course – or so my controlling parents had insisted. And God help me, I'd almost listened to them. It had become a habit by that time.

Until Dixie had arrived, raging. Because selling Wits' End would have meant selling her out too. I'd come with Dixie to Wits' End that night and hadn't gone back.

I turned to face her. "I'm not my parents."

"Yeah, you are. Everyone is. Oh, you've been good at fighting it, but come on! You've stuck your nose in three murder investigations because you thought you'd do a better job than the police."

"That isn't why." I ran my palm along the butcher block counter's edge. "The sheriff asked for my help."

She arched a brow. "Oh, really?"

"She did!"

"News flash: you're not in control. None of us are. Horrible things happen in this world which we have no control over. All we can do is remember what counts and keep moving forward. So, what counts for you?"

And that was the problem. Wits' End counted. Dixie counted. How could I take the blame and throw either of them to the wolves?

"You're right," I said. "I need to think."

I walked out the kitchen door, Bailey trotting behind me. We crossed the lawn and sat on the gazebo steps. I closed my eyes and focused on my breath. I felt my lungs fill and empty. I felt the pulse of my blood slow.

Be present.

The trickle of water from the UFO fountain was a calming murmur. A warm breeze glided across my skin. I opened my eyes.

Gran's roses danced in the light breeze. The sun had begun to drift behind the western mountains. It set ablaze the fringe of marzipan clouds and glinted off the UFO in the shingled roof.

My reluctance to fall on my sword was about more than saving Wits' End and Dixie. I wasn't that noble. I was worried about myself too and about leaving Arsen. That was the future.

But it didn't exist. It might never exist. What could I save in the here and now?

"What am I going to do?" I whispered to the roses.

Wits' End. Dixie. They were what counted.

I raised my head. Of course. It was obvious. It didn't matter what happened to me in the end. If I took the fall for the panic, I'd manage. I always managed. I didn't know where I'd go, but there'd be somewhere. My heart cracked. But Dixie? How would this affect my cousin?

I stood.

Bailey at my heels, I walked to the picket fence. I stared at the empty A-frame next door, dark and lifeless. There were more awful things happening in Doyle than my little problems.

What could I do here and now?

A curtain fluttered at an open, upstairs sliding glass door.

My spine straightened.

I stared at the open door. I'd take the blame if I had to. But I wasn't going down without a fight.

CHAPTER 25

"Stay," I told Bailey and clambered over the low, white-painted fence.

He made one, low, mournful yip, but didn't follow.

I shoved aside thoughts of who might see me. The curve of the bowl-shaped court and the thick trees obscured me from the neighbors. The light was dimming. The only people with a clear sightline were the stoners across the street. And I wasn't worried about them.

Rufus, on the other side of the colonel's house, might see me, but only if he was walking his dog.

I walked up the front steps. Hands trembling, I tried the door.

Locked.

Well, I'd figured as much, but I would have felt dumb if I hadn't tried the front door.

The porch wrapped halfway around the side of the cabin facing Wits' End. I walked around its corner and to the spot where the wooden railing met the shingled wall. Bracing one hand on the wall, I climbed the railing and stood on its top.

I could just reach the upstairs porch with the open sliding-glass door.

"This is a bad idea," I muttered. But I stretched and grasped one of the upstairs porch railings. I swung my feet up. In an inelegant wriggle, I slithered onto the small porch.

Heart thumping, I opened the glass door wider and slipped inside.

I smoothed my clothes and looked around. I stood in a master bedroom — the colonel and Mrs. Fitzgerald's. A simple quilt covered its king-sized bed. Rustic furniture decorated the room.

Since I didn't know what to look for here, I went downstairs, to the kitchen. If there'd been foxglove in here, the sheriff would have surely taken it away. But I searched the cupboards and tiled countertop and found... nothing.

I returned upstairs to the master bathroom. There was nothing suspicious in the drawers or closets that I could see. No weird medicines in the bathroom cabinets. No secret caches of alien artifacts.

I cocked my head, listening. When I didn't hear anything, I walked into a smaller room next door. Stuffed animals lined the narrow bed. They must have belonged to Clare once. But she hadn't lived as a child in this house. I was surprised the practical colonel and the even more practical Marion had kept the toys, much less made up a bed for her here.

The drawers were filled with old books and toys. On an impulse, I looked under the bed.

A dark shape lay jammed on the side near the window.

I rose and walked to the other side of the bed. Nose wrinkling, I reached beneath it and touched something rubbery. I yanked it out. A gray alien head stared back at me. "Yeow!" I fumbled the thing and clutched a hand to my heart. It was only a mask.

The mask wasn't dusty, its rubber supple. And it explained the face I'd seen at my window... if I'd fallen into an episode of *Scooby Doo*.

I dropped the mask on the bed and did a double take.

A white owl stared out at me from the pile of stuffed animals.

I breathed slowly to quiet my galloping heart. It was just another stuffed animal.

But it didn't look like a toy. It looked... real.

I pushed aside a nearby polar bear.

The owl angled against the pillows. A black metal spike stuck from one clawed foot.

I pulled the owl free from the pile of toys. It was real. And dead. And had been stuffed by a professional taxidermist. But what was it doing on Clare's bed? I studied the bird. It had been a beautiful animal in life, but taxidermy was just creepy.

A board creaked inside the house.

My head jerked upward. Holding my breath, I strained my ears.

Silence.

The sound could have been the house settling.

Or maybe I wasn't alone.

I'd been in here too long. It was time to leave.

Gripping the owl, I tiptoed to the bedroom door.

Another creak.

I froze.

That wasn't the house settling. Someone was on the stairs. And it wasn't Clare. She was in the hospital.

My hands grew slick on the white feathers. I mouthed a curse. There was only one door leading from Clare's room, and it led to the hall in full view of the staircase.

I was trapped.

But did the intruder know I was here?

Mouth dry, I licked my lips.

Another stealthy creak.

He had to know he wasn't alone. Otherwise, why was he tiptoeing up the steps? Movements jerky, I looked around the room for a weapon, an exit. The small window had a sheer drop down onto a gravel path. It was way too long a fall.

Footsteps padded down the hallway.

I hadn't made a plan for getting caught. I hadn't come up with an alternate exit strategy. And I should have.

But I could do this.

I raised the owl over my head.

One... two....

CHAPTER 26

Three...!

Swinging the owl like a club, I whirled into the hallway. "Back off!" The owl exploded in a flurry of ivory feathers. It soared over the stairway banister and clunked down the steps.

Arsen dropped his fist at his side.

I gaped, heart thundering. "You?"

He brushed a feather off the shoulder of his blue golf shirt. "Sue, you nearly gave me a heart attack."

"You're free." I hurled myself into his arms.

Arsen was free, and he was okay and that was all that mattered. I kissed him, electricity humming through my veins.

Breathing heavily, we untangled ourselves.

"You're back." I panted. "I'm so glad you're back."

"I thought you were a burglar," he said.

"Technically, I am. What happened? Did they charge you?"

"Emmery came to his senses. I was let off with a warning."

"But what are you doing here?" I leaned closer. In spite of the sheen of sweat on his neck, he smelled like soap. Lightly, I ran my hands down his arms, assuring myself he was really here.

"I was going to ask you the same thing. I saw someone moving around upstairs through the curtains. There was no car was in the driveway. It didn't look right."

"How did you get inside?"

"Open window. Bottom floor."

Rats. Why hadn't I seen that?

"You?" he asked.

"I've been looking for evidence."

"Find any?"

I pointed down the stairs. "Owl."

"Was that what it was?" He peered over the banister. "I think you killed it. But what's that got to do with anything?"

"I think it's the white owl Clare has been seeing."

His brow furrowed.

I stepped away. "I also found an alien mask."

He followed me into the girlish bedroom, and I pointed to the mask atop the bed.

"Did you touch it?"

"How do you think it got on the bed?"

"Wait here. I'll be right back." He vanished out the bedroom door, his footsteps clattering on the stairs. A minute or two later, he returned with two plastic bags in his hand. Using one as a glove, he deposited the mask into the second, larger bag. "For the police."

"Maybe we should leave it and let the police come get it?"

"Do you want to wait here for them? Because knowing our luck, if we left it here, it would be gone by the time the cops arrived."

"Good point," I said glumly.

"So, Clare's been putting us on."

"Not necessarily. I saw Emmery's father, Rufus, in here earlier today. I assumed he was collecting Clare's clothing for her stay at the hospital. He left with a small bag and didn't look like he was trying to hide anything."

"Huh."

"And Danella's been in and out of that house a dozen times. She could have snuck in just like I did."

"But wouldn't leaving the mask there have blown the whole scheme?"

"Maybe it wasn't meant to be found. Or maybe it was meant to make Clare look guilty."

"I just— it seems extreme. I mean, she's her mom."

"As extreme as hiring a detective to follow her?" I snapped and grimaced. That had been a little harsh. Arsen didn't know. Not even Dixie knew this part of the story.

"Danella did that?"

I blew out my breath. "No. Not her. Me. My parents." He didn't know. And I wasn't being fair.

"I'm confused."

I forced a smile. "My parents hired a detective to follow me when I moved to Wits' End."

He blinked. "Why?"

"Because I'm screwed up, okay? Because my entire family is screwed up. Including me."

"No, you're not."

"I am. I run a UFO B&B that I didn't even create. I don't talk to my parents, because if I do, they may suck me back into their lives, and I can't. I can't do it again." My eyes heated. "I... delude myself into believing the sheriff and I are besties, that I can actually solve crimes."

"There's nothing wrong with you, Susan."

My throat closed. "No, Arsen. There is. I thought Dixie—" I shook my head. How could I explain it?

Someone who'd always been independent couldn't understand. I could barely understand it. A big part of me didn't want to understand, because I was ashamed. Ashamed of all those lost years. Ashamed of all those "yeses" when I'd meant no. Ashamed of not being with Gran at the end.

"Dixie called to tell me Gran was failing." I sniffed. "But it was tax season, and my parents had said leaving was impossible." And to them I'd said yes. My pulse pounded in my ears.

"What are you talking about?"

"I wasn't here for Gran when she died," I said unevenly. "I was weak. I was so used to letting them tell me what to do, I just kept doing it. Afterward, I told myself I hadn't believed it, that I'd thought Gran had more time, that Dixie was exaggerating her illness. But the truth was, I'd been a coward."

Because when Gran had left me Wits' End, I'd gone along with my parents again. I'd agreed to sell it, because I didn't believe I deserved it.

Until Dixie.

The gray shadow touched my shoulder, and my knees buckled. The shadow wasn't my parents. It was the truth. This is what I'd been trying to avoid. And truth wasn't relative. It was real, and it was coming for me. It would always come.

My chest tightened, my breath thinning. I didn't deserve Wits' End or Arsen or Dixie.

The truth was awful.

"Susan, you're in the colonel's house. You're with me."

Warmth enfolded me. I fought against it.

"Look around," he said.

Dots swam in front of my eyes.

"You're at the colonel's. We're together. I love you, Susan."

The world was spinning and I couldn't breathe and I didn't deserve to breathe and how had I even thought—

And then I was in my own black-and-white sitting room. I sat in Arsen's lap on the couch. A soft blanket wrapped around me, and Bailey pressed against my hip.

Control. I drew in a deep breath. I needed to take back control. Control drove the shadow away. And I was safe. I was here, with Arsen.

Now really was all that mattered.

Arsen's muscular arms enveloped me. He pressed his lips to the top of my head. "Dixie did tell me, but I didn't believe."

I lowered my head, unable to meet his gaze. Of course he didn't. He was too good. He'd never do something that terrible, and so he wouldn't believe it of me. I shifted, trying to pull away, but his arms were iron bands.

Bailey whimpered and burrowed closer.

"So," Arsen continued, "I went to see your parents."

My head jerked up. My hands fisted in his golf shirt and turned clammy.

"What? When?"

"This morning, after the sheriff let me out."

"You've been free all day and didn't tell me?"

"You didn't want me to meet your parents. This seemed like my best chance."

"That's—" What I deserved. "All right," I said dully. "What happened?"

"They offered me money."

"To do what?"

"To bring you home and leave you there."

My throat closed. After a moment, I said, "Clearly, the second detective they hired didn't do a very good job investigating *you*."

He laughed lightly and brushed a strand of hair from my face. "No. I don't need their money. But I guess it might have looked that way last year, when I was working as a trail guide."

I winced. "I'm sorry."

Bailey nudged me and knocked a white throw pillow to the floor.

"Don't apologize for your parents." His voice hardened. "You're not responsible for them."

"What else did they say?"

"It doesn't matter. We'll put aside the fiction that they're accountants–"

"They are!"

He gave me an odd look. "Sue, I don't understand everything about that situation, but I think I understand enough. And so did your grandmother."

My gran. Tears burned my eyes. I'd disappointed her so badly, and she'd done so much for me – was still doing so much for me.

He chuckled. "The only thing I can't figure out is how she managed to pry you loose every summer. What did she have on them?"

"No idea."

"Did Dixie ever tell you what your Gran's final words were to her?"

Final words? "No."

"You should ask."

A loud bang rattled the windows. I started, gripping Arsen more tightly. Car alarms bleated.

Bailey jumped to his feet and barked.

Arsen stiffened.

"Stay here." He lifted me up and deposited me on the velvety couch. Arsen strode from the room.

Bailey trotted after him, the beagle's collar jingling.

I sat there for a long moment, love tangling with relief. Arsen knew the truth, and he wasn't running. He'd said he loved me, and this time it wasn't a throw-off comment. He loved me, and I loved him…

And I still hated being told what to do.

Lurching from the sofa, I walked into the kitchen. The porch door stood open. I rushed outside.

Arsen and Bailey stood in the yard and stared at a green-streaked twilight sky. Sirens echoed through the pines. Arsen held his phone to his ear.

I jogged down the steps.

My neighbors streamed from their homes and pointed at the clouds.

In the court, one of the stoners – Dunk – dropped his phone to his side. He arched his back and howled.

The sound raised gooseflesh on my scalp.

"Dude! We're having a riot!"

I hurried to Arsen. "What's going on?"

He shook his head. "All right. Thanks," he said into the phone and hung up.

"There's been an explosion," he said.

My breath caught. "Where?"

"Town hall."

I felt the blood drain from my face. "Mrs. Steinberg works there."

"It's after five. I'm sure she's gone home."

"Why would you be sure of that? She's crazy! Everyone's terrified of her. She does what she wants."

He grasped my shoulders. "The volunteer fire department called me in. I've got to go."

"No," I said. "We'll go." After everything that had happened, I wasn't letting him go that easily.

He hesitated and took my hand. "We will."

CHAPTER 27

We drove through thick and acrid air towards the wail of sirens. On Main Street, a wall of stopped traffic blocked our path. Arsen swerved between two pickups. He parked his Jeep beside a wine tasting room, its metal shutters pulled fast.

We jogged toward the glow lighting the night sky. People clutching backpacks and suitcases fled in the opposite direction.

Fire and police vehicles clotted the street around Town Hall. Flames licked the brick building's dome. Smoke billowed from its lower windows.

Chilled, I glanced at the nearby rows of old-timey wooden buildings. One spark could send up the entire street.

"There's my crew." Arsen motioned toward a group of men in heavy overalls spraying water on the fire. His volunteer department was backup only, usually called into service for forest fires. That they'd been called this evening spoke to the seriousness of the fire. My stomach spiraled sickeningly.

He kissed me lightly. "Are you going to—"

"I'm fine." I smiled tightly. "Go."

He squeezed my arm, kissed me again, and jogged toward the volunteers.

Pressing one hand to my mouth, I stepped beneath the eaves of a 19th-century restaurant. Had Mrs. Steinberg gotten out of the building? Was anyone still trapped inside?

"I should have guessed you'd be here," a familiar voice said behind me.

Agent Manaj stared, impassive, at the fire. Soot streaked her cheek. Wisps of dark hair escaped her chignon.

"Are you all right?" I asked her.

"Fine. What's the word?"

"Nothing. There's no word. Were you in there?" I pointed at the smear darkening her cheek.

She rubbed it absently. "Not for long. The fire alarm went off, and I got swept up in the evacuation."

"Did you see Mrs. Steinberg?"

"Who?"

"An older woman, likes to wear black. She works in town records, in the basement."

She gave me a long look, then shook her head. "No. Friend of yours?"

"Of my grandmother's. I mean, yes. She's a friend."

"Then, let's find out what's going on." She stood on her toes and peered over the crowd. She pointed. "Those two. Come on."

I followed her through the chaos. Staring, pointing people mingled in the middle of the road, heedless of passing cars. Along the street, business owners clanged shut their metal, fireproof shutters.

Danella's cameramen stood outside the police tape by Antoine's Bar. Mahir filmed the burning building.

"Bob?" I said. "Mahir?"

Mahir lowered the camera from his shoulder. "Susan. What are you doing here? Were you in there?" He eyed the FBI agent.

"No," I said. "What have you heard?"

"They say the fire started in the basement," Mahir said.

My stomach tightened. I braced one hand against the rough, wood-slat wall. "Oh, my God."

"What's wrong?" Bob asked.

"Do you know if everyone got out?" I asked.

Mahir shook his head. "No idea. We got here after the shouting started."

Tears stung my eyes. This was awful.

The historic building seemed a lost cause, and Mrs. Steinberg... She was part of my Gran's generation. If she was gone, it was the end, the real end, of an era.

Surely if the old woman had gotten out, she'd be here making cryptic comments about conspiracies? I closed my eyes. This wasn't helping. I had to stay focused.

Swallowing, I pulled my planner from my bag. I flipped to my notes on Clare's "visitations." "Were you filming on March 31st?" I asked.

"March 31st?" Bob asked.

I opened my color-coded calendar and pointed at the date.

"Oh, yeah," Bob said.

"You were?" I said.

"No," he said. "I was surfing with a friend of mine in San Clemente."

Manaj rolled her eyes.

"What about April 23rd?" I asked.

Thunder cracked above us. I glanced up hopefully. But no rain fell.

Mahir nudged his colleague. "April 23rd. That was the woman in Nebraska. Remember that snowstorm?"

Bob shuddered. "Snow in April. How do people live like that? I mean, I get the whole, *we love having seasons* thing, but shouldn't April be spring? Spring's a season, right?"

"And Danella was with you?" I asked.

Bob gaped. "Do you think we'd go film someone without her? In a Nebraska snowstorm?"

"And you're sure about the date?" I said.

"I'm sure," Mahir said. "You can check the weather report if you want. It was a freak storm. I think some cows froze to the ground or something."

"Oh yeah," Bob said. "The Nebraska cowsicles. Let's go. We've got to get a better angle."

He and Mahir moved into the crowd.

"Satisfied Danella couldn't have pranked your client?" Agent Manaj asked.

I stared. "How did you…?"

"I read your investigation planner."

"What?" I sputtered. "That's an invasion of privacy."

Her dark-eyed gaze bored into mine. "You know what they say about turnabout and fair play."

"I have no idea what you're talking about," I said in a high voice. Last year, when Manaj had first come to stay at Wits' End, I *might* have snuck into her room and rifled her top-secret FBI files.

But it had been for a good cause.

"Relax. I'm not going to arrest you." She clapped my shoulder. "You're a little nuts, but you're a good egg, if I can mix my metaphors."

"Go wild," I said weakly.

"Best you return to Wits' End, where you're out of the way, and it's safe."

She strode toward Sheriff McCourt, standing on the fender of her SUV.

Jayce Bonheim stood woodenly nearby in a tight, gray t-shirt and jeans. The café owner watched the fire.

Maybe she'd seen Mrs. Steinberg. I trotted to her. "Jayce!"

The coffeeshop owner didn't move.

"Jayce, have you seen Mrs. Steinberg? Jayce?" I touched her arm.

She turned her head slightly toward me but couldn't seem to drag her gaze from the fire. "What?" she asked in a dreamy voice.

"Mrs. Steinberg," I said with forced patience. "Have you seen her?"

"No."

I stepped between her and the burning building. "Jayce, are you ok—" Her expression was slack, dazed. But she didn't look hurt, or as if she'd been in the fire… "Oh." I was an idiot. Of course she wasn't okay. Ground had burned down last year. This fire must be bringing back all sorts of bad memories. "Jayce." I grasped her arms. "It's okay."

She stared past me.

I tugged on my purse. What did Arsen do with people who were freaking out? "You're safe. You're on Main Street. Ground is safe."

She didn't respond.

"Red! Look for the color red. Where do you see it?"

"Red," she repeated dully.

I blew out my breath. The "red" technique worked for Arsen. But it wasn't getting me anywhere. Okay, what got me to focus during an anxiety attack? Arsen did, and he wasn't here. Getting back to the present helped me.

Then there was anger.

"I have a bone to pick with you, Jayce Bonheim. You're new hand lotion stinks. Literally. I mean, sure, my hands were soft and silky as a baby's butt. But that's not the point. They smelled manky. Your lotion is manky," I said, hoping to jolt her out of her malaise.

Dry thunder rolled across the darkening mountains.

She blinked. Her nostrils flared. "Manky?"

"I thought it would smell like coffee. It left me smelling like rotting parsnips."

"Rotting?" Her green eyes flashed. "It's–" She blinked, swayed. Her expression cleared, her eyes regaining their focus. "Susan?"

"It's okay." I smiled, relieved. "The same thing happened to me earlier. If I had an idea you…" I trailed off. Not everyone wanted to admit to debilitating anxiety. "Well, I wished we'd have talked sooner."

I steered her onto a sidewalk and sat her down on a wrought-iron bench.

Jayce clawed a hand through her thick, mahogany hair. "Sorry, what were you saying? Oh, and I promised you another jar. I'm sorry, I just haven't had time to make more."

"It's okay." But why *had* it smelled so awful the next day? That didn't seem like Jayce's style. "What would make your lotion smell like rotting parsnips?"

"Parsnips? Nothing. I mean, I don't put anything like that in my lotions."

Glass crashed from Town Hall.

"Anything like what?" I asked in a strained voice.

"Like hemlock, or any of the other–" She bit her lip. "Sorry, what am I saying?"

"Hemlock smells like parsnips?"

"Yeah, it does. But I don't know why that came to mind. I guess because there was an outbreak of wild hemlock in the Sierras last year. They had to close a park along the Truckee river. They were worried foragers might confuse it for parsley. Forget I said anything. Hemlock. Ha! I mean, the smell could have been anything. But definitely not hemlock."

She leapt to her feet. "I've got to…" Jayce hurried down the sidewalk toward Ground.

That was a little abrupt. But it's hard to be at your best in a fire that could burn down the entire town.

I pulled out my phone and typed hemlock and lotion into the search engine. And got an error message. No signal.

The entire town must be on their phones because of the fire. Ground had wi-fi, but Ground was closed. Antoine's? It might have a connection.

Dodging gaping Doyleites and tough-looking deputies, I crossed the street. I clambered onto the raised sidewalk in front of the bar. Raucous music and laughter flowed from its batwing doors. At least one group of people wasn't panicking.

I checked my phone. "Thank God." I had wi-fi again.

Hurriedly, I typed the words into the search engine.

"Hsst! Hs–" The sound dissolved into hacking.

I followed the coughs around the corner of Antoine's Bar.

Mrs. Steinberg leaned on a wooden post and bent double, her shoulders quaking.

"Mrs. Steinberg!" Laughing with shaky relief, I hurried to her. "Are you all right?"

She straightened. Soot lined the creases of her wrinkled face. She brandished an e-cigarette. "Fine. About time you lost the fed."

"The fed? You mean Agent Manaj?"

"Damned snoop." She sucked on her e-cig and coughed some more.

"Should you, er, be smoking right now?" I was already getting a lungful from the fire at Town Hall.

"Antoine and I go way back," she said. "He won't mind. Now, what did Manaj say?"

She'd nearly been killed, and she was still focused on her conspiracy theories? Exasperated, I crossed my arms. "Nothing, really."

"I saw her in Town Hall."

"You don't think she set the fire?"

"No, young Susan, I do not think she set the fire." She pressed a gnarled hand to her chest and barked a cough. "I think she knows more than is good for her. Much like you."

"I don't know what I know," I grumbled.

"Well, you know that so-called psychic hasn't been gaslighting her own daughter."

"You knew the two were related?"

"I know a lot of things."

"Well, I wish you would have told me."

"I've told you it's dangerous to–" She raised her head and sniffed. "That's not smoke. I've wasted too much time here."

"But–"

"Go home, Susan. Go home to your roses and your dog and be happy." She tottered around the corner of the wood-slat building.

"Mrs. Steinberg..." I rounded the corner and stopped short, scanning the milling throng. The old woman had vanished.

I braced my hands on my hips. Where the devil had she gone? She must have gotten lost in the crowd. It was dark, and she was wearing that black dress. But I shifted, uneasy.

CHAPTER 28

I pushed through the roiling crowd. The glow from Town Hall distorted the throng's shadows into wavering, demonic figures.

"Well, get on it," she sheriff snapped to a uniformed deputy. The deputy hurried toward the burning building.

I hesitated. Maybe I had been deluding myself about the sheriff and my detecting abilities. But this was important. "Sheriff?"

McCourt turned and glared. "This is not the time—"

"Are you sure it was foxglove that killed the colonel?" I blurted.

She eyed me. "Why? What—"

Thunder rumbled, echoing across the granite mountains. The sheriff and I looked up at a blackening sky, empty of stars.

"What have you heard?" she asked.

"Hemlock," I said.

"And this is why civilians should leave policing to the police. According to the coroner, who's got the only opinion that counts, it was foxglove."

I slumped against a lamp post. So much for my hot lead. "Oh."

Her face spasmed. "No one's blaming you, Witsend. People grow foxglove all over Doyle. I've got it in my garden. It was just your bad luck that yours happened to be growing next door to a murder victim."

Another boom, farther off. I glanced toward the mountains but saw no answering flash of lightning. But of course, the lightning came first, then the sound.

"Sheriff—"

"Stop, Susan." She raised a hand, palm out. "Just stop."

I gripped my purse strap between both hands. "But I found—"

"Later. In case you haven't noticed, Town Hall's on fire. The highway is blocked by three accidents. There was an alien sighting at the hospital. It caused a stampede."

"Was anyone hurt?"

"The cafeteria espresso machine was DOA. A pregnant woman went into labor, but that might have happened anyway. I can't swing a cat without hitting a firefighter, and that damned FBI agent—"

The radio on her collar crackled. She cross-grabbed it and bent her chin to the device. "McCourt."

A blitz of panicked screeches and numbers flowed from the radio.

McCourt said a word I'd never heard her utter before. She leapt into her SUV. The sheriff flipped on the sirens and fishtailed the car. She screeched to a halt in front of a trio of gawkers. McCourt leaned out her window. "Get off the damn road!"

The pedestrians stared at her for a moment, then scattered.

More slowly, she drove down Main Street. Other car doors slammed, deputies leaping into their SUVs.

Soon only the sightseers and firefighters were left. And me.

I huddled beneath an awning, my eyes watering from the smoke. Whatever disaster the deputies were running to, it couldn't be helped by me. My gawking was getting embarrassing, even if my boyfriend was one of the firefighters.

I edged through the crowd and came to a stop beneath Ground's overhang. The front of the coffeeshop was dark, but a faint light gleamed from the kitchen in the back.

I glanced toward the eastern mountains. Those were rain clouds. Now if only they'd move west, dampening the dry tinder of Main Street.

I dropped into one of the metal chairs on the sidewalk. Digging out my phone, I connected with Ground's wi-fi. Jayce had said hemlock might have caused that smell. According to the internet, hemlock could be absorbed through the skin and lungs. But I didn't find anything about it causing hallucinations.

If there was hemlock in Clare's lotion – and that wasn't a sure thing – then it wasn't responsible for her seeing aliens. Plus, there'd been that alien mask I'd found, and an alien had stolen my lemon curd. But while it had startled me, I hadn't fallen apart like Clare. But I hadn't been the victim of a gaslighting scheme for months either. I rubbed my phone against my chin. There was something here, something important.

My finger skimmed across the phone's screen, and I searched for more information. *Hemlock lotion* didn't give me any results. *Hemlock ointment…*

Flying ointment.

Also known as magic salve, lycanthropic ointment, and witches flying ointment is a hallucinogenic ointment attributed to medieval witchcraft. Detailed recipes for the ointment have been found dating back to the early modern period. Francis Bacon listed the ingredients including: "the fat of children digged out of their graves, of juices of smallage, wolfe-bane, and cinque foil, mingled with the meal of fine wheat." Small children aside, typical ingredients include belladonna, hemlock, mandrake, and wolfsbane.

Involuntarily, I glanced at Ground's red-paned windows. Flying ointment? Lenore had mentioned that. And Dixie had said Jayce was…

I shook my head. *Nah.* That was crazy thinking.

But Jayce did know a thing or three about herbs.

I wavered, then stood and knocked on the door.

After a minute, lights brightened the coffeeshop's interior.

Jayce answered the door. "Susan? What's wrong?"

"About that lotion—"

In the street, a woman cried out.

Jayce's head jerked up, her eyes widening. There was a collective gasp, and a crash of thunder echoed through the town.

I turned and scanned the sky. An uncanny greenish light burst across the clouds, turning them waxen. Thunder boomed.

And in that moment, understanding came, too late.

"They're coming!" someone shouted.

Shrieks filled the streets. A horn blared.

A car swerved around a pedestrian and knocked a planter onto the sidewalk. Green matter and earth spewed toward us.

Jayce yelped. We both leapt backwards.

From somewhere came the sound of shattering glass. A dog barked frantically. Other dogs took up the cry.

The sheriff's fears had come true. This was a panic, a true panic. I should have been terrified. A part of me was terrified. But the gray shadow that stalked me wasn't nearby now. A cold, clear clarity descended.

"Oh, no," I breathed.

Because in that flash of lightning, I understood. Someone was coming, and someone else was in terrible danger.

CHAPTER 29

Jayce clawed her hand through her thick hair. A thick cloud of smoke bloomed, billowing down Main Street, and she blinked. "Look, I've got to get to the hospital—"

"So do I," I said quickly. "Can I hitch a ride?" My face warmed. "Sorry. Is everything all right?"

"It's— It's fine. I'm meeting Lenore there."

"Is she okay?"

The lights on Main Street brightened and went dark. There was a collective gasp.

Dry thunder rumbled, and we glanced again at the mountains to the east. Another greenish light flickered over its highest peak.

A screech of tires, the rending of metal. Curses and the blare of horns floated through the darkness.

"She's fine." Jayce eyed me. "And... yes, you can have a ride. My truck's parked in the alley. This way."

She let me inside and locked Ground's front door behind us.

We hurried through the empty coffeeshop and out the alley door. Jayce locked that too.

We climbed into her gunmetal pickup and drove down the alley.

"The sheriff said the highway was blocked," I said. "Car accidents."

Jayce made a frustrated noise and turned the pickup down a residential street. "I know some shortcuts, but we can't avoid the highway forever."

I checked the map on my phone. "The highway's a solid mass of red all the way to Angels Camp." The map froze, the signal vanishing.

"We don't have time," she muttered.

I shot her a curious glance. "You're sure your sister's okay?"

"Yes. She's visiting someone." Jayce bit her bottom lip. "But Lenore hates hospitals," she said shortly. "What about you? Are you visiting someone?"

"Clare Fitzgerald." I just hoped she was out of ICU. "Excuse me." I dialed the hospital and got one of those out-of-service tones. "Dammit. The cell service must be overloaded. My service is cutting in and out." And I should call Arsen and tell him where I'd gone. The service bars vanished from the top left corner of my phone, and I groaned. "And now I'm out again."

Jayce rounded a bend and stepped on the brakes.

Stopped cars lined the highway. Two men shouted at each other in the road, the veins in their necks bulging.

"Nuts to this." She turned sharply and drove onto the shoulder. The truck tilted sideway. Pine branches scraped against my window.

"Jayce, I don't think—"

She made another hard turn, aiming the truck's headlights straight down a grassy slope.

I squeaked in alarm and grabbed the door handle. The pickup bumped and slithered down the hill and onto a dirt track. She accelerated, and the pickup fishtailed, then roared down the rutted road.

"Lenore must really hate hospitals," I croaked. The F-150's headlights bounced across thick stands of pine.

"You have no idea. This logging trail—"

"Isn't it a hiking trail?"

"It is now, but it was a logging trail—"

"Oh my God." We were going to run over a hiker at this speed.

"—and it should take us pretty close to the hospital."

We skidded around a sharp turn.

I gripped the door handle more tightly. "Jayce, maybe we should slow down."

"No one's hiking here tonight. Not with that storm coming."

A flash illuminated the road, turned the spires of pines into a photographic negative.

A pair of backpackers appeared in her headlights. She swore and slammed on the brakes, rocketing me against the seatbelt.

Glaring, the hikers edged off the road, and we passed.

She smiled, sheepish. "Well, there won't be *many* people on the trail tonight."

I gulped.

We flew over potholes. If I hadn't been wearing my seatbelt, I would have hit the ceiling on more than one occasion. The road narrowed, branches whipping the truck.

"Fun, huh?" Jayce grinned maniacally. How had I not seen this before? She was insane.

I checked my phone. Still no signal, and no chance of calling the sheriff or Arsen.

A boulder rose before us. The pickup lurched to a halt.

Jayce unsnapped her seatbelt. "We walk from here."

I stepped from the truck and looked around. Trees crowded close, the only sound the ticking of the F-150's cooling metal. A chill breeze blew down the mountain, rustling the trees.

I shivered and hurried after Jayce.

The truck's lights flicked off, plunging us into darkness.

Jayce paused, nodded. "Okay, I can see again. You?"

I could see Jayce, but only because she was right in front of me. "Not really."

"Don't worry. I've got a great sense of direction."

Pursing my lips, I nodded.

I love living near forests and mountains and lakes. But unlike Arsen – and Jayce, apparently – I wasn't comfortable *in* forests and mountains and lakes. The wilderness is great – through a window.

I stumbled over a stone. It rattled and pinged off invisible rocks and fell silent.

The path branched. Jayce hesitated and pointed at the left fork. "Up this way, I think."

"You think?"

People got lost in California forests all the time. I didn't want to become one of them.

We walked on and on. Sweat dried beneath my thin blouse. We came to another fork.

Jayce paused, her head bent. "This way."

I followed, thinking of every bad thing that could happen to us. Getting lost. Getting eaten. Getting lost and eaten. "Be in the present. I am in the present," I sing-songed quietly.

"What?" Jayce asked.

"Nothing." I ducked my head. "Just talking to myself."

The ground sloped upward, and I breathed harder.

"There it is," she said.

"Where?"

And then, there it was. We emerged into the hospital's parking lot. The tall, glass building glowed with bluish light.

Thunder rumbled.

"Come on," Jayce said. "Let's get inside before the storm breaks." She jogged across the parking lot, and again, I followed.

The hospital's sliding glass doors whooshed open. We trotted into a maelstrom of shouting, jostling people. The thickest group stood in front of the reception desk, and my stomach sank.

"Lenore!" Jayce shouted and hurried toward a lounge area.

The bookstore owner faced the wall. She stood between a painting of an alpine lake and the entrance to the hospital lounge, as if she couldn't decide to admire the painting or go inside. She didn't turn, even when Jayce grabbed her shoulder.

I glanced again at the desk. I didn't know what room Clare was in and didn't like my chances getting through the mob. But it had to be done. Steeling myself, I strode toward the crowd.

Danella walked past me and to the bank of elevators. She pressed a button, shook her head, and darted through a door to the stairs.

My breath, which had only just begun to steady, quickened again. I scurried to the stairwell and peeked inside.

Danella's footsteps rattled on the metal stairs.

Quietly, I shut the door behind me. I tiptoed upward, making sure she was exactly one landing ahead of me.

A door clicked open above.

Taking the stairs two at a time, I grabbed the door before it could close. I edged into a pastel-green hallway.

Danella vanished around a corner.

I followed her past an abandoned nurse's station.

She turned another corner. I sped up, rounding the corner in time to see her disappear inside a room.

Heart thumping, I went to its open door.

Clare lay in the bed, her eyes closed.

Danella leaned over her.

I bumped the door. It glided open and banged into a rolling, metal tray. A plastic pitcher tumbled from it and to the ground.

Danella jerked upright. "You!"

I grabbed the empty pitcher and replaced it on the tray. Why did someone leave that here?

Clare blinked and yawned. "How long have I been sleeping? Susan?"

"This is not a good time," Danella said to me, her mouth crimping.

"No," I agreed, "it isn't."

She grasped Clare's hand. "If you've come to tell her the truth about me, don't bother. She knows I'm her mother."

"It's wonderful," Clare said, "meeting you, having someone in my life again." Her eyes welled with tears. "It's also made me realize how important Marion was. She was my mother too, and I... I never really appreciated her."

Danella glared at me. "So, there's no reason for you to be here."

"Sorry. There is," I said. "Clare, we've got to get you out of here."

"Out of here?" Danella planted her fists on the hips of her jeans. "Are you kidding me?"

"It isn't safe." I gave Clare what I hoped was a meaningful look. *Listen to me.*

"It's a hospital," Danella said.

"It's chaos," I said. "Clare, you've been gaslighted. None of what you think you've been experiencing is real. I mean it is real, but it isn't what you think—"

"And now you insult me, my work, my beliefs," Danella said. "This is ridiculous. I'm getting a nurse." She stormed from the room.

"Good luck with that," I muttered. The nurses had their hands full. Someone had even left a bottle of laundry detergent on top of the room's wardrobe. It was totally unprofessional.

Clare sat up, shifting her back against the headboard. "What's going on?" The collar of her white hospital gown slipped, and she adjusted the thin cloth.

I drew in a breath and released it. How to explain so she'd believe me? "In the movie *Gaslight*, the bad guy tries to make his wife think she's crazy. He wants to institutionalize her and get power of attorney over her estate. He makes all these small, odd things happen around her. Then he pretends it's in her imagination."

The detergent bottle seemed to stare reproachfully.

"No one thinks it's in my imagination," Clare said hotly. "My father and stepmother were murdered."

"Someone is making you look guilty and unstable."

"Guilty? Of what? Of—" She paled and sat up. "The sheriff thinks I killed my parents?"

"Did you take the drugs that made you collapse?" I reached up and grabbed the heavy bottle from the wardrobe. It was missing a cap. *Unprofessional!* I looked around the room.

"No," she said, "of course I didn't! I don't know how the drugs got—" She bit her lip.

I returned the detergent to the top of the wardrobe and eyed her. "Don't you? Because deep down, I think you had your suspicions. You had them all along. It was why you went along with bringing me into the investigation. You wanted a witness."

"N-no." She pressed a hand to her mouth.

"Emmery's always been controlling, hasn't he?" I asked gently. But Clare's tough-as-nails father hadn't made her malleable. It had toughened her up. Clare wasn't one to be pushed around, so she'd needed to be broken first.

I should have seen it sooner. Emmery had displayed the classic signs – jealousy, over-concern for Clare, quickness to take offense. The speed they'd become involved had been a warning sign too.

"And your father saw it," I said. "That's why he didn't like the relationship. It had nothing to do with Emmery's father."

"My dad never liked Emmery. He told me he was no good, but—what did my father know? He hardly spent any time with us. And I love Emmery."

"Do you still?"

She turned her face to the window and didn't reply.

"Clare?"

"This *is* my fault," she whispered. "All of it. He did it. He killed my father and Marion…" She swayed in the hospital bed.

"No," I said. "It's Emmery's fault. And your father would want you to fight."

Clare swallowed. Her expression hardened. She threw off the blankets and swung her legs from the bed. "We've got to get out of here."

I released a breath. She believed me. I'd done it. "Where are your clothes?"

She pointed at the wardrobe.

I jerked open its doors, and the bottle on the wardrobe wobbled. Grabbing a pair of jeans and a t-shirt, I tossed the clothing to Clare. "Here."

She pulled on her jeans beneath her hospital gown. "When Emmery suggested bringing you in to investigate, I thought I was wrong. That I was imagining he was trying to control me. I felt so guilty about ever thinking—"

"That I was behind it all?" Emmery asked from the open doorway. His hand rested casually on his holstered gun.

CHAPTER 30

Clare and I froze, mannequins in a hospital tableau.

"You bastard," she said.

Emmery drew his gun and sidled into the room. He closed the door behind him. "It was a mistake bringing you into this, Susan."

"Then why did you?" I asked over the pounding of my heart. We had to get out of here, get away from the deputy.

My gaze darted around the hospital room. Rumpled bed. Chair too heavy to throw as a weapon. Swivel table. Wardrobe.

He shrugged. "I figured you'd see aliens under the bedsheets too."

"So that's why you stole my lemon curd?"

His expression flickered.

"It didn't work," I continued. "The sheriff has the mask. I found it in the colonel's house. It may not have your prints, but it will have your DNA on it. And the owl will too."

Clare gasped. "I remember. I saw the owl on my bed that day. It flew at me, I swear, and then..." She rubbed her temple. "It's so confused."

"That's because Emmery's been drugging you through that coffee lotion," I said. "There was hemlock and I'm guessing other things in it that Jayce didn't put there. He must have added something so it would absorb through the skin." He could have killed Clare. He could have killed me when I'd tried the stuff and had my own crazy visions.

"It *was* nice to finally be able to use my botany degree," Emmery agreed pleasantly.

My gaze darted about the room, looking for an escape. But the windows were shut fast, and Emmery blocked the door. We were trapped.

Stall. "How did you manage to vanish so completely that night at Clare's? One minute you were playing alien, the next you were gone."

"Ah." His gaze shifted. "I'm nimble," he said. "I got on top of the carport and laid flat. All I had to do was wait for the right time to slip away to my car. I didn't mean for things to get this out of control, Clare. But you wouldn't listen. I really do love you Clare."

"You killed my parents!"

"Your father was a bully. And Marion wasn't really your mother." Facing me, he edged toward her.

Clare flushed, her hands fisting in her white hospital gown. "Yes, she was.

Something you'll never understand."

"Why did you kill her?" I asked. "Was Marion in your way too?"

"In a manner of speaking." He stopped at the foot of the bed. "She knew the colonel didn't like me. She didn't like me much either. I knew she'd never give up control of Clare's estate as long as I was in the picture. Marion saw me rummaging in their refrigerator the morning the colonel had his heart attack. She said things to me that made me realize she knew I'd added the foxglove to the colonel's green mix."

I released a breath I hadn't realized I was holding. "You added it to the greens, not to his juice?" *Stall for time. Think of an out.* But there was no out. We were on our own, unless Danella returned with help. And I wasn't that lucky.

"It was easier that way. The colonel, being the colonel, had pre-washed and dried his greens. He'd even segmented them into neat, juiceable bunches. Very efficient. But it meant he didn't look at them very carefully when he was adding them to his blender."

"And he poisoned himself." My voice cracked. He was insane. And the only reason he was telling me was because he planned to kill me too.

"I don't know why Marion didn't tell the sheriff what she suspected right away." He shook his head.

"I do," Clare choked out. "She came to me, asking how well I really knew you. I defended you."

"She didn't trust what she'd seen," I said. "She didn't want to hurt you, Clare."

"How did you poison my mother?" Clare's voice filled with tears.

"I juiced the foxglove, extracted the poison, and added it to that awful fake creamer she puts in her coffee."

"You're a monster," Clare whispered.

"I just wanted to protect you," he said.

"Protect her?" I asked. "You could have killed Clare with that lotion."

"I would never have killed Clare. I was careful."

Careful... I glanced toward the wardrobe.

Clare's chest caved. She collapsed against the bed. "So, you just made me think I was crazy, made me hallucinate, made me think I was being abducted by aliens and haunted by owls—"

"You were always careless. You wouldn't let me protect you."

I sidled toward the wardrobe. "And if she depended on you, that would make it easier to get your hands on the colonel's money. Your father always felt the colonel had cheated him out of an opportunity. Did his resentment rub off?"

His face spasmed. "This had nothing to do with money." He turned to her. "Clare, you've got to believe me. It's always been about you, protecting you. I need—"

I shoved the top of the wardrobe. The heavy cupboard creaked, its end scraping the wall.

Emmery whirled. "No!" He threw one arm up, catching the wardrobe. His knees buckled. The gun skittered across the floor.

"Run!" I shouted and picked up the gun.

Clare scrambled over the bed. We bounced off each other racing out the door.

Behind us, there was a crash.

I dropped the gun into a medical waste bin, pivoted, and slammed into Danella.

"Where are you—"

"Run," Clare screamed.

Danella turned and ran alongside her daughter.

We turned a corner, headed toward the elevators.

"Stairs," I gasped. We were running from a cop. He could arrest us, cuff us, put us in his car in full view of a hundred nurses, drive us to a nice quiet location...

Clare flung open the door. She and Danella rocketed through into the stairwell.

Not daring look over my shoulder, I followed.

We raced down the metal steps, our footsteps echoing.

"It's Emmery," Clare half-sobbed. Her hospital gown flapped around the hips of her jeans. "He did it all. It's always been Emmery."

Running footsteps clattered on the stairs above us.

Clare grabbed a metal door and yanked it open. She ran through.

Danella waited by the door, and I sped past.

I turned to her. "Danella?"

"Go!" Danella pulled the door shut.

I swore and kept moving, told myself that Emmery wanted Clare, not Danella, not me. That he wouldn't hurt the psychic.

I stumbled to a halt.

But what if he did? Danella was a guest, my responsibility.

And you don't abandon guests to psychopaths.

"Dammit." I turned toward the stairs.

A wild-eyed man in a cowboy hat grabbed the arm of my shirt. "You're the UFO woman. I saw you in the store. What's happening? Are they here? Is it time?"

I yanked my arm, but he held fast. "Let go. I have to go."

"They're coming. Aren't they?"

My head throbbed, my pulse beating in my ears. We didn't have time for this!

People pressed around us and shouted questions. "Is this an invasion?"

"What do the aliens want?"

"What do they look like?"

I jerked away, but the cowboy didn't let go. "Stop it," I said. "They're not—
"

The stair door thumped.

My heart stopped. *Emmery.* How could I stop him? He'd overpower us both, and the hospital would cheer him on. Unless...

"They're here," I shouted. "And they look like us. There's one in the stairwell now, dressed like a sheriff's deputy."

Emmery burst, stumbling, through the door. Gelatinous, purple goo coated the top of his head. It streamed onto the shoulders of his deputy's jacket.

"Alien!" the cowboy bellowed.

Women screamed and scattered.

Emmery blinked and rubbed the back of one hand across his eyes.

The cowboy lowered his head and charged. He rammed Emmery, lifting him off the floor. He slammed Emmery against the wall, then dropped him, limp to the tiles.

Emmery slid sideways against the wall and collapsed in a heap.

The door creaked open. Danella crawled from the stairwell.

I ran to the psychic. "Danella! Are you okay?"

One eye was red and swelling. Blood trickled from her nose. "Is she okay? Is Clare safe?"

I looked around the swiftly emptying reception area. Clare was nowhere to be seen. The glass doors slid open, and Clare and Sheriff McCourt strode inside, scowling.

"She's safe," I said. For now.

"Thank God." Danella peered up at me through her swelling eye. "Or Goddess."

"Are you badly hurt, ma'am?" The cowboy lifted her to her feet.

She studied his tall, muscular form and smiled unevenly. "I'm better now. Nice rescue."

He nudged Emmery with his snakeskin boot. "Dang. He bleeds purple."

I knelt beside Emmery and drew one finger through the purple goo, sniffed.

Detergent. The purple gel was the detergent from the wardrobe.

I hoped it stung like hell.

CHAPTER 31

Arsen sprawled on Gran's black velvet couch, one arm wrapped around my waist. "I never liked that guy." Soot stained Arsen's marvelous face. His hair, thick with grit, stood on end. Bailey's head rested on his thigh.

The sheriff stopped pacing and glared down at us. "You never liked him? He blew up my station!"

Thunder rumbled, rain drumming the eaves. In the corner, Dixie shifted on the ebony ottoman.

I gaped. "Blew up? When? Why?"

"I was wondering why the fire department had to leave us volunteers to manage the Town Hall blaze." Arsen yawned. "Though the fire was mostly out at that point anyway. So, Town Hall was a diversion?"

Sheriff McCourt raked a hand through her hair. Her curls were limp and damp and darkened by smoke. "Looks that way. We're still investigating."

Silent, Manaj leaned in a corner of the sitting room, shadows folding into her black clothing.

"What are you talking about?" I asked, my head drawing back. "What does the fire have to do with Clare?" Clare, who was safe upstairs in her own room, next to Danella's. The two still had a lot to talk about.

"It has to do with the evidence Deputy Hernandez collected on the hill above the colonel's yard."

"What evidence?"

"Never mind what evidence, but now that we know what Emmery was up to, odds are good it points straight back to him murdering Marion Fitzgerald. One of the turkeys must have dragged it there," she said.

"I don't understand," I said.

"No," the sheriff said. "As usual, there's a lot you don't understand. I'm still trying to put it together," she muttered.

In the corner, Agent Manaj shifted but said nothing.

"What happened?" I asked, carefully not looking the FBI agent's way.

"Emmery Berghoff is what happened," the sheriff said. "He created a timed incendiary device, which triggered a fire in the garage bay so he could take what we'd found. Fortunately, after that leak of your video, I stopped trusting my own deputies. I'd already moved the evidence, so he didn't get his hands on it, and that's all that matters."

"So Emmery leaked the video?" I asked.

"He minored in computer science," the sheriff said.

"How did you know Emmery was behind it all?" I asked.

"I didn't," she said. "It was only when I heard your story about the drugs, the alien mask, the attack, that I started looking at him as a suspect." She kicked the corner of the rug flat. "At least one of us had the measure of him. I owe you, Susan. You did a good job."

Huh. Maybe I wasn't so delusional after all. "I should have seen it sooner," I said modestly. "It struck me as odd that he would take Clare, who was obviously on edge, to a creepy circus. His story of getting attacked there made him look like he was the victim too. But of course, it was only a story."

"That damned circus," the sheriff said. "Between the panic and the pickpockets—"

"Pickpockets?" So, I hadn't imagined that arm?

"The circus was crawling with them."

That little man had stood awfully close to me on more than one occasion. Good thing I hadn't had my purse with me when we'd first met at Wits' End. "So was Emmery really attacked at the circus?"

"No," the sheriff said. "He said that, as you guessed, just to ratchet up Clare's tension and make him look innocent. But that circus *is* a den of thieves. I couldn't get them on anything this time. Fortunately, they're moving on."

I frowned. "But if you only figured out it was Emmery later," I said, "why were you at the hospital?"

"To check on Deputy Hernandez."

"Is that who Lenore was visiting?" I hoped he was okay.

"Connor Hernandez?" Arsen's muscles tensed. "Was he hurt?"

"Smoke inhalation," the sheriff said. "But the doctors say he'll be okay."

"Was Emmery working alone?" I asked.

McCourt eyed me.

"Interesting question," Agent Manaj said. "Why do you ask?"

I cleared my throat, embarrassed. "Well, I mean, setting the fire seems kind of complicated—"

"Yes," McCourt said stiffly. "He was working alone."

"Did he confess to stealing my lemon curd?"

Manaj studied her fingernails.

"Yes, he took your lemon curd." The sheriff's chin jutted forward.

"Why?" I asked.

"To make you think you were crazy too."

"And One-armed Frank's cows?" Arsen asked.

"Found wandering in the mountains," she said. "Are you all satisfied?"

"Yes," I said.

"Good, because I have work to do." She bent, grabbing her hat off the black coffee table, and mashed it on her head. "I don't suppose there's any sense in asking that daffy medium to keep her mouth shut?"

"Probably not," I said.

"I figured as much. I had a long, hard talk with Tom Tarrant. He's going to do another podcast, saying today's was a joke, an ode to *War of the Worlds* that went just as wrong as the first radio show."

"He will?" The whole town would hate him. I tried to feel bad about that. But Tom was good looking. People would forgive him. They always did.

It was super annoying.

"The press can take it." The sheriff grunted. She turned her hat in her hands. "The riots have died down, but people will be looking for answers from someone they trust."

"I guess you'll be busy then," I said, rueful.

"Not me, Susan. You." She strode to the door.

"So, what was the evidence he was after?" Dixie asked.

"When all this settles down, I won't let you know." The sheriff strode from the room, the kitchen door swinging in her wake.

Manaj shot me a sympathetic look. "So that's that."

"I can hardly believe it," I said. "Was anything about Emmery real?"

"He was really your neighbor's son," Manaj said, "and a really bad guy."

"But—"

"The colonel's death had nothing to do with his work with the Air Force. And whatever happened in Doyle this week was an outbreak of nothing more than human nature."

I squinted at the FBI agent. Had she put emphasis on the word *human?*

"So, you really were here because of the colonel's suspicious death and his work at Area 51?" Dixie asked.

The FBI agent eyed Dixie. "People will believe what they want to believe, and say what they want to say, regardless of the evidence."

Dixie stiffened. "Why are you looking at me?"

Manaj smiled. "No reason." She nodded and strode from the room. The door swung behind her.

I rested my head on Arsen's shoulder.

"Do you get the feeling there's more going on than they're telling us?" Dixie asked.

"Like there really was something alien going on?" I asked. "No. No, I don't." Could there really have been aliens running around Doyle?

Nah.

"So Emmery killed the colonel, Mrs. Fitzgerald, perpetrated a UFO hoax, stole your lemon curd, *and* set the sheriff's station and Town Hall on fire?" Dixie gave me a sly look. "That took some planning. He was quite the multitasker."

I ignored the jibe. Just because an evil lunatic was an effective planner didn't mean planning was bad.

"The sheriff wasn't a bad multitasker either," I said. "With the town in a panic, most of the deputies were on calls rather than at the station when the bomb went off." Emmery had been willing to go so far to cover his tracks. There was no doubt in my mind he wouldn't have stopped at me, and I shivered.

Dixie rose and stretched. "You got that right. My police scanner was going crazy. There were so many calls, it was hard to keep track of what was going on."

A snore erupted beside me. Carefully, I turned. Arsen's head angled against the back of the velvet couch, his eyes closed. The poor guy. Fire-fighting must be exhausting.

So as not to wake him, I gently disentangled myself. I pulled a throw over him and followed Dixie into the kitchen.

Another boom of thunder rattled the house. I glanced toward the door to my sitting room.

"Clare's safe," Dixie said. "Emmery's arrested. And Danella's Clare's birth mom. Anything else I should know?"

"Not that I can think of. But..." My insides jittered. *Forget the stupid lemon curd, forget the alien.*

"What?" she asked impatiently.

I hesitated. "Arsen told me to ask you... What did Gran say to you?" I said in a rush. "Before she died, I mean."

"I was wondering when you'd ask."

Guiltily, I looked at the wall clock. It was after midnight. I swallowed. "I guess I didn't think I had the right to ask," I said in a low voice. "Not after what I did."

"What you did?"

My eyes heated. I met her gaze. "Not being here for Gran at the end."

"That was your parents."

"No. Me." If I didn't take responsibility, I'd never be able to forgive my parents. I'd never be able to be free. "I let her down. She was the one person... She was always there for me. She managed to get me out of that house every summer so I could taste some freedom in Doyle. Gran made sure I knew there was a different way to live. That I didn't have to be what my parents told me to be. And in the end, when she needed me, I betrayed her." My throat thickened, my words choking. "And I can't tell her how sorry I am."

Dixie didn't speak for a long time. She cleared her throat. "Save Susan."

"What?"

"Save Susan. She's in terrible danger of losing her soul. Save her."

I stared, uncomprehending.

"That's what she said at the end. It's why I came to get you." Dixie looked away. "I loved her too."

And Dixie *had* saved me. Dixie. Arsen. Gran. Gran had even set crazy old Mrs. Steinberg to watch me. And I had everything I needed.

Water drummed on the eaves.

I brushed tears from my cheeks.

The shadow touched my shoulder and vanished, and this time, I knew it was for good.

Note from Kirsten

If only the sheriff hadn't given Susan that pat on the back, Susan might have finally realized McCourt didn't really want her help.

But what fun would that be?

Besides, Susan caught another killer, making the streets of Doyle…

Who am I kidding? The streets of Doyle will never be safe.

Especially since there's more to this story than meets the eye.

I'd written the Wits' End series as a counterpoint to the Witches of Doyle cozy mystery books. The witches see the events in Doyle (aka Murphy's, CA) from a magical perspective; Susan, like most Doyleites, doesn't. But I decided to challenge myself and try to tell the same set of events from the two different points of view. *Fate*, book 6 in the Witches of Doyle series, overlaps the events in *Close Encounters of the Curd Kind*. The witches have their very own murder to solve, and Susan gets unwittingly tangled up in the mystery.

So, if you'd like to read the "flip side" of this story, watch for *Fate*, coming in November, 2019.

CHERRY COBBLER COFFEE CAKE

Ingredients – dough:

2-1/2 to 3 C all-purpose flour
1/4 C sugar
1 pkg (1/4 ounce) active dry yeast
1 tsp. salt
1/2 C butter
1/2 C milk of your choice (2%, soy, almond, whatever)
1/2 C water
2 eggs
1 large can (21 ounces) cherry pie filling
Ingredients – glaze:
1/2 C confectioners' sugar
1/4 tsp almond extract
3 to 4 tsp milk of your choice (2%, soy, almond, whatever).

Directions for Coffeecake:

Note: You'll need a cooking thermometer for this recipe, because you want to be sure not to burn the yeast. That will prevent it from rising.

Combine 1-1/2 C flour, sugar, yeast and salt in a glass or ceramic bowl (avoid aluminum or copper bowls, as these are reactive vis a vis the yeast). Cube the butter. Using a small pot or saucepan, heat the butter, water, and milk until the temperature reads 120°-130°. Remove from heat and beat the liquid into the dry ingredients until well mixed. Add eggs and whisk until the mixture is free of lumps.

Gradually mix in remaining flour to the mixture until you have a soft, sticky dough (you might not use all the flour). Cover the mixture with plastic wrap. Leave it to rise in a warm place until it doubles (Susan likes to warm it on a heating pad). This should take approximately 40 minutes.

Grease a 13"x9" baking pan.

Stir the dough (it will collapse, but don't worry about this). Spread two-thirds of the dough into the baking pan. Spread the cherry pie filling over the top of the dough, spreading to the edges of the pan. Drop tablespoons of the remaining dough over the pie filling (filling should not be completely covered). Carefully cover with plastic wrap so it's not touching the batter and leave the cake to rise in a warm place for approximately 30 minutes, until it doubles.

Preheat the oven to 350 F.

Bake 35-40 minutes or until the coffee cake is golden brown.

Remove the pan from the oven to set aside to cool. Now it's time to make your glaze!

Directions for Glaze:

With a fork or whisk, mix the confectioners' sugar, almond extract and slowly dribble in enough milk or milk substitute to get the glaze to a drizzling consistency. Drizzle the glaze over the coffee cake while it's still warm.

LEMON CURD

Ingredients:
6 T unsalted butter, softened at room temperature
1 C sugar
2 large eggs
2 large egg yolks
2/3 C fresh lemon juice
1 tsp grated lemon zest

Directions:

Note: You'll need a cooking thermometer to this, because you DO NOT want the curd to boil. You will also need plastic wrap for the cooling process.

In a good-sized bowl, using an electric mixer beat the butter and sugar for 2 minutes. On the slowest speed mix, introduce the eggs and yolks (eggs and yolks, meet sugar and butter!). Beat 1 minute. Mix in the lemon juice. The mixture now should look frighteningly curdled. But don't despair. This will all even out in the cooking.

Cook the mixture over low heat in a medium-sized, heavy bottomed saucepan until the lemon curd is smooth.

Increase heat to medium. Cook, stirring constantly, until the mixture thickens so that it leaves a path on the back of the spoon. This will take about 15 minutes. DO NOT LET IT BOIL. The thermometer will read 170°F.

Remove the curd from the stove and stir in the lemon zest.

Pour the curd into a bowl. Lightly press a sheet of plastic wrap to the surface of the lemon curd. (This will prevent a skin from forming).

Cool the curd in your refrigerator. The lemon curd will continue to thicken as it chills.

Transfer to jars or a plastic tub and seal tightly. The lemon curd will keep in the refrigerator for up to a week and in the freezer (in a plastic tub) for up to two months.

EASY CINNAMON ROLL CASSEROLE

Ingredients:
1 pkg. of 12 cinnamon rolls, frozen, with cream cheese frosting. (Note: these pre-made and unbaked rolls are generally found in your supermarket's freezer section).
4 eggs
1 C milk (or milk substitute)
3 T granulated sugar
1 1/2 tsp vanilla extract
1/2 tsp ground cinnamon
1/4 tsp ground nutmeg

Directions:

You'll be prepping this the night before for baking in the morning. (B&B owners love this sort of thing).

Spray a 9"x13" casserole or baking dish with non-stick cooking spray (preferably butter flavored). Quarter the frozen cinnamon rolls. Evenly spread the pieces in the bottom of the casserole dish.

Reserve the cream cheese frosting from the package for later.

Whisk the remaining ingredients (aside from the cream cheese frosting) in a bowl. Pour the mixture over the cinnamon roll chunks. Cover the baking dish with plastic wrap. Refrigerate overnight, for at least 6-8 hours.

The next morning, preheat your oven to 375 degrees. Remove the plastic wrap from the dish. Bake your casserole for 35-40 minutes or until the top is lightly browned.

Remove casserole from oven. Frost using the cream cheese frosting from the cinnamon roll package. Serve warm!

Join the Society

Escape with *Fortune Favors the Grave*, a free novella in the Tea and Tarot series, by joining **the Ravenous Society**.

Plus, society members will get other free short stories and exclusive reads. Sign up and become a member today!

If you have trouble with the image above, click here: **https://www.kirstenweiss.com/ravenous-society-cozy**

Here's a bit from Abigail about *Fortune Favors the Grave*:

Some people have the cockeyed idea running a tearoom is an elegant and genteel profession. *I'd* thought it would be elegant and genteel.
Some people haven't met my business partner, Hyperion Night.
In fairness, I can't entirely blame Hyperion for embroiling our tea and tarot room in a murder. After all, he was chained to the San Borromeo pier when California's most famous psychic, Trevor Amalfi, was killed.
And yet, here I am. And here we are. Embroiled.

Fortune Favors the Grave is an exclusive *Tea and Tarot* novella only for Raven(ous) Society Members!

ABOUT THE AUTHOR

Kirsten Weiss has never met a dessert she didn't like, and her guilty pleasures are watching Ghost Whisperer re-runs and drinking red wine. The latter gives her heartburn, but she drinks it anyway.

Now based in Colorado Springs, CO, she writes genre-blending cozy mystery, supernatural and steampunk suspense, mixing her experiences and imagination to create vivid worlds of fun and enchantment.

If you like funny cozy mysteries, check out her Pie Town, Tea and Tarot, Paranormal Museum and Wits' End books. If you're looking for some magic with your mystery, give the Witches of Doyle, Riga Hayworth and Rocky Bridges books a try. And if you like steampunk, the Sensibility Grey series might be for you.

Kirsten sends out original short stories of mystery and magic to her mailing list. If you'd like to get them delivered straight to your inbox, make sure to sign up for her newsletter at kirstenweiss.com

Made in the USA
Middletown, DE
26 July 2020

13517713R00116